Canyons

J. D. Levy

Copyright

This book is dedicated to the memory of

A. Dewey Jensen

TABLE OF CONTENTS

Prologue

Kate awoke to find herself face down in a urinal. Someone was fumbling at the clasp of her bra. A furtive glance to the right was met with a pair of beat-up cowboy boots.

I am being raped!

What was she supposed to do? She couldn't think right; it was as if her mind was a jellyfish riding a wave, breaking on the stony shore; all was tumultuous and without a sense of up or down—without balance … terrified.

She screamed.

A filthy, greasy hand clamped itself over her mouth.

"Shut up."

For the moment her bra was left alone, and then the hand returned to fumbling with the clasp.

How had she gotten here?

Must have something to do with the pain on the left side of my head.

The urinal stank, like … a urinal, and it was disgusting.

She screamed again, not words and not meaningful sounds, just a loud, painful scream.

The hand clasped over her mouth again.

"I said shut up."

It was a disgusting hand and she wasn't going to scream again. Here she was, about to get raped by an unwashed man in a filthy bathroom and all she could think about was how dirty and grimy her assailant's hand tasted.

The hand busied itself with her bra again. She cringed as she felt the hooks snap into place.

"There," said the voice.

Clasped?

Involuntarily Kate huffed out a small expression of surprise, of confusion.

"Huh?"

"That's right, silly girl." The boots shifted and she felt a pair of strong hands reach under her and lift her as if she didn't weigh a thing. "I am rescuing you."

It was then that she saw the bodies of two men slumped in the urinals next to her.

"Yes that's right. Now keep still little one, I don't need The Man coming down on us. Don't want to be 'splaining this to no one."

She reached up and clasped the neck of the man who held her. It was a strong, thick neck, hairy. She hadn't seen his face, she couldn't still, and she didn't want to. He was beautiful, he had to be, *he was rescuing her*.

Tucson, Arizona

Mid-twentieth century

Kate

Kate put her hand on Rob's chest. His kisses were good; he had good lips—full, soft on the top, firm underneath …but there was little else that would stick with her about this evening. Kate already had forgotten the name of the restaurant they'd dined at and she would soon, hopefully, forget Rob's phone number; she very much hoped he would forget hers. He was *so* not her type. Actually, she thought, suppressing a giggle, he was her father's type, her father's type for *her*. Well, sort of; she doubted that even he would be able to stand Rob for very long and would certainly grow weary of him as a son-in-law—that made Kate laugh, which Rob mistook for an elevated level of interest in him. He pulled her closer.

"Can—"

"No." She interrupted, hoping her breathing didn't betray her. His kisses *were* good.

"C'mon, Kate, you know you'll like it."

That did it, such a lame line; not even a little her father's type - she ought to close the door in Rob's face just for that pass.

"I said no." More firmly this time.

"Yeah, sure. Don't call me anymore, then."

Rob turned and hurried down the short stack of stairs that climbed up to her little house on a street comprised mainly of little houses near the center of town; things take care of themselves, always—he wasn't going to call her … and she had already forgotten his number.

Kate turned, entered her home, closing and locking the door prior to heading into her room without stopping to mix a drink as she was want to do before bed; sleep and Kate were not the best of friends these days. The night-tide hours she spent trying to lose the events of the day to dreams, and long spates of wakefulness in the middle hours of the night were a testament to her inability to reconcile what was mostly a dull, pointless life with what it was she thought she should be doing, which in an odd sense was what she was doing now, only it should be better, it should be more; more of everything—basically what she was doing now but with excitement, with purpose. Some of her restlessness had to do with money problems that dogged her and some with her father and his behavior specifically toward her; but in the end, didn't she control the nature of the relationship with her father?

Tonight she thought she just might settle down, relax and have a good, healthy sleep. Maybe it had something to do with saying no and being firm about it; maybe it was because she was really tired. Regardless, it was time, she was tired, and work would be calling her much sooner than she would like. Sometimes she wished work would threaten not to call her anymore, either; that was another number that she'd have no trouble forgetting. Well, except for the fact that Guy was intimately tied to her work; he was her supervisor. Now, he was one fella whose number she'd remember—if only she could get it. Ah well, maybe tomorrow; so much time, so little to do.

Tucson had been very good to Katelyn Stein for all the years she had lived here, which were basically all the years of her life. Good that is except for that one time in the bathroom, in the park, after; well, there was no reason to go *there*. Born and raised in Tucson—never having lived anywhere else. By the time Kate had been born, Tucson had already become one of the designated free cities, with an unplanned economy and a local government. But there was a price to pay for that freedom: lack of resources, energy shortages, no federal government support whatsoever—the free cities had lost the major part of their populations to the industrials on the eastern and Pacific coasts … where planned economies and federal management ran amuck. The industrials had their benefits, food in abundance, albeit high in carbs and low in nutrition; energy, clothing, medical facilities aplenty … all readily available at second- or third-rate quality, creating a cheap prison of convenience for those who lived there.

It was morning; Kate turned up the radio to drone out the sound of the engine of her car. She had to get another, and soon. Not that this one didn't drive well; it didn't, really, but no worse than most of the cars that her friends drove, it was just that hers was so much older, and the older electric cars tended to make more noise, something about the brushes getting worn or something like that.

She did have to be careful with the radio, though; there were always new stations coming on-line and many could make a woman, or a man, a *sensitive* man, cringe with embarrassment—entertainment today was a constant battle between taste and sensitivity on one hand, and abhorrent decadence on the other. Straight-laced she was not, but neither did she need all the body's sexual functions and physical traumas thrown in her face at a quarter to eight as she drove to work.

She skipped through the channels, holding on one but for a moment before deciding to go on or give it a listen. She had made some mistakes and tuned into some really awful stuff. Drat, sometimes it was just easier to turn the damn thing off and listen to the brushes. Besides, she was only a handful of minutes from work and that was actually a good thing; free cities with universities or college campuses held up better than their surrounding communities—they still drew in some outside dollars. The heartland cities, without some type of ties to the government, were not so lucky, growing more impoverished every day. The private sector had been minimized, and the remaining business was dependent on government and its institutions, and no institution brought in the dollars like a university or a military base, of which Tucson had a prominent enough number to survive even the flight of all remaining capital. But the crappy little urban communities that surrounded the campus sucked; family life was boring, full of heartache and aggravation.

The best jobs were on the campus. Not only was the work fairly easy, but the pay was decent too. Hers was a good job; Kate was in the planning department, and she was responsible for determining the correct allocation of physical resources for new construction, renovations, and tenant improvements—carpeting, tiling, the number of tables, chairs, desks, photocopiers, even wall jacks and ceiling fixtures fell to her. Since the university was always getting money, there seemed to be no end to the construction that was going on, both new and renovating existing structures. Kate had a couple of part-time people who worked for her, and when a large project came on-line, or several smaller ones got going at the same time, she could boost her employees to full-time on a temporary basis for up to a month at a time. She had, in her own little world, a bit of power.

Uniformed security waved her through into the parking lot nearest her office without much of a glance, which was too bad; she was young and a little double take would be nice. She pulled her long black hair back into a tail, looped a couple of ties around it, checked her appearance in a little hand mirror she carried in the console, and stepped out of the car, smoothing down her skirt before heading into the Planning and Facilities Building. In addition to the relative ease of work, the decent pay, and good hours, there was another thing that Kate liked about her office. Guy worked there; tall, with auburn hair cropped short, a tight face—and butt too … totally twenty-eight. Maybe today he would ask her out, then again maybe not. The last date they had been on had gone rather poorly. Granted it had been six weeks ago and Guy had been traveling since then, but with her father gone now, perhaps things would go smoother. Max, which is how she often referred to her father, Max's behavior had always been inappropriate, but what he had done in front of Guy last time was beyond anything he had ever done within the confines of their relationship; for him to dress down her date was unconscionable, even if Guy had been being a bit of an ass. She'd had lots of dates who had acted the ass and she was okay with it to a point, as long it didn't get out of hand. No, she was glad Max was gone. As she headed into the building her initial thought, well, actually, her only thought, was that, hopefully, Guy was going to take another chance on her.

Kate took the steps hurriedly, steadying her purse with a free hand, as she grappled with getting to the fourth floor while keeping a composed appearance. The elevator was out again; it seemed to be working less often than it did work—an odd state of affairs for the building responsible for campus facilities.

Her office was at the opposite end of the hall from the stairs and she had to pass Guy's office on the way. Guy wasn't at his desk when she arrived, which wasn't unusual; the boy, much like the elevator, was out more often than not. In actuality, though, he was the director of construction for the university, and he did little work. His father was a big shot somewhere, either on campus or off, she couldn't remember; it was said that Guy owed his job, and lack of need to really work, to whatever it was his father had done prior to and since bringing Guy into the world. Granted money wasn't everything, but look what a lack of it had done for her family—well, between her and her father, anyway, and the small house they shared. Things might have been better when her mom had been alive, though she had only been ten at the time. Since her mother died it was all Kate could do to keep her door locked when the two of them were home alone together Living out of the house had helped with that somewhat, but her father was so dependent on her emotionally, that she couldn't help but return home on a regular basis, and to his intrusions.

But Guy wasn't really out; when she entered her office she found him sitting on the edge of her desk flipping through one of the many magazines that she kept on a table next to a couch; Kate used the couch for reading when she needed to get the most out of the material ... sitting with her legs curled up beneath her in a quiet setting provided the best environment to get the job done. It was a little disconcerting to see Guy sitting in *her* office flipping through *her* journals; it wasn't so much that he was in her office, unannounced and uninvited, he was, after all, *Guy*, and, *ahm*, her supervisor—it was not so much what he might discover about her from what she was reading. What was disconcerting was what he *could have* found if she were less diligent in screening the materials she brought into work to read. Her choice of reading material was of course her own, and nothing like censorship was imposed at her place of work, but as in other segments of society, what a person chose to read gave others *opinions* about you, and the journals that she didn't bring to work were far more controversial than these industry journals.

"Hello, Kate."

That deep, even voice of his, coming from the well-proportioned body beneath his short-cropped blond hair and blue eyes, so dreamy and so much like his father; she had met Guy's father once on a chance visit of his to the Planning Center.

"I was looking for you and knowing how punctual you are; figured it'd only be a minute or two till you got in, so I figured I'd wait it out for you. Don't mind?"

Kate feigned a calmness she did not feel and hid the nervousness she did feel.

"No, not at all, Guy, you're welcome anytime." *Only, you haven't chosen to do so before, and in fact, you've pretty much ignored me these past six weeks.* "What can I do for you?" She thought she saw his flash of a secretive grin, exciting in part, and unnerving.

"Well, you know, or probably you don't, hmmm."

Looking down, he picked at a piece of fuzz on his pants; Kate couldn't help but think this was a dramatic touch on his part, to draw out the "revelation"—again she found his behavior both exciting and unnerving ... he was so premeditated. Then, with a snap of his head locking his eyes on hers, and with a faint, sacrosanct smile he continued.

"I have been asked to put together a team going forward. Up top has decided we are a bit overstaffed, and asked me to select a team to go forward, a smaller team, of my best and most trusted personnel. I have been making the rounds, checking in with those that I want to have come with me, er, go with me, and see how they felt about it. Now," he said, and raised his hand as if to forestall questions or a hasty acceptance of his offer, "now before you say yes, I have to tell you that we will be working harder, as a team, doing what we have to, to make us so valuable to the university. Newer tasks will probably be assigned to us, some of which will be a bit outside of what we have done before, but they will be planning in nature. Sorry I can't tell you more, but basically I am offering you a chance to keep your job, move ahead, at the cost of a bit of hard work and expanding the types of duties required of you. Now, what d'ya think? In or out?"

Guy flashed her a warming smile and bobbed his shoulders slightly, a shy little habit he had when he was stretching himself socially, an endearing shy little habit.

"Well, given the *'opportunity to keep my job'* part, I would say in."

"Yeah, is that the only reason?"

Again that knowing grin, almost a sneer. Kate decided not to take the bait. She was willing, but she wasn't easy, at least not often.

"For the most part."

"You mean there are other parts?"

"Perhaps."

Guy gave her a fresh smile and let a moment of silence hang in the air.

"Well, Kate, I'm looking forward to working with you again." He grinned. "Oh, and by the way, not everyone will be coming with us; with our reduction we will be down to five. Can't say who the other three will be, and it wouldn't do you or anyone any good speculating who is going to be with us. In other words, this is kind of confidential. Anyway, we will be moving to the fourth floor, the five of us, just us, so we will have lots of room. Bye."

"Bye," Kate answered to his back; he had already bounced up and was out the door.

Kate took a seat behind her desk and busied herself with some papers, and then quickly lost interest and turned her chair so as to look out the window behind her. It wasn't a particularly great view; over the parking lot and the back of the football stadium—long in disuse and disrepair …but she could see the mountains standing tall in the distance. She wondered idly what kind of view she might have from the floor above. *Probably more of the same.* Perhaps she should see if she could get a room facing south. There wasn't much in the way of mountains in that direction, but there weren't any buildings either, nor parking lots adjoining abandoned stadiums.

Kate suddenly felt very uncomfortable. The whole conversation with Guy had been disconcerting on the whole; just the opposite of what she would have thought. The whole thing bothered her, though, but she couldn't say why … there was something, something, what? It almost seemed that he was taking advantage of the misfortune of others to get closer to her, but truly he needn't have done that for she'd have let him closer on his own accord. She didn't like the fact that her co-workers were going to lose their jobs, nor did she like the apparent lack of sensitivity shown by Guy to the impending disaster in *their* future. With jobs as hard as they were to come by in Tucson, losing a position such as the one at the Planning and Resource facility was no small matter; many of these people could be forced to relocate to find comparable employment—which was no small matter either.

Ech.

Kate grabbed her purse from the couch; wanting to be anywhere but in this office she opened her door, walked down to the end of the hall where sat Mary, the receptionist, probably soon to be Mary the *ex-receptionist.* Kate mouthed to her that she would be out for about an hour, and then piped up and said, "I am going to LP."

"LP" was the Lunar and Planetary Building, the renovation of which was the only real project going on at this particular time; she frowned—cutting back did make sense if LP was the only real project going on. Kate spent about a fourth of her time at LP—there was always plenty to do … examining the renovation process, checking the floor plans against the work, correlating future work with the planned allocations of resources. Kate was very hands on, a big reason that she had been able to learn so much in a field to which she was so new when she took the job. It had been this effort on her part that allowed her to move up from a clerk in the Planning Department to become one of the senior planning consultants, though now it appeared that it might just be her cute ass that allowed her to keep the job; Guy did not seem the type to do anything for anyone based on merit—there had to be something in it for him, and in this case she was fairly sure what was in it for him was her. Kate was okay with this; she might not be really clear on what it was she wanted out of life, but she was very clear on what she enjoyed—at the moment, a love life or leastwise a little romance seemed an enjoyable prospect indeed … what else to do in a dusty little town such as this.

It was a large job; the LP Building was four stories high, and the renovation involved gutting the top floor to install a large bank of atmospheric computers that were going to analyze data on the atmospheric conditions in the northern hemisphere. A rather pointless endeavor in the years since the project had been envisioned, having lost most of its relevance before the renovation even had made it to the design stage. Climate change and global warming research had become a tad chaotic, to put it mildly, in the aftermath of what had come to be called the Kyoto Farce, formerly the Kyoto Accords. The *accords* became a *farce* with the inexplicable failure of the environment to conform to the models of global warming and climate prediction. The Atmospheric Hotspot Monitoring Project, or AHMP, and the reason for the LP renovation, was supposed to scan for violations of the Kyoto Accords, 2029 Revision, but now … well, apparently AHMP was simply going to observe the planet's atmosphere in the hopes of discerning any sustainable trends regarding temperature changes in the atmosphere that surrounded planet Earth. A far cry from the hype that launched the project so many years ago, amid the fanfare of the coming catastrophe and predications of calamity; AHMP was to be the first in a series of disaster alert centers—a data center to feed teams responding to disasters precipitated by temperature spikes that were to strike the Earth like lightning amidst a monsoon. There turned out to be only minimal warming and it turned out that there were no heat spikes precipitating calamities; today no one wanted to be associated with AHMP, as was the case with most currently active atmospheric calamity research.

No one except Kate, that is.

Regardless of the type of work to be done by AHMP *in* the LP Building, the frontline renovation work of the building had fallen to Kate about three years ago. It was a big-time assignment for a young woman with so little experience in project management, but at the time, because of the checkered association as one of the last of the grand Global Warming Projects, no one wanted to be associated with it. Well, Kate was associated with it, and the renovation was coming off extraordinarily well, landing her and the project on the cover of *Plant Planning Today*, a small but highly acclaimed journal in her field.

Now whenever she felt down she'd enter a world of steel beams and ductwork, of plumbing and wiring closets, all the features of a building under development, which was what she felt about herself, under development; Kate was developing, but into what? That was the question that she supposed weighed on her, sending her spirits spiraling down when she least expected it. It was good to be out here away from her office; every hour she spent someplace else was one less hour she need spend with her peers before the ax fell; she just hoped it would not be too bloody.

Max
(eighteen years ago)

It was a humid day and the line was long, colorful, but long. But they knew that going in. What had promised to be a long wait was resolving into the exhausting activity of taking one's place in the queue. Rides, attractions, events, shows, refreshments, this park had them all; this and more came with the price of admission—which was free. Free and definitely appreciated by the seemingly endless thousands that had poured into the park this June morning, which was slowly becoming a June afternoon. But Max, Karen, and daughter Kate were loving every minute of it. Really, in spite of the crowds, heat, and the wait.

Yes, it would have been better if it were cooler, or if the lines could snake through air-conditioned buildings; fewer people in attendance, that would be better too. But for the man who taught at a community college two hundred and forty days a year and four hundred miles from here, the woman who was his wife and who was dedicated to her nursing job at the hospital, *and* their seven-year-old with pigtails, a summer dress, and the ubiquitous cotton candy stick in hand, this was the next-best thing to heaven—at least for today.

Morning sailed into afternoon, and afternoon coasted into the evening tide. In the park there was even less division; it was families, most with children, all having a good time. Here, there were no ideological conflicts; all parties were in cultural agreement regardless of race or ethnicity; here, style referred to a preponderance of clothing rather than a form of titillation—and gay was an adjective rather than a noun … outside this platonic, some would say sterile world, style meant titillation and gay was a noun. Rightly or not, many of those gathered at the park would describe the world that surrounded the park as decadent.

But such ideological polemics were outside of Max's take on the world; this family-oriented, platonic, *sterile* world was much to his liking. Seven years ago Max rarely gave social values a thought. Kate's addition in his life put *easy* into his mind, and easy, *in his mind,* above all else was predictable; he was to find that prancing about with these twenty thousand other young adults and their children was very predictable.

The Stein family spent the day frolicking, eating, and at evening, as the last light lingered in the sky, exploring a small forested canyon which ran through the western section of the park; it was a very large park. They stayed on into the evening and when the sky darkened there was live entertainment in the centrally located amphitheater. It was a rock band that Max liked when he was younger, though Karen had never heard of them. There were two opening acts which neither Max nor Karen had heard of, and the musical sets were interspersed with speakers and small skits, aerobic acts of strength, a little magic, and an electronic show which was really a parody by a young man who had invented a machine that could do anything except something useful. The showman called it *The Machine That Can Do a Hundred Different Things Some of Which Might Even Be Useful* and promptly demonstrated that nothing useful at all could be done with it; dramatizing the government's propensity to do everything but that which was useful along the way—it was funny and allegorical, though most of the material went over the heads of those present; since many were young, half asleep, or couldn't care less.

The music began in earnest and the refreshments moved from the soda and cotton candy of the amusement park to the beer and wine of the concert venue.

The shows over, the rides closed, the concessions sold out, the Steins left with the thousand others returning the short distance to their cars that took them to their hotels along the water, or homes if they lived nearby. The Steins spent extra for upscale digs, but this being their annual vacation the expense was well worthwhile; ten minutes from the park and other great attractions, walking distance to the beach—in spite of Max's tenacious desire to avoid spending money, it was easily worth it. Tomorrow would be more of the same, and the day after that, and the day after that. Eventually they would return to what they did the other three hundred and fifty or so days of the year, but for now they slept the deep sleep of the exhausted *and* truly contented.

Karen died when Kate was ten. She died after contracting a particularly nasty case of the flu that settled on the planet about thirteen or so years ago. She was one of perhaps two hundred million individuals worldwide whose symptoms included the extreme condition of death. Healthcare workers were especially susceptible to becoming infected; such was the nature of the profession—but they also had the lowest rate of mortality of any infected group, mainly due to their familiarity with the symptoms and the close proximity of medical care. But that didn't save Karen. She died, and Max and Kate became The Family.

Max put all his effort into being a good father to Kate and he met with mixed results; he often thought that getting mixed results was darn good considering all the opportunities for downright failure that came his way. On the positive side, Kate stayed in school while Max kept his job teaching, by then at the local university, which in itself was a bit of a stretch; Max wasn't true university material—universities, historically, and certainly in his time, were bastions of Socialist thought … Max wasn't a Socialist, he wasn't really of any particular political persuasion, but he most definitely was not a Socialist. Max was known for having once remarked that rather than providing financial assistance through the Unwed Teen Parent Scholarship program (or UtePS, as it was called), the aid would be better spent rewarding teenage girls who didn't get pregnant. Fortunately for Max, his stand was so far off the mark, beyond the pale as it were, that no one took him seriously; he was either sick, kidding around, or playing the part of the provocateur. That was fine with Max; he didn't really care what they thought, but he also realized that he probably wouldn't have his contract renewed after the end of the year.

In spite of his fears and misgivings his relationship with Kate, at least at first, went along fairly smoothly; Max fumbled the boyfriend thing rather poorly and ended up backing off from the hard-core protective stance he had taken—the last thing he wanted was for Kate to be setting up dates on the sly because she couldn't trust him not to interfere. But his effort to disengage himself was a failure in ways he hadn't expected and his relationship with Kate took an unexpected and troubling turn.

As soon as she had been accepted, Kate moved out of the house to go to college. Though she chose to attend the local university

21

rather than leave the area, she decided that she would not attend from home. Max saw less of her almost immediately and over time he saw less of everyone, that is, except Daryl, a relatively recent acquaintance of Max's. Daryl was writer, about twenty years Max's senior, who was now out of favor with the government, but for a long time prior, had been a popular political writer and commentator—his fall from grace coinciding with his move to Tucson, though his relocation was a symptom of this disfavor, not the cause.

Max met Daryl during Kate's high school years, and he was a man with whom Max was to develop a lifelong acquaintance, though late in their respective lives this acquaintance might be. The relationship *had* to be one of acquaintances, as neither Max nor Daryl was particularly susceptible to developing friendships; Daryl had but few friends, and Max had, well, none actually. Oh, he had friendly acquaintances among many of his students and a few, very few, among his fellow faculty. Max rightly understood, but misinterpreted the fact that friendship went beyond enjoying the company of another, of caring for another, or helping another out. Max had many of the aforementioned types of relationships on and off during his life; friendship, however, was different, though not necessarily more. The best that Max could figure was that true friendship involved opening one's self up to an ill-defined trust, coupled with a commitment that absence over time would not impinge on this trust, this openness. But that was not what Max was all about; for him, relationships were built on regularly recurring *shallow* events and activities, though not shallow in a negative sense. Over time and distance his acquaintances became strangers; there had been nothing beyond the immediacy of the moment to sustain the relationships.

Daryl became a good and dangerous acquaintance; over time, Max shared things with Daryl, things that he wouldn't tell anyone else, things that he was ofttimes afraid to even think of to himself—things of a highly personal and controversial nature that in the deteriorating tolerant political climate could well get Max and perhaps both of them arrested. But still Max considered Daryl his friend, and Daryl felt likewise.

Within a year of Kate's college graduation, Daryl moved out of town and Max saw less of him as well. Now Max had lost his wife, and his daughter, for all intents and purposes, had disowned him, or so it seemed—and his last good acquaintance had essentially disappeared. With no one close to talk to, this closed person clammed up about everything; Max made himself small, small in his outlook on the world, small in his circle of "friends," and small in the impact he had on the world around him. In the end, Max had been correct, his contract was not renewed at the end of the year; they had grown tired of him and while they didn't see him as a threat per se, it was past time to give Max's position to one of the faithful, one who would shore up the dyke going up around intellectual America. He returned to teach at the community college as much to have a job as for his love of the classroom—and there were no further incidents or problems reported. No problems, that is, except with his daughter; guilty about the attention he was paying to her and the form that attention took. Love was one thing, but what he was doing was entirely something else.

Over time, Kate survived her father's attention, her tedious studies, and her various relationships, doing well for herself in the process; she avoided the culling by the Socialists in the university, many of whom were actually yesterday's Conservatives—it was odd, everything was turned on its head, but one did what one had to in order to survive and in this case survival had meant going along with a burgeoning and communal Socialist development … and she graduated from college with relatively good marks. She took a job locally, which was another thing turned on its head; she hated her father for what he had done to her, but couldn't bear to bring herself to leave him.

So she stayed on in Tucson, rented a small house that he didn't know the address of, and worked during the day and played at night; she played the role of the recently graduated young girl of twenty something, enjoying her freedom to do as she pleased while self-monitoring to make sure she didn't get out of hand. It was a lifestyle she thought would suit her just fine for the indefinite future.

(today)

Max put the pencil down and rubbed the knuckles of his left hand with his right; it wasn't arthritis, the doctor said so, but all the same it could hurt fierce. His head hurt more, though, from fatigue and worry. Could he blame her if she never came home again? How could he do this to her after having done it so many times before, each time promising her, and himself, that it would be the last. He just couldn't help himself.

He couldn't, and that was the full of it; he loved her and couldn't keep himself from expressing his love the way he did. Wasn't that what fathers did? Some, anyway? Besides him?

He would set things right with a letter, he would. It had worked before; after the other times—he would write her and tell her how sorry he was and it would be better now and she would come home and things would be fine. True, avoid him she would, at least at first, refusing to be in the same room with him, such was to be expected, at first. But soon enough she'd let her guard down and they would be together only to have him lose control and then it would start all over again. In the morning she would be gone.

Max was finishing the letter when the phone rang. It was Paul, an acquaintance, a good acquaintance, actually, a student asking him for a drink.

"Were?" " … Yes, I know the place" … "No, I have no one here. If I did I'd either excuse myself from them or not come" … "Yes, even for you" … "OK, a half hour will do it" "Bye."

Paul was insecure. Max's closest acquaintances now were his students; they were a decent enough lot, to be sure, but it was more than that. They didn't challenge him, at least not in the sense where he would either endanger himself in a risky conversation, or risk jeopardizing his own moral fortitude by denying a core belief to avoid a risky conversation. Of course the fact that he felt no need to evaluate any of his life in their presence helped, too. His explanations on any topic were considered complete, if not authoritative. Max knew they were neither, but it was okay; at least he had some way of interacting with other people in a personal way that was not threatening at the same time. Students. But they were a tough nut emotionally, and he was not always able to distance himself from some of the needy ones. But Paul was just Paul, and Max liked Paul, because Paul was easy; insecure but easy.

The lounge Paul had selected was a fifteen-minute walk with a mailbox on the way, so he'd drop the letter in as he walked past. The evening was pleasant though cool, much as he thought it would be. Max turned up his collar a bit and evened out his stride as he headed east on Second Street.

"Can I trouble you for a light?"

A shadow stepped out of the darkness; a man in a waist-length leather coat, a baseball cap riding high on his head, a short-cropped beard hugging his chin and running up to each ear.

"Certainly. Nice evening, huh?"

"Perfect."

Max held the light for the stranger, who studied Max carefully over the flame. The light made his eyes glitter ever so slightly, and Max found himself oddly allured to their sparkle. They seemed friendly yet mocking at the same time; so alluring, in fact, that he never heard and didn't sense a second shadow coming up behind him, nor the blow to the back of his head that sent him reeling to the ground; knees buckling, he crumbled forward, the side of his head whacking the concrete of the sidewalk, the cigarette spinning away from his slack jaw.

The stranger with the glittering eyes threw his cigarette to the ground and crushed it with the toe of his boot.

"Nasty things."

"Hunh," was the only reply that he got from his companion, the brute in the brown shirt who had cold-cocked Max. "You're sure he was the right one?"

In the dark, without the flame, his eyes no longer glittered. "Shut up."

Then the two of them went to work on Max.

Daryl

The mountain makes its own weather; it was true, the mountains did make their own weather, and as of late it was wetter, and warmer. There were many for whom the warm rain was attributable to man's environmental stewardship, or lack thereof, and was a symptom of a process that was killing the entire planet. Daryl couldn't quote the science, but something that man had done, though what exactly was a little vague, had affected the *environment*—the exact definition of which still eluded mankind … even after eons of language development.

Huh?

Daryl couldn't help himself from thinking like this; random wandering thoughts—sometimes even talking like it … Daryl was a writer and he was always writing, be it with pen and paper, in his head, or his voice. For Daryl every moment was grist for his literary mill. His life filled pages dull, complex, vague, and exciting, depending on the chapter his character was in. It was enough to confuse Daryl, who had developed this mysterious way of looking at life and the world.

Anyway, it was a generally, though not necessarily universally, accepted fact that man had done something destructive to the environment and caused the weather to be warmer; or wetter—or was it *warmer and wetter?* It did rain frequently here, but it was not due to man's destruction of the environment, *it was the atmospheric physics of high places.*

That it was warmer was never in doubt; the politics as to the cause is what resulted in so much anxiety and pain. Government mandates on fuel requirements, household energy consumption, the kind of light bulbs that could be used, government-controlled thermostats—heck, even Christmas displays were designed by an unassailable government … a government seeking to use every available tool to control people's lives.

Daryl stood on the ladder, hammer by his side, a good nail in his left hand; his breathing slowed, his vision returned to focus. He would be here for a while, and until he thoroughly thought this through, he was pretty useless for anything else—but he needed to get this picture hung … for the prestige and for the harmony of his little life, he needed to get it hung before Cassandra returned.

Though an odd duck, Daryl lived well, actually, with his wife Cassandra and their two dogs, a matched pair of black and yellow labs. He didn't have an income any longer, but that hardly mattered; writers were not paid per say, they were provided with a stipend from the government, a stipend that was based in part on how politically conforming their work was and in part based on its popularity. Writing a conforming work that made it into limited print would find the author leading one kind of lifestyle; writing the same conforming work and having it find wide distribution would have its author living another lifestyle, the high life, as high as any of the powerful and mighty. While quick to make it to the top, a writer's position was more tenuous than most; a wrong word, a flat scene, a dullard chapter, and he could be bounced down as quick as he had up—up and back, down … and maybe up again or perhaps imprisoned.

But you had to be an active writer to participate in any of this, which Daryl was not. His good fortune, and a small fortune he did have, stemmed from the time when incomes were real, when a writer was paid for the quality of his work, was paid as the books sold. The author wrote, the publisher published, the public bought, and Daryl got two dollars on the head, and he sold tens of thousands, hundreds of thousands of books, over the course of a life. Then, too, there were investments, back when Americans could and did own America, before "America" owned the Americans, and Daryl had had a knack for investing.

In the years leading up to his "disappearance," a disappearance not without good reason, Daryl had been taking his earnings and first buying land, then building a house on that land, in a very secluded spot of southern Arizona, right smack on top of the mountain, outside of a dingy little city called Tucson. Out of the way and out of sight to those who had an interest in finding him and not for anything good, of that he was sure.

In his early years Daryl wrote a series of political essays highly critical of the dangers inherent in the growing accumulation of power by the government; the essays, originally published in various political journals, were eventually compiled into a book—it was hot stuff at the time, and though the government was relatively benign, his criticism centered on what would happen when a reactionary group of individuals took the reins of a centralized government bureaucracy.

The government soon changed hands and a more "active" government came to power; his verbiage became more intense and critical—the intensity of his criticisms matching the aggressive methods that the Social Democrats were using to establish their program and their hold on the reins of power. He went on the literary attack and made even more enemies along the way.

What exactly did that mean, *more enemies?* Was Daryl shot at? No, but he did get a pie thrown in his face at a public speaking engagement. Daryl had his supporters and detractors, and for the most part his detractors limited their criticisms to scathing articles in op-ed pages of Socialist journals; there was very little in the way of personal threats and Daryl never really feared for his safety—a first. But over time, leading Conservative authors, speakers, educators, and politicians began to feel pressures of a less subtle and a more direct nature. They began to be arrested.

Now it was the morning of October twenty-first, many years removed from the days when the youthful firebrand first penned his works raging against the machine. The rays of the early morning sun danced a facet of rainbow colors prolifically across the walls of polished pine and across everything else in the room; his hand, the hammer, the assorted odds and ends of living-room furniture—the faceted rainbow would soon be dancing across the painting as well, provided he could get it hung in its spot. His wife was responsible for the hanging crystal and all the colors of the rainbow dancing across the room … a silly touch, her touch, but he couldn't blame her, much. It was his life they were leading, after all; his glory when he had been a successful writer—now his disgrace with the resulting anonymity and isolation following his fall from grace.

In this small community he was known affectionately as *The Professor;* a gray-haired, well read, and mild-mannered man, the prototypical retired professor—it was erroneous but useful … a retired professor from a college never named. The townsfolk never thought to ask where he had retired from and probably wouldn't have asked if they had thought to; it was a keep to yourself kind of place, which suited Daryl admirably—he had a feeling he wasn't the only one who had a past to hide … and this was a great place to do just that, hide, with the wind, the trees, the cool mountain air and deep canyon shadows. *All* was as he wanted, and no one here had the slightest interest in him beyond that his account was kept current at the local grocery mart and that he kept his walk free of snow for the mail delivery. Daryl had paid cash for the house, under his wife's maiden name, so all was on the up and up; the tax man billed and collected his due without ever realizing that it was flowing in from a man on the government's watch list. Daryl was visible without being known; it was his wife who was invisible—she had stayed in his shadow for so long that she, to the outside world, was no one.

To Daryl she was everything.

She was also out to the town center when a knock came at the front door, startling Daryl and causing him to miscue his hammer stroke, striking his thumb rather than the nail. Cursing silently to himself he climbed down the ladder, threw a frustrated glance at the oil painting of a mountain-high frigid lake at the base of snow-covered peaks, wanting to, but not blaming his wife for his hammer-struck thumb.

Daryl crossed over to the foyer boxing the home's entryway; by habit and caution, he put his eye to the spy hole and studied the young man standing on the other side of the oaken door, the operative word here being *young*. His visitor could not have been more than seventeen or eighteen; a visitor to the Howe home was a rarity in and of itself—visitors under forty were unheard of. He rested his forehead against the door and thought to wait him out, let the young thing leave. A moment passed, then another, then a *long* moment, followed by another knock and then a voice; more surprising still, the voice was using his name.

"Mr. Howe? Mr. Howe? Sorry to disturb you, sir, but he said that I could, Max, that is, he said … " there was a pause and Daryl furrowed his brow. *Max*, Daryl thought quickly, *Max … Max?* "He also said that you probably wouldn't let me in, at least not right away. But he hoped that you wouldn't keep me waiting too long. He did say *that,* that is, about letting me in. I mean about not letting me in and then letting me in."

Daryl wasn't sure what he had just been subjected to, but it seemed to be a variant of the English language; Daryl hadn't seen Max in years, at least six, maybe seven, and even then he hadn't considered Max a close friend, more like an acquaintance. Yet for all that, Max obviously knew Daryl well enough; Daryl was going to open the door, just as Max said he would—make the kid wait and then open the door.

Daryl opened the door.

In the doorway stood the very epitome of young maleness; lanky, short blond hair, a wiry, *empty* grin, blue jeans, and a T-shirt. The boy was tall for his age, or so Daryl thought; he hadn't actually seen a seventeen-year-old male in maybe two or three years—really.

"Why did Max send you to me?"

If the boy was taken aback by the direct question and Daryl's forward manner he hid it well. "He didn't send me, well, not exactly. Do you know him? I mean Max?"

"No, I have never heard of him. That is why I opened the door when you said he *didn't* send you." A blank look of confusion was all Daryl got in reply. "Never mind. What did you say your name was?"

"I didn't, but it is Paul, sir."

"Paul, *Paul*. Okay, Paul, I am going to ask you again and either you are going to give me a straight answer, in your case, maybe just a well-thought-out answer, or I am going to close this door not caring a whit for who sent you. Now, why did Max send you to me?"

"Max-once-told-me-that-if-anything-ever-happened-to-him-and-I-found-out-about-it-I-was-to-find-you-at-this-address.   "That-is-I-was-to-find-you-at-this-address-if-he-was-still-alive-which-I-think-he-is."

This juggernaut of words, fanning out in all directions as if Paul were catching his thoughts one at a time and putting them to words before they flew off on their own, came to an abrupt end, followed by a pause. An anxious look came over his face.

"You *will* help him, won't you?"

Daryl looked the boy level in the eye, no not a boy, he could see it now, probably twenty-two or -three, gay, that was for certain. Somehow it contributed to his younger look; *slightly effeminate?* Daryl didn't know why, but for some reason gay men always looked younger than they were. Maybe they were more content with life.

"Well, you do know Max, I'll give you credit for that much, at least. But you probably don't know why he sent you to me, right?"

He took Paul's lack of response as an affirmative. "To tell you the truth, I'm not sure either. Or maybe I am. Max once told me that he didn't trust any of the faculty members, not even a little bit; maybe that was his way of saying he trusted me. It still might not do him a whit of good, though. Maybe you ought to tell me what happened to Max."

"I don't know, at least not for sure. I know he's been having trouble with his daughter, and we met that night."

"You were with him?"

"Actually, no." Daryl wanted to roll his eyes but forced himself to keep a straight face. "We were going to meet, but he didn't show up, and I went to his home and he wasn't there."

"Hmmm."

Daryl turned away, rubbed his chin, and *hmmm*'d some more, stroking his chin. He turned toward the youth. "So, how does this mean that Max is in trouble?"

"He hasn't returned my calls since yesterday."

"It's Sunday, you know. So he didn't call you over the weekend, what of it."

He motioned the young man into the house, nodding him over toward a chair near the coffee table, indicating that he was to sit.

"It's late morning. I can offer you coffee, tea, liquor, though if you take the alcohol I shan't be indulging with you. Food: I have some cheese, bread, other refrigerated stuff. Sit."

Paul sat, not asking for anything, nor did he think Daryl expected him to.

"You don't understand, he would call me, he always returns my calls, and promptly too."

Daryl gave the lad a quick searching look. Could Max have a thing for him? No, not Max, the straight-laced bastard, besides he had loved his wife too much and now his daughter. But it was only his wife's *memory* now and … Daryl shook his head. He must be getting old to ponder out such idiosyncrasies to the very end. Or perhaps he was just being Daryl, who pondered out everything till the very end, idiosyncrasies or not.

"He would have called you?"

"Yes."

"You're sure?"

"Yes."

"Positive?"

"*Yes.*" Now Paul pinned Daryl with an irritated look.

"Okay, *okay*. He needs help, on that we agree, but am I the one to see that he gets it?" Daryl drummed his fingers on the tabletop. *Missing people*, what was he to do? *He* who was of the nonexistent in the first place. It wasn't as if he could go down to the local police and fill out a missing person report. In fact, without knowing where Max was, how could he be of help?

"Hmmm."

"Does that mean you'll help?"

"Does *hmmm* sound like *how can I help you?* No? I didn't think so. *Hmmm* means … well, it means *maybe*. But this particular maybe is a yes, so I guess, yes, I am going to help. Now, *who exactly are you again?*"

Daryl decided that Paul would spend the night, and sent him off on a tour of the property and the surrounding meadows and groves, with instructions to end his outing at the bottom of the hill at the grocery mart where he was to charge a six-pack of beer to Richards, Cassandra's maiden name. Paul didn't question him on this, and Daryl didn't offer an explanation—Daryl sensed that it was more a matter of it being over Paul's head than respect for Daryl's privacy … though certainly not dumb, Paul seemed to be a bit unaware of what went on around him. Nice kid, though.

They dined on burgers, Daryl's favorite food to make, juicy with lots of onion and tomato, on a soft bun. They ate in silence on the south porch, in the last of the sunlight, enjoying a cooling breeze and the quiet of the forest broken only by the air pushing through the pine nettles; it was a clean sound, a cleansing sound. After a while Paul, it seemed with some effort, began an attempt at a conversation. Daryl had been intentionally providing the silence to see what Paul did with it and he was mildly amused and a tad impressed when Paul picked up the gauntlet.

"I know you, or heard of you, or I mean heard that you wrote things, books."

He looked expectantly at Daryl, who continued eating, making no attempt to help the young man along, flustering the already skittish and indecisive lad. He instead took another sip of beer and bite of beef burger and hid a wan smile.

"Max, he had some on his shelves. We read a couple in class a couple of times. You are daring, Mr. Howe."

Daryl inclined his head and put his burger down on his plate, the first time he had done so since he had started eating.

"Daring, huh, that is an interesting choice … hmmm, why do you say daring?"

"What you write, some of the things you say. Didn't people go to prison for that?"

"If they can find us, yes. But that doesn't mean that I'm brave; I wrote when people did not go to prison for their ideas, for penning their thoughts to paper. Of course that does not make me a coward, just as it does not necessarily make me brave. But daring … "

He glanced up at the tops of the pines surrounding the house as he stroked his beard with his thumb and forefinger. "Yes, I suppose you could call it daring. One doesn't need to be brave to be daring, just oblivious to danger. Anyway, what is it you do, Paul?"

"I study, a student, at the university."

"Take classes from Max?"

"Max doesn't teach at the university."

Daryl gave the lad a long look from beneath his bushy eyebrows. The boy had to be dysfunctional; an overused term, for sure, but what else could be used to describe him, since he didn't function right, as it were.

"Boy," he said with a slight irritation he was trying to hide, "boy, that doesn't answer the question."

"I took classes from Max when he did teach at the university. He taught history, you know, and philosophy too. He would read, on occasion, from the books you wrote. The books you wrote that he owned, that is. Max said it wasn't possible to get your books anymore."

No, thought Daryl, *he supposed not.* He had lived away from reality so long that he didn't even know what it was any longer, what was real. Seven years. He had really done Max a disservice, Daryl had. He left him, left a man who had lost his wife and was in the process of losing his daughter; he left him with little fanfare and less explanation. He turned his back on Max, but Max had not returned the favor. Max had taken the trouble to track Daryl down, he took a big risk by using his, Daryl's, books in class, and when the chips were down he placed his hope in Daryl's sense of, of what? Morality, humanity? *I am a shit,* thought Daryl, and now it was seven years later, and seven years too late to be the friend to Max that he should have been, the friend that Max so obviously needed.

"Ahmm,"—Daryl cleared his throat—"he read from my books, eh? Well, what do you know about that. No, don't tell me, *that* was not an invitation for an opinion on your part, but tell me this, which ones did he read?"

"Many, sir, he read from *The Politics of the Social Democrat's Policies, Fallacies of the Left on the Right,* and *To Kill a Mockingbird, Revisited.*"

Daryl nodded, yes, that would be Max, obviously trying to thread together a political point based on the resources at hand; but of all people to draw upon it had to be me, thought Daryl. But given Max's predilection to utilitarian existentialism, how could it be otherwise. In his mind's eye he could see where Max was going with this; damn him too, and damn his moral tenaciousness—he was abusing Daryl's work.

But Max has been arrested, or so it seemed, and this could not be a good thing; misfortune should not be the karma equivalence to creative usurping, and Max was likely in real trouble, and he was counting on Daryl to do something, anything—but that anything good could come of this was as unlikely a scenario as one could imagine … the arrested outcast, being saved by the man who didn't exist, fetched in by the gay liberal arts student.

"Max's point, my dear fellow?"

"Point?"

"Look, you sat in his classes. He discussed things. At a certain point he read some of my works, and probably works by others … the point he was trying to make. What was it?"

Paul gave him a quizzical look.

"Okay, you're in class, you sit down. Max starts a lecture, the topic … "—Daryl gestured openhanded to Paul.

"Freedom of choice," Paul piped in.

"Okay, freedom of choice. Of choice in what?"

"Ethics."

"Ethics what? To choose to be ethical?"

"No, not really, not that. Let's see. Anyone can be ethical in a world that will allow for ethical behavior. Yes, that's it. Not to be ethical, but to choose, to intentionally choose."

"Intentionally choose? As the opposite of not intentionally choosing? Boy, what you say doesn't make sense. Maybe I was wrong. Maybe you won't be spending the night."

Paul looked at him with a silly grin until he realized from Daryl's glare that he just might be serious and, as such, got serious himself.

"You know, a man can choose to be ethical, or not, if such a choice is allowed, if other people are also choosing. But in a society where there is no ethical behavior, such as in a fascist society, maybe there is no choice, no one is being ethical, everyone is participating in the atrocities. What Max was getting at is the freedom of choice to see beyond what is beyond acceptable behavior. And how one does this. That is what Max meant. But it is more than that."

Paul's voice had begun to ring with the timbre of one who understands what one is talking about even if they don't realize it.

"The pain around him should be enough to cause him to choose to go against this society, should be enough to give himself the freedom to choose to be different in a world where no difference exists."

"And likewise," added Daryl, "give him the freedom to choose to go against a government when he sees the pain that the State's policies place on his fellow man."

That is what Max tied together, the precept underlying all Daryl's anti-government rants; *one had to first choose to see* and then act—Daryl had always gone directly to the "act." There was a quick stiffening of Paul's back and he gave Daryl a startled glance.

"You took his class too?"

Daryl was slow to respond, and when he did so, he felt that he was choosing his words carefully, though in the end what he said was a rather mundane, "No, but you can take what I wrote and make a class like that."

Which is just what Max, bless his God-fearing heart, had done.

Paul looked silently at Daryl, who was no longer seeing the young man; his thoughts were on Max, who apparently had moved beyond the hack instructor Daryl always took him to be. The reality of why Paul was here, of what had befallen his old friend and apparently star pupil, was taking hold of him; what was going on here? Was all this payback for his absence over the past seven years? One small turn in the big wheel of karma?

Max

Canyons; dull granite gray and the harsh black of charcoal—pit colors, a mosaic of canyons … a network of darkness spread across the floor.

A criss and a cross; grouted tiles on a cold, stained floor.

Max lay on the tiled floor, his breathing labored; his hair was dirty, his clothes torn and damp, his face swollen—one eye sealed shut with dried blood.

This was the life he had been living for the last two weeks, and yesterday had been the worst; where his left eye tooth had been, there was now an empty socket of inflamed, tender, hot flesh—the cold of the tile floor seemed ease the pain, but he worried greatly that the dirt might go to infection in an open wound. The sour tang of blood filled his mouth and blood trickling from his nose pooled on the floor; his toes wiggled and his knees flexed, or at least he sensed they would. He wanted to roll onto his back, but he dared not—maybe he wasn't alone, most likely he was being watched. If they were going to beat him awake they would have done so by now; of course that didn't mean that they wouldn't beat him if they knew he was awake. Best if he lay still; even relieve himself in his pants—not the first time. A warm sickening feeling spread beneath him but he kept himself still just the same; he would smell bad till they hosed him down—even the guards didn't like the smell of urine, though it seemed such a part of their lives.

Max dozed again, maybe; without a clock he was never sure if he had just briefly closed his eyes or had slept half the day away. The first thing he used to do upon wakening was to look at the clock and see how long he had slept; sleep didn't seem complete without a context to put it in—how long had he slept? Should he feel rested? How long could he go without sleeping again? It was strange that the world of dreams, where time matters not, was so bounded by time.

Kate wouldn't have anyone looking out for her now, at least no one that she could trust like her father, which was why he had to get out, and soon. To be sure, she was a grown woman, knowledgeable in worldly affairs, but she was still a child; he knew that someday she wouldn't be, only that day hadn't come yet. It would be hard to get out of this place, especially feeling like he did, but he needed to get out. *Kate needed him*, regardless of what he had done in the past.

Everything was turned around here and stealth meant pain; a brutish awakening meant a meal, or a hosing down, or perhaps a visit to the infirmary—a rude awakening held no surprises … but stealth meant pain. They entered in quiet for one reason and one reason only, and that was to beat a sleeping prisoner to consciousness; few things are as terrifying as waking to a beating, to be hauled from the relative safety of sleep, to all of the worst that exists outside of the human being—*sleep deprivation* was an archaic form of torture, mistakenly practiced since the dawn of oppression … beat a man conscious a couple of times and he will give up sleeping of his own accord, howling in pain at its replacement.

But Max was awake, and as such he steeled himself to the blows that would most certainly rain down on him, but not overtly; showing them that you could play the game would encourage them to ever greater brutality and have them change the rules—in this place, things always went from bad to worse.

Then his side exploded in a blinding flash of pain as the toe of the guard came crashing into his ribs. Max grunted and coughed, wheezed and tried to catch his breath without breathing; breaking a rib would do that to a person.

"You snot-sucking bastard!"

Again with the toe of the boot; Max thought he might lose consciousness while pretending to sleep. A rubber truncheon came slapping across his buttocks, causing Max to jerk up off the floor, and flop like a lifeless rag doll.

"You slimy sack of shit, you've soiled yourself, from the smell of it."

The world seemed to be spinning and then it was as a blast of water caught him in the neck, wrenching him around on the slick floor and slamming him into the far wall, which was not as far as he thought; the ice-cold torrent subsided his pain a bit and with the air flailing in and out of his lungs he knew at least his ribs had not been broken.

"I … I …. " But he could not speak and in fact didn't know what to say even if he could have formed speech.

"You what?"

The water stopped as quick as it had begun, and Max risked his first glance around the room. Two, which was two too many. One holding a pressurized hose as thick as a man's forearm, the other holding a length of rubber pipe in his right hand and slapping it into his left palm; both uniformed in the green of the security forces, a style somewhere between military attire and that unceremonious cut of clothes known as business casual. The man leading the charge was lean and mean, with short-cropped, stiff blond hair. The one with the hose had the stupid look that comes from letting brutality do one's thinking; short, stout, with a thick mass of short black hair and an uneven beard from a week's growth. Both were younger than Max, but that was not unusual; it was the younger ones who tended to power in this new climate of cultural diversity.

Diverse though they might be, brave they were perhaps not; something of Max's previous thoughts of fight and flight on his face betrayed him.

"Don't even think about it," said the tall, thin one as he slapped the rubber pipe down into his left palm. "I'd kill you as soon as spit at you. Besides, where would you go? You're locked tight in this wing even if you could pass that door."

But his cruel face betrayed some doubt. Max straightened his back some, *and against all* survival instincts looked his goaler right in the eye, this *goaler* who had beat him incessantly for days, ridiculed him with every word, but had yet to ask a single question. Max could sense the man calculating in his own crude way; evidently the odds did not come up in Max's favor—he saw his goaler take a step back while at the same time reach down and press a small red button on a black device attached to his belt. Max stood up, soaking wet under the glare of the lights in the tiled room that was his cell; Max knew, weak and as beaten as he was, that he had just showed them that he could play a counter move in the game—for good or for ill, soon enough the rules would change. Standing there soaking wet, under the glare of the lights in the tiled room that was his cell, Max waited as the pieces on the board were being reset; unlikely as it may be, this round somehow went to the bruised and battered Max Stein.

Kate, I'm coming for you.

"One count of sexual assault on a minor; one count of statutory rape." The voice firm, authoritative, and new. The right hand tossed the indictment onto a pile to the left. "These charges can have you detained for the rest of your pitiful life."

"The charges are false."

"Oh really? We have a signed affidavit from the victim."

Max didn't know what to say about that, he knew what this man said was true, he had already seen the document, it had been shoved under his face at the time of his arrest; his formal arrest, not the sucker-punch-beat-up he had received the night he had been *detained.*

"It, ah, was signed under duress. She would never have signed such a statement willingly."

"No?"

"No."

"Well, it says right here … well, why not." The right hand had picked up the indictment from the left pile and pass it into Max's hands. "Go ahead, read it, there, at the bottom, where it says *'and of my own free will.'* That is your daughter's signature, is it not?"

Max had to admit it was. He was still wet from the hosing he had so recently received, and he still smelled of urine. His left eye was swollen from a previous beating, but he could read just the same. Scanning the affidavit he saw the term "intercourse" mentioned several times, and oral sex, skirt, and trousers … it read like a short pornographic encounter, of which the most disturbing part was that he and his daughter were the main characters.

Max looked furtively around the room.

"We never did this."

"Then why … "—he took the indictment, putting it back on the pile of papers to his left—"then why does she state that you did?"

Why did she? That was the question, why had she betrayed him like that? Had he hurt her that much? Honest to god it was never the plan. But why did she betray him; that was the question he avoided facing in his cell during the cold, dark hours alone and during the innumerable beatings he had received in the company of the first jailer and his squat guard. Fear, disbelief, denial; many things he could attribute to avoiding the question. But not here, not in this room; not with this thin, intelligent, mean face sitting across from him.

"I never did these things." It was as much a denial to the interrogator as it was to himself, *to Kate;* then, hoarser, "What is it you really want of me."

39

"There is nothing *'else'* that we want of you, it is all right here, everything I need is right here." He tapped the document with his left forefinger, left hand. "Everything I need to send you away."

"Without a trial?"

That brought a snicker of mirth from the prosecutor.

"You think yourself special? A trial by a jury of your peers? Yes, I know, the Fourth Amendment, or some such nonsense, pertains only in cases where there is an element of doubt as to the guilt or innocence of the victim. In your case … why would a daughter accuse her father if the truth weren't found to be in the accusation?"

Why would she indeed? But instead he kept silent. How far the greatest legal system the world had ever seen had strayed from its original intent; now it was no more than a shabby mirror of the Socialist dictatorships that rose and ebbed across Europe, Asia, and Africa. America had been one of the last democracies the world had left to show, but as the State grew in power, so correspondingly did freedom shrink and with it the due process that at one time had been the envy of every free man on the planet.

"Have you anything you would like to add to the record of these proceedings? Depending on what it is, I will either add it to your file or not."

The prosecutor eyed him critically, waiting … waiting … waiting for what? For Max to throw himself at his feet and declare his innocence? For the protestation of the error of his ways? It was clear that he was about to lose his freedom, perhaps his life, based on a lie, on the statements, seemingly, of his daughter, statements about things that never transpired.

That he should lash out at someone, something, was clear, but what? This prosecutor before him? That would accomplish what? They would kill him, of that he had little doubt. Shout, swear, threaten? In this soundproof room, in the midst of this concrete and steel structure, who would hear him? Such a dilemma had faced all who in this room were to have their lives destroyed on trumped-up charges. *Who* to appeal to and, in the end, who would know that such an appeal had been made?

Without an answer forthcoming from Max the interrogator lowered his gaze, directing it to the paper in front of him; he began scratching at the fields with a pen—filling in the blanks. The silence was disconcerting; the courses of these two men drifting apart, their ports of destination moving away as would two spots on an inflating balloon.

"Sign."

Unceremoniously he pushed the paper across the desk to Max; slowly, with great reluctance, Max picked up the paper which seemed to weigh pounds, tons even, and began to read it to himself, only half paying attention; his mind drifting back to that afternoon in San Diego when his wife Karen was alive and Kate was a little girl—so much had been lost, so much never to be regained. Did it really matter where he went from here?

He signed.

"You will accompany the guard to the platform, you are done here."

"Platform? What platform?" asked Max agitatedly, his efforts at contesting the indictment for the moment lost in the transition.

The guard laid a meaty paw on Max's shoulder, who slung it off with a shake.

"What—" he managed to get out before a palm strike between his shoulders sent him reeling forward and gasping for air as he hit the interrogator's desk chest high, losing his wind. The guard again grabbed him by the shoulder, rougher this time, turning him to meet a fist head high and crumpling him into a pile on the floor while the prosecutor casually shuffled his papers back into order.

"Take him."

Max awoke lying face down again, but this time he was not on a cold tile floor and he wasn't alone; he was on the mid-tier of a three-story bunk and there were many men seated around him. The space was small and had the stink of closely confined bodies. It was warm and it was moving; the room was moving—he was in a boxcar on a train. He was awake and in pain and while not at all inclined he moved a little; his senses were sending out feelers—unsure what data they would collect.

"The bitch rises."

"Bet she wonders what's on the menu at the whistle-stop," toned in a second voice.

Then it all deteriorated into ribald jesting and obscenities. Max easily blocked out the tremulous din.

Oh Kate, where are you? What will become of my baby in a world that produced this.

He was only now realizing just how dangerous and mean the world could be, a world which Kate may well find herself trapped in at any time. Max opened his good eye; the other, swollen and rebloodied, hopefully would open soon of its own accord. He could see, and hear, and think, and that was something; he was no longer in the dark—answering men like this in the dark could be a mistake … indeed, it could be deadly. Bad humor in such close and evil confines could turn to murder in a breath.

He was in one of three small compartments, walled with wood on three sides; metal bars opened on the fourth, facing a narrow hallway. There was a small barred window across the hall and from the flashes of shadow and brightly reflected white, Max assumed that they were passing through a snow-covered forest of some sort; it was too damn quiet outside the carriage for city buildings to be casting the long shadows into the compartment. He was in a cell on wheels.

"Eh, what you in for," asked a thin man, short of stature, in a ragged peacoat and pants, who was sitting next to him on the edge of the bunk. He offered Max a cigarette, which he accepted, grinning ever so slightly, split lip and all; it was the first decent, human gesture anyone had made over the last several days—several days which at the moment seemed like the only life he had ever known. A smoke would be good; besides, he needed to think for a minute; to answer that he was incarcerated as a child molester would not do—so he decided to tell him the truth. "I, I … I'm not sure."

"Harrumph." And a *smile*. "Join the group. Half of us don't know themselves, or if they do they're not saying, and the other half can't believe they will actually be spending the rest of their miserable lives in this stinking place. *They* usually just answer the question with a blank stare. Go on, it don't bite."

His scarred hand held out a match for Max to take a light. Max leaned forward and in a moment a thin trail of smoke and a cough were leaving his messed-up lips.

"Not much of a smoker, eh?"

Max waved him off for a brief moment. "No, but it feels good."

"Right."

They sat and smoked in silence, which was interrupted by the entrance of a couple of guards into their compartment; lunch.

Lunch was served from a pail, the inmates passing metal bowls through the grating to be filled with a barley type soup with some meat in it. Max realized that this was the first hot meal that he had in almost two weeks; one can get by, get used to, even, the lowliest of rations so long as there is enough variety and a bit of nutrients in them—a little bread, some cheap vegetables, and spoiled fruit had sustained him through the beatings and the seemingly endless loneliness.

Except for the initial taunts, a quietness had taken hold and the eleven men in the way-too-small cell sat and ate for the most part. They didn't seem bad men, at least not crazy bad; though he could well imagine it otherwise—there would be little to shield a man in this cell of a boxcar from the wrath of truly hardened criminals if it came down to it.

Following lunch, the thin man sidled up to Max, again offering another smoke which Max waved off. The man shrugged and took one for himself.

"Know where we're bound, old man?" he asked softly.

The use of the familiar took Max for a start, though in truth he *was* old, leastwise older than these others; most looked in their thirties, a couple maybe a bit older. A pair of his co-travelers took a quick interest in the start of the conversation but soon went back to staring at the ceiling or picking at their nails, or some such thing.

Instinctively, Max lowered his gaze. "No. But you do?"

"Yes, a lumber camp, just outside of Flagstaff. You taken in Phoenix?"

"Tucson."

"Hmph. Just as well. Cells is more crowded in Phoenix. Not everyone lives to get sentenced, if you take my meaning."

"Ah, yes … I do." Max frowned. This was truly a shitty world.

"America, where are you now, don't you care about your sons and daughters …"

It was a line from a song his parents had listened to when he was a child; as with most snippets, he couldn't remember the name of the group who did it, but these old, odd snippets had a way of surfacing during the most appropriate times and circumstances.

"Got a family," asked the man, though it was more of a statement than a question.

"Yes, how'd you know?"

"You got that look about you, that's all. Most come in, many is scared, many regretting their loss of women, wine, and money, but only the family ones have the *'worried look,'* as I call it."

"And I have it, the worried look?"

"Shit yeah, you got it, and not just because you're thinking they be needing you. Something else has you too, I can tell. Something ain't sitting right when you was taken."

"No …" Max answered slowly, a bold conversation bordering on the risky for sure.

"No, no, I don't want you to tell me, that'll only make it worse. You see, then you'll be wondering if I'm a gonna betray you and whatnot."

"I'll take that smoke now, if you're still offering."

"Always." He reached into his shirt pocket and pulled out a pack that had but few of the twenty remaining; they were of the cheap government issue, which is basically all that had been seen outside the coastal cities for more than a year now. Max let a light stream of smoke out, this time no cough.

"You know you'll die."

"Huh?" It was almost as if the man had commented on Max's shoes.

"I said you'll die. You've not the back for logging, I can see that. Not that you're not strong, no, I am sure you are, but you haven't the back for it. Back needs to be supple to swing an ax all day. Strong, muscular backs, they take too much fuel. Strong, muscular backs strike hard, but that cuts both ways." He grinned. "Yours will break, or be broken. I've seen it before, yes'm, I have."

Max rolled the cigarette between his thumb and forefinger; he doubted not for a second that this fella had seen others die, mayhap he had taken a few lives himself. Max didn't know what to think about that. Over the years the world had gone from a place he had been comfortable in, that he knew well, to a world ill at ease with itself and one in which he found himself in jeopardy.

Fifteen years ago he had a job and made a living; his familiarity with death was a teenager's memory of his fallen grandfather, an open-casket funeral, and of course his wife, always his poor dead and lost wife. He didn't think of her much, though not for lack of love for he loved her well and still did; it was that thinking, reminiscing , just wasn't Max. His relationship to her death was like that of a tree that loses a limb; forever damaged, it goes on and becomes the best tree it can, growing tall, reaching for the sun, providing a home for the animals in the forest. Max hadn't killed anyone, indeed he'd never even seen another killed in anger. But what was once a distant concept now hovered around the core of his being; if a career criminal with blood on his hands told Max that he was likely to die, well, he believed him. He tapped the ash from the end of his cigarette.

"I don't want to die."

"No, of course you don't, n'er met one who did, though there was that aunt of mine who prayed constantly for the day when she could leave her body and travel to who knows where, though it t'waint here. Going to heaven, she was certain of that. But I really don't ramble, really I don't, so I guess I'll be stopping before you start thinking that I do."

Morbid, thought Max, *locked up with a crazy criminal, to spend his last days.*

"But I like you. I like the way you haven't a clue why you are here w' the rest of us sorry lot. If people don't know why they are locked up, I mean truly don't know, then that means they didn't do it, right? What's more a shame than a man dying for that which he don't even know what he's dying for." He fixed Max with an evil grin. "It'd be easy for me to fix it so that you don't die." The eyes above the evil grin twinkled, or so it appeared; in the bad light it was hard to know for certain what was twinkle or what was crazy. Crazy or no, Max wasn't going to let this opportunity slip; he gave this man the look his wife said earned him more money and love than any man of his birth had a right to, a slight sideways glance with an easygoing smirk.

"I'm listening."

"Listening, ha! You should be speaking highly of me, or at least thanking, that is."

Max ignored this last jibe. He only had the stomach for so much bantering, especially as shitty as he felt and with his life at stake.

"How would you do it?" he asked cautiously, with equal parts hope and disbelief; in order to go on living he had to believe that salvation was ahead for him, he just hadn't expected it from this quarter—yet there was no sense that this man's claim would amount to anything.

"By keeping you from the hard site, the hard place."

This got Max's attention. Yes, that would work, unlike magic escapes or invisibility potions, this had a down-to-earth sound, *feel,* to it; it was simple enough, and it wouldn't mean struggling day to day just to live, leastwise not on a hill full of trees—out there he could die and his grave might not ever be found. His sideways look became a steady gaze. Max let the silence work for him.

"You know, I grease this asshole's hand and that's it, and in the end you'd be sitting comfortably while some other slug takes your place and dies. I help you and not one less person dies, just different people, that's all."

Hmmm. That brought Max up short for a moment. He hadn't really thought of it that way, though he supposed he should have; just what was the cost of survival?

"How?"

"Oh, yes, you would want to be knowing that too. Well, I am not going to tell you, but it will be soon, mark my words. You keep an eye on me and you will see it when it happens. Otherwise you're too stupid to try and save."

"And you?" Max wasn't sure that he really was concerned with his conspirator's well-being, but something inside made him ask.

"Me what?"

"Do you keep yourself, ah, *greased?*"

"Well, that is an interesting question. Sometimes I do and sometimes I don't. See, I don't mind the logging, 'as its advantages, it does. The big dicks, they don't like to step outside much, 'specially when it gets cold. So being out there actually be good for my health in a way, much harder to get into trouble, much harder to run afoul of the camp rules, those known and those unknown. Plus I like the air, it don't stink,"—that claim, from a chain-smoker in rags, brought a smile to Max's lips—"and I knows how to look like I'm working hard when I'm not. Then for a spell, I'll get myself inside, get myself good.

"Don't pay well for a man to be inside all the time, though. It attracts attention and makes a lot of people wonder what it is that fella has that's so valuable that they keep him close. Man can get killed for that, or at least develop enemies and the like."

"Yeah, and how about me? You're talking about me sitting inside all the time."

The thin, edgy man looked at Max for a long moment and for a moment Max didn't think that he was going to answer, but then he did, soft enough, ratcheting the level of their conversation down a notch to avoid listening ears.

"Well, I said I'd save you, not baby-sit you. Once you're inside, you're going to have to do some of the work yerself." He paused, then said, "But there is more. You got that intelligent look about you, you look like a man who could *figure out* how to stay inside. Mind you, it might not help much, but at least they won't be thinking that you're giving handouts to the bosses. That happens and then other people want some too, even if you don't have to give what it is they're thinking you're giving. And if you can't pay …. "—he made a slicing gesture across his throat with his finger.

Max nodded. "Okay, I got you. I'm smart and have nothing to give to no one."

"Right. Might not help with some of the lot. There's some that don't like peoples smarter than they are, but at least you wouldn't draw the attention of the greedy type. Some o' *that* kind will kill ya for a cigarette if they thought they could get it clear."

Sheesh, thought Max, not for the first time, *and this is twenty-first-century America.*

The train rattled on and the shadows flew by the barred window, afternoon moved to evening, and soon it was night. Max stretched out on one of the several tiered bunks that slept two and sometimes three. There were two more compartments like his in the boxcar, twelve to a compartment; his convict buddy said there were probably sixty boxcars like this one hooked to the train. Nearly two thousand roughed-up, worked-over men heading to slavery and some to death. It seemed that the north would swallow them whole, making way for the next caravan, and the next, and the one after that. Somehow Max felt that once one had made this trip, they'd make it again and again if they ever made it out alive.

Jack

It was a short step up to the covered porch fronting the width of the old adobe house. Since it was set back from the street sixty feet or so and nestled between two businesses—with no storefront windows or signs—Paul couldn't even begin to guess the nature of the business that was transacted on either side of this old house.

Jack was older than Paul by fifteen years; small of stature, shorter than Paul, but a stocky, solid man—sporting jeans, a black T-shirt, and a narrow-brimmed leather hat, he lifted the large brass knocker on the front door. It was shaped like a saguaro, of course, and fell with a solid thud against the wooden door. The door opened and before them stood a woman, shorter than Jack, her long hair black running to silver—thin of face and a slender build. She smiled at Paul but it was Jack that she addressed in a feisty voice, with her hands on her hips.

"I could say good to see you again, and I will, so good to see you, but perhaps I don't really mean it. Perhaps I am just honoring the formalities you can be such a stickler for. You had best know that things have not improved since you were here last, so it won't come as a surprise when I tell you I know that you are either bringing trouble with you or likely to find it here, either way, one or the other."

"Yes, I know *that*, Marie, but *is* that any way to greet an old friend? Besides, it couldn't be helped, my coming by, that is; you know I need to see you three or four times a year."

"Need or want?" interrupted Marie. "Bah, no matter, for you it is probably a bit of both, no doubt. Staying the night? At the apartment? You know Ted's been using it lately?"

"Yes. I sent him a letter and an e-mail, so I am hoping that one or the other got through and that he is expecting me."

"I don't think Ted will be hanging around if you're coming. You might be on the same side of the aisle, but that's about it. He is not taken by you."

"Yes, and I know that. He will be gone." Jared frowned. "He hasn't a girlfriend, has he? That could make a difference in what he decides to do, or goes, you know."

"That, I can't say, as I haven't seen Ted since the last time you were here. Thing is, last time you were here alone."

She stepped back from the doorway into a clean but sparsely furnished room, though not having invited her guests in yet.

"I know why you come to town, so I don't need to hear that, but I do need to hear what you have come to see *me* about and what it is you have here with you."

"Mean *who*," said Paul with a slight frown. Jack was right, she was an *odd* bird, that he could sense already.

"Yes, sorry. Paul, Marie. Marie, Paul. Paul is a student, helping me out. He was referred by Daryl, so don't go asking about things you don't need to know, anyway."

Paul gave Jack a sideways glance, wondering if the man always took on the idiom of whomever he was talking to; he should keep an eye out on that one. Traits like that, well, they could mean a lot, understanding them, that is. Or they could mean absolutely nothing.

"Okay, but why are you here? And you know very well that if I didn't ask about things that *'I don't need to know about'* I'd be a lot less use to you."

Jack nodded in deference to the reprimand.

"Well, it's an odd one. ... Let me begin with that. A fella by the name of Max Stein has vanished and his disappearance seems political; it looks a lot like a 1C, Child Molestation." A quick glance to Paul was a hint to Marie as to the source of the information. "Apparently he was arrested, taken at night, his place tossed, the heinous charges, no one in the know, as to his fate. Odd part is that this particular fella has never come up on our radar, which makes the whole thing kind of fuzzy like. Anyway, it's my job to keep up on intrigue and odditics, and this one qualifies, certainly. At least it is too much of a mystery to pass up."

"A mystery, yes, and dangerous too."

"You think?"

"I think that everything is dangerous these days, particularly if it involves you. I think that things have gone past dangerous when outspoken people disappear, and I think it well beyond dangerous when folks see the natural order of things as rebelling against that which you reb—."

"What, better to let it stand?" interrupted Max.

"No, not stand. Evil should never be left to stand. But you are playing a role with a losing hand, with cards specifically selected for you, and you're in a hole so deep, and you are so busy feeling righteous about being in that hole *and* digging yourself out that you don't see beyond the little patch of earth you are hammering against. It matters not how you play the game, and it matters not whether you win or lose, for you can never win. What would victory look like to you, have you ever wondered this? You will march from Tucson and take the nation by storm? Replace the ruling party in Washington?

"How has it that oppression and rebellion against that oppression have become the natural order of things? No, don't answer; I am not looking for an answer, especially from you, to a question I am intimately familiar with."

"Well, if I'm in the hole, then so are you."

"Ay, you might be right on that account, Jack."

Her look softened, and Paul felt as if he were watching a woman who could mold the environment around her, as if the world's difficulties of the last twenty years or so had been but incidental blips on the road of life. As if on a turn of her phrase they had all been shuttled to a simpler place in a simpler time.

"Why don't you and Paul here come on in and I'll fetch us some cold lemonade. October though it is, it is also too hot to be standing out on the porch bantering about the wisdom of acting, as we are compelled to do."

Jack gave her a perfunctory nod; holding the screen door open he followed Paul directly into the main sitting room, no foyer or entryway here. A bedroom was off to the right, which could be seen through a half-opened door, and the kitchen was partially hidden behind a wall to the back. Overall, small but tidy, airy and relaxing. The furniture was worn but not threadbare, overstuffed but not tacky. The place was comfortable and smelled like … home.

"Ahm … so, Marie … what say you about this fella I am looking for?"

"Looking for? I thought you were after information, not the actual flesh, and besides, you know damn well where to look. North, where they send all the 1Cs."

Jack frowned and toyed with his glass, he sank low in the chair, his knees just shy of eye level … this wasn't really getting him far. He looked over at Paul; another problem—to be dealt with later. Jack shook his head, which Marie took as frustration with her answer.

"Jack, I will find out what I can about your man, but if you want to talk to him, you're on your own. You have no idea why he was arrested?" She glanced at Paul, who gave a slight shake of his head. "Did you ever consider that perhaps he did just what he is accused of? 1C charges are only a cover to get politicos shipped off all the quicker. There are those who have done the heinous acts that 1Cs are accused of; they were arresting perverts long before they began arresting people for political beliefs."

Despite her levelheadedness, Marie couldn't help but live in denial, wanting things to be bright, happy, and on the up and up. She was an old woman who took everything to heart; things were bad and bad needed to be challenged and defeated, but maybe it wasn't all so contrived, maybe the times were not as dark as they seemed.

For Jack it was darker and he pressed her harder. "He had no priors."

"Yes, and that means what, exactly? No men have priors prior to the first time they run afoul of the law." Marie was trying to hold on to her skepticism, but some of the conviction in her voice had been lost.

"He was taken secretly at night and beaten, badly. That much I have been able to discern."

Now Marie looked into her glass and was silent. There wasn't much she could say to that. The real ones, the truly criminal element, just didn't get processed liked that; it was only the politicos that were beaten hard and fast-tracked out of town, and quietly too. But one had to be a heavy to fall into that class of folks; out-and-out raking of common politicos was still a bit beyond the pale, even for this administration … even in this day. But if that were true, if this man Max were such a heavy, how is it that Jack didn't know of him, more to the point, why didn't she know of him. Marie screwed her face up a bit.

"Does this concern him?" She nodded in Paul's direction, a stern glint in the eye of the woman who a moment ago seemed so matronly.

"Yes. There is something that I haven't told you," Jack replied slowly. "Daryl sent him, Paul, over to me. It is through Paul that I got wind of this."

"Daryl sent him, huh?"

"Yes, I am afraid so. I didn't want to play the Daryl card for your help, and more to the point I am not pursuing this on Daryl's account, so don't go charging him on this one. He is a good man, Daryl is, you know it and I know it, but he was only the source of the information, well, actually Paul is the source, but Paul was directed to Daryl by Max, and in turn was directed to me by Daryl. Be that as it may, the pursuit of this fella is my idea, my responsibility. If this goes south I want it on me, not Daryl."

"*Your* credit is not as good, son. The cost on this one could be quite high."

"I know, but it is what it is."

"I'll find out what I can, and quick too. I know you'll want to be getting back to that seedy little ranch of yours."

"Marie, it is not seedy, but you wouldn't know that, would you? Why don't you take a ride out sometime? The trip would sit well with you."

"Me? That's a joke and you know it. Why, it's been near five years since I ventured as many blocks from my abode here. The grocery mart, the bar."

"Yes, I know, the laundry, the library … it's all right here, your own little world. Believe me, Marie, I have heard this story before."

Paul and Jack took their leave a short time after that, after Paul mostly, gave Marie what he could for her investigation, which wasn't much, really, beyond Max's name, along with his address, place of employment, and the like; the really useful items, such as Max's friends and acquaintances, hobbies and hangouts, most of all his political affiliations—for those, Paul was of little help.

They left on foot together; Jack hadn't the slightest idea as to how to part company with this young man, boy almost. Paul had slept on Jack's couch last night, it had been too late to send the poor boy home by the time Paul had tracked Jack down, and Jack was beginning to wonder if he hadn't made a mistake on that front. Despondent and flighty by turns, the lad didn't seem to have a life to move on to, or toward. It all made Jack very nervous; he hadn't the time or disposition for a *puppy*, and worse, the boy could be a plant;

maybe there was no Max Stein, or if there was, maybe he was off on a cruise, not arrested. Paul had been hanging close to Jack and by this time had seen way more than was right, yet nothing indicated that he was any more than he claimed. But still, best to see the young one off, and soon.

"Have you known Marie long?" Paul asked, more out of boredom than from any real interest.

Jack answered without taking his eyes off the road. "Many, and more years, it seems, though in reality it is but a handful."

Quiet ensued. They hadn't really enough common ground to carry a conversation and Jack took this as the moment he was looking for.

"Look, I'll call you when I hear something. I know this fella was a friend of yours and that makes it more difficult for you, but I am sure things will work out. Max's arrest just doesn't add up, which is good because as far as I can tell, he wasn't taken for anything in particular, which means that he might be free, even as we speak."

Jack didn't believe a word of it; it was the humane thing, to reassure one's fellow human being. They mumbled some words of parting; Paul thanked Jack for his help and for allowing him to stay on his couch. Help Paul, Jack would, but on ideology there was no match; Jack had never been a strong draw for the gay community, and Paul would not be joining the Conservative movement anytime soon. But you never knew. There were many levels to people, and Jack *had* been helpful and compassionate, as a good human should.

Enough of intrigue and politics. It was a beautiful day and a short walk to where he had parked his truck. Jack was half tempted to blow off staying in town tonight; it wasn't the drive that kept him in town more nights than not—it was more of a mindset … Jack focused better on the action, the conspiracy, and intrigue, when he was living in it. Then there was the safety factor to consider; patterns of behavior were sure to trip a man up, and a daily run into and out of town would eventually raise someone's suspicions; a few days here, a few days there, really mixed it up nicely—he could be a rancher or a city boy, depending on the need. Jack basically lived below the radar; he was careful in his acquaintances, he moved slowly, had money to spare, and he was meticulous—as such, managed to keep a very low profile and was truly no one to the authorities. It was not so for some of his Conservative brethren; a day was coming, and soon, of that

Jack was sure, when the more outspoken of his clan would pay dearly, perhaps with their lives. Of this, Jack had little doubt. But an hour's drive, no more, would bring him home to Ellen, a warm and loving wife. *That* was something that every man should have, and something he ofttimes thought he was crazy to ever separate himself from her even for one night.

He was at the corner café having a cup of coffee when he learned of Paul's arrest. It was a rainy, blustery day; the end of October. It had gotten dark early. Jack fingered the note in his pocket, feeling the crease of the paper beneath his thumb. Paul had been arrested, though on what charge Charlie had not said; it wasn't unusual for Charlie to decide what information was important to the reader— Charlie was psychic that way, or more precisely, a pain in the ass that way. Charlie might not know why Paul had been arrested, or maybe she did but decided that wasn't something to tell Jack, at least not in this note; Charlie's selective dissemination of information could be most infuriating. Well, a man must work with the tools that God gives him, and God had given Jack *Charlie Hutch*.

The note had been discreetly slipped to him via a courier as he was crossing the street to the café. Such methods of message delivery, while not unique, were rarely used, and again was a trademark of Charlie. The use of a courier for delivering a message got Jack thinking about the cell phone he had owned for a while, many years ago, but had later given up. There was a time when virtually no one was without one, and there were people who had two, three, or even more. But the damn things were so insecure; prone to intercepts and governmental and criminal eavesdropping— the technology had died even as it was being touted as irreplaceable. They were gone now, or almost, and so was the associated industry; with only the very wealthy able to afford the truly secure and private devices, there were few wireless transmissions to eavesdrop on.

Jack took a deep breath, a mind-clearing breath. He needed to. Marie had yet to locate Max, if indeed he truly existed, which Jack was beginning to doubt to some degree, and now the arrest of Paul made the picture that much more perplexing.

In all likelihood it was as Paul had presented; there really was this fella Max who had been arrested who *had* instructed Paul to go to Daryl should anything happen to him. If all this were true, then Jack was doing a disservice to the young Paul. There wasn't much Jack could do even if he wanted to. He couldn't storm the castle gates with Charlie, Marie, and a handful of half-baked anarchists.

Max decided to do nothing; there wasn't anything he could see that could be done. He crushed Charlie's note in his pocket and not for the first or third time, wished mightily that he hadn't become involved in this mess.

Sometime later, three, four days or so, Jack was back in town, after spending several nights on his ranch. He headed back to Marie's to see what she had uncovered regarding the Max. Unexpectedly, for he hadn't told her about his decision regarding Paul, or even about Paul's arrest, Jack encountered her wrath nonetheless; Marie really did have a way of finding things out, most anything, it seemed—her fists on her hips, barring the door to her abode, she tore into him.

"How could you make such a decision on your own."

Startled, he asked, "My own?"

"Yes, your own."

"Well, why should it be any different? I often make my own decisions regarding *my own actions*." He had been caught and it was best to hide behind bravado.

Marie blithely ignored it. "Maybe *your actions*, but not necessarily *your* decision. What makes you think it was your decision to make? Who made you the arbitrator of the actions we take?"

"I am not … I never … hell, Marie, if you knew about this, you could have taken an action on your own."

"That's just it, not on my own. There is so little that any of us can do *on our own*, we are nothing on our own. It takes the involvement of so many seemingly little and seemingly powerless people to even give us a ghost of a chance of improving our lives and the lives of others." Then, with her finger jabbing at the front of his chest, which would have been his nose had she been tall enough, she said, "Are you part of the team or not? Or do you view everything as an isolated little toad? My actions, your actions; what about *our* actions?

"You walk around in this town like you are somebody, a big-ass somebody, but you're not, not really. There are many in Tucson who can step into the role you have. Mostly anyone is replaceable if you have a good team behind you." Marie sighed. "If we don't start working together, how can we ever hope to defeat a group as well organized as this government is? No, don't answer that, for it was not a question—leastwise, not one that I have an interest in your answering. Now tell me, how is it that you decided not to help Paul."

The pit in Jack's stomach was enough to know that even he wasn't going to like his answer, but he gave it anyway, or thought he was giving it.

"We can't help everyone, there are too many. Besides, it is risky, dangerous. Even the little that we can do … it is not like we could have broken him out of prison."

The steady look Marie gave him was not one of disagreement, but it was certainly not one of acquiescence either. They both knew that though legitimate, it was not the true answer. Jack grimaced.

"I chose not to do anything, anything at all, because I didn't think him worth the effort. *Any effort*," he added softly.

"Well, honesty becomes you, but that may not suit you well, for Paul *was* telling the truth. There is a Max, he has been arrested, and he has been sent to one of the lumber prisons up north."

"Truly?"

"Truly. Not that I expect you now to go running off after Paul."

Jack moaned dejectedly. This didn't change anything that he could have, would have, done. But the knowledge that a wholly innocent boy was in store for … for … *what, exactly?* Jack didn't know; he was not sure that he wanted to know or that anyone truly knew. They had only recently started taking people solely on a political basis; the options in such cases in terms of punishment and incarceration were myriad. That did not bode well for Paul, or Max, or *any of them*, for that matter. The future was getting bleaker, darker; they hadn't figured out where the light switch was—hell, they didn't even understand what kind of room they were trapped in. Today's interpretation of the law meant no one was safe from arrest and the trauma that came with it; tomorrow's interpretation and associated trauma might be completely different. Or so it seemed.

"This changes nothing as far as Paul is concerned, though I wish him no ill."

"How kind of you," she said with sarcasm, and meant it. "As I was saying, I do not expect you to go running off after Paul, for as you said yourself, he is but a young gay college student and not worth the risk to you or your organization. I won't bemoan you that, as you say, you can't save everyone. Perhaps you can't save anyone." Again

56

the level gaze. "But you should know this: Max has been sent up on child molestation and rape charges."

"A pedophile? But that is exactly how they are railroading 1C politicos."

"Yes. Or maybe not. The accuser is his daughter."

Jack grimaced. "Do you know what is going on here?"

"You mean with Max, or why the world seems to be turned on its head?"

Jack nodded in the affirmative, *both*.

"Oh Jack, my boy," even though he was near forty, Marie ofttimes referred to him as *"her boy"*; Marie was well past old enough to be his mother. "This has been going on for years, it has been a slow process, this erosion of civil rights. Don't let the events of today forget your knowledge of history. You know what I am talking about. What you are missing, in your thinking, is the understanding that today's events are not arbitrary, nor random, nor unplanned. Far from it, Jack. This is only yet another step in a well-thought-out and planned direction that none of us want to go."

"My head hurts."

"A lot more than that is going to be hurting before this is done."

"Right ... but now, I dunno."

Jack paused and then with conviction, smacking his fist into the palm of his hand, his voice rose in irritation, though at what he couldn't exactly say, there was so much he was irritated about. "I am going to get this Max out, get him down here, and find out just what he is all about ... politico, rapist, or just a man in the middle of a mistake. Then," he said more softly, "he will get what he deserves, good, bad, or indifferent from me, er, from us." He answered her withering look by repeating, "From us."

Charlie

Jack walked over to the wall-mounted phone; he was not taken by staying in town and if he were to spend the night here in this tiny two-bedroom flat, then he wasn't about to do so alone.

"Charlie? Yeah, it's me, Jack." A pause. "Yeah, I know that. Look, can you be here? … No, don't take the car, that is an invitation to being stopped if there ever was one. Stay on the side streets and keep to the shadows. … Yes, I know that you know that. Maybe you can bring Mike and Linda. … Oh well, they'll be back. Leave them a note, but we got to meet. Daryl," Jack said, looking down at the note in his hand, "he needs to be taken care of, but how, I don't know. … Yeah, bye."

Jack cradled the receiver and looked down again at the note.

The bear is coming down the mountain, to see what he can see, and what do you think he saw?

An old child's rhyme or close enough, yet also plain enough in its implications. This note at least was not from Charlie, yet its author seemed to have as little inclination as Charlie when it came to providing information; *the bear* was of course Daryl, who was obviously coming down from the mountain—while the note didn't say why he was coming down, the reasoning was plain enough. Max's disappearance, Paul's subsequent arrest; none of this had any bearing on Daryl's life; the best course of action for the man was to stay in his mountaintop retreat and let the little people down below slug it out in the trenches. But after almost ten years of aloofness, the man had decided to get involved. It had to be the immediacy; damn Max and Paul, though not truly, but still, if they hadn't dragged the old man into this mess of theirs, he would have been oblivious to what was going on and would simply be adding yet another day to his list of long days of … well, Jack really wasn't sure what Daryl did. But his getting involved was going to be a real pain in the ass for Jack. Having the man in town would mean nothing but trouble for him, of that Jack was sure; it was like letting a fox loose in an old English hunting ground—sooner or later trouble would brew itself up.

Max had a corner apartment, actually all the apartments were; two units on the bottom, two on the top, his being the top right. He pulled a bottle of scotch from the upper shelf in the kitchen and poured three fingers in a glass that was sitting on the counter; it was his scotch glass, and it lived on the counter just below the cabinet that held the scotch—the scotch and the glass were home tonight, as a good roommate was. Tonight, as he did most nights, he downed it in one gulp, feeling the fire burning down his throat as the warmth spread out across his chest and into his limbs. He thought it over and poured another three fingers and let the glass sit; with all the other preparations he was making, it seemed a good idea.

He paced around the sitting room with a glance at a couch, an overstuffed chair, a television on a small TV stand—between the TV and the kitchen was a small table with two chairs. A small place, two bedrooms; just what Jack needed on those nights that he stayed in town, though he didn't enjoy the solitude and spent as little time alone in the flat as possible—guests, coconspirators, and friends, were about at all hours of the day and night.

He opened the door on the second knock, after first using the peephole to make sure that it was Charlie. Actually it made little difference who it might be, as Jack couldn't possibly affect the outcome of any encounter at this point; had it been the gendarmes, Jack's refusal to unlock the door wouldn't even buy him the time needed to make good going out the kitchen window.

"Hi, Charlie."

The embrace was quick but still he loved the scent of her long black hair. It was a tad on the thin side but that only added to her allure. Working with her would have been a whole lot more interesting had he not met his wife Ellen first. But Charlie was as warm and friendly as she was creative and smart, which is what Jack needed just then.

"Good to see you too, Jack."

She planted a quick kiss on his cheek before they drew apart and she stepped into the flat; Jack took a quick look over the patio rail, up and down the street—deserted as it always was this time of night. He followed her in, admonishing himself for letting his eyes briefly come to rest on her butt.

"Right."

Jack, getting down to business, pulled a second chair to the table; Charlie grabbed the first, passively aggressively ignoring the chair Jack offered her. She was like that seemingly every chance she got— she grabbed a glass of her own and the bottle of scotch.

"What is going on right now? I've been out for a couple of days and you're better tied in here than I am. The faces seem to keep changing and I never learn half the names, anyway."

Charlie shook out of her light jacket.

"Yes, I *am* better tied in than you. I had a chance to check with a cohort of mine on the way here. Seems that someone unpleasant has gotten wind of Daryl's pending arrival, picked up his scent. Though who it is we don't know, nor as to how close they are to him."

She said this with a sacrilegious smile, never one to rest on formalities or the seriousness of the situation. She was a tight, diminutive girl, light skin with black hair—veritably exuding sexy. Charlie *liked* being appealing; not risqué, but appealing—she liked being desirable but not desired … she was a very mixed-up girl of twenty-nine who had grown up in a culture where casual sex was the norm, but it never was for her. She lost her virginity more out of obligation than desire. She had a three-year affair with a man two years her senior; she hadn't another one, though she had once or twice hooked up and didn't like that at all. Yet she didn't dwell on any of this; she was confused only by what others thought of her in this regard; as to how she regarded herself, she was not confused.

She playfully poked him in the ribs.

"But it is fairly common knowledge that the cat is out of the bag and that he is on his way here. Maybe you should try staying about more often rather than hiding out on that so-called farm of yours."

"Ranch."

"Huh?"

"It is a ranch and I am not hiding out, *and* you know that. I have to make a living. We can't all exist on our good looks, you know."

"Oh, that would be *good looks* and my daddy. Though if he knew just what his only daughter was up to, cavorting around with the right-wing likes of a nut job like you … "

Charlie paused and took a sip of the scotch, grimacing as she did so, her face a funny, scrunched-up little ball with a small pug nose.

"Brrrrr, how can you drink this?"

Jack ignored the rhetorical question.

"Does he?"

"Huh? Does he what?"

"Know the politics of his only daughter."

"*Of course, and he loves me anyway, great bighearted Liberal that he is.* Of course not. Why trouble an old man's revelry with such petty concerns. He knows that I've gone back to school, studying something, anything, and that makes him happy. He is past sixty now and likes to remember days when he meant something. Not that his life now is bad, it isn't, but he is a bit out of touch. Which is just as well. I don't think he would approve any more of the Progressives than he does of us. It's just that, well, you know, he is, or was, the opposition in his youth, against the established order. He was a Liberal before I was born and I don't think he would like where his efforts have ended.

"Then again, maybe I am wrong to keep him in the dark about my political persuasion. After all, maybe he would support us if he knew the facts. He was a supporter of human rights before he joined, what was it … the Deemon-crats? No, that doesn't sound right. Hmmm …" Charlie chewed her lower lip as she was wont to do when thinking something through and the answers were not coming easily.

"It was the Democrats, and back then they were in opposition to the Republicans. Time for that later, if you ever see him again, or when. It has been how long now? A year? Two?"

"Not that long, but probably a year, yeah. I owe him a visit. Maybe soon."

"Leave the politics when you do go."

"Huh?"

"You heard me."

Charlie ignored the last. She was quiet for the moment, thinking perhaps on the political maze into which they had so willingly stepped. Could it really cost her life? She felt a freight train of introspection coming on, but instead she checked it and drifted back to their main concern, Daryl.

"Still, after all these years … they track him and fear him? *If* that is what this is. I dunno. You know, we say that they are stupid, but they are not a bunch of idiots, not really, after all, they *run* things."

Jack wandered over and poured yet another glass of scotch, though not quite three fingers. It had been one of those days which was heading quickly to being one of those nights. He looked Charlie over; she was too confident in her thinking, she must have it right— Daryl was still in the system and his trail had been picked up somehow … no sense wasting time in querying Charlie on her story. She just knew too much, had a way of finding out without even trying. While Jack could hunt and peck at a spot on the wall to garner the smallest bits of information, and while Marie leaned on her sources hard, and who'd believe it of that frail old lady, Charlie seemed to pick up data like a lint comb in a warehouse. Sometimes he thought that maybe she was prescient and things just sort of came to her like visions. Jack hastily gulped the scotch before his thinking got out of hand.

He nodded in agreement.

"It is *so* much more satisfying thinking that the people you hate are inferior. But you're right, they're not, not really; I mean after all, they wrested power from some of the best that our country every produced."

"Yes, but they haven't wrested power from you, Jack." She gave him a light, playful tap on his cheek with her forefinger.

"Right, how can they wrest something that doesn't exist."

"Oh, I don't know about that. Give yourself a few more years; I am sure that you will put something on their plate."

Jack simply grunted at that remark. "Oh, I doubt that. I take a dim view of advancing anything of importance anytime soon. Preaching equality opportunity over cash handouts never was a winning proposition. Just look at the history of the last thirty years or so."

"But that is unsustainable, Jack, and you know that very well."

"Know it? Shit, I know it, but at the price of our freedom and prosperity it can." He raised his palms as if they were a set of scales, raising and lowering each palm as he said, "Free lunch, work for a living; free lunch, work for a living. I am already doing everything I can to bring about the end of the illusion. You know it, I know it, Daryl certainly knows it, Marie …. Every good red-blooded, or should I say red-bloodied Conservative knows this, but what of it? We can only make a case from the shadows and that only makes us look … shadowy."

Jack's grin was rueful. Charlie lightly put her hand on his arm.

"You know things will change; they always have, given time."

Jack studied her with a level gaze; *things will change,* implying a corresponding improvement that rarely materialized, the refrain having become the mantra of an up-and-coming generation of intellectual youth. They were so optimistic in their beliefs, and he just wanted to slap them around; for them, things were always getting better and they were always looking for signs to support that—*it* was always just around the corner, or just over that rise ... the long-awaited resurgence, the turning point.

Jack loved all these young 'uns, and he hated to be the one who kept them from pursuing their dreams, but the way they went about it, well, it was more likely their demise that they would attain than any dreams of plenty.

Charlie turned the conversation about and brought him out of his fog.

"So what's with this Max dude? Is he cute? Why are you so secretive about him? I mean you haven't given in to your cover, have you?"

Jack shot her a withering glance; he played the gay man in public to avoid arousing suspicion. Gay men were hardly considered a threat to the Social Democratic Party, what with the LGBT community having been endowed with so many social and legal advantages under the Socialist government; a gay man was considered a party man—or a party woman if she was lesbian ... or as the joke had it, a "Partying Man."

"Well, have you?"

"Hardly. You'd be the first to know, honest."

"Oh, bull. Ellen would know way before me, unless you have some hidden feeling for me you would like to share?" She ran her hand down the side of this cheek, which he carefully yet firmly took by the wrist and removed.

"If I did, you'd be the first to know that too. Anyway, he is too old for the likes of me or you, for that matter." Jack gave her a level gaze. There was no telling, ever, what was on Charlie's mind.

"So why are you going after him? I mean, you are trying to free him, right?"

"Yes, I don't know." Jack lit a cigarette. Charlie made to speak, but Jack waved her off. "You've been talking to someone; I never mentioned Max to you. No matter. I am doing more than just going after him, I have him."

Jack studied the play of emotions on Charlie's face; she was so easy to read yet she thought she was like a closed book. Right now he read surprise, as he had expected, but also, oddly enough, worry, written all over the pages of that cute face framed with that darling black hair.

"Yes, I know, I'll get myself killed if I keep acting as irrational as I am today ..." said Jack, trying to put words to her thoughts, or what he took to be her thoughts, "taking chances for dubious ends." He took another drag of smoke and then used the cancer stick as a pointer of sorts, pointing in the general direction of north. "North," he said, turning the conversation back to her question, "he is mine now, in the north, and he will be here soon. Then we will get some answers."

Charlie took the cigarette from Jack's hand, took a pull on it, handing it back. "I like the taste on occasion. But can you believe him?"

"Hmmm, believe what?" He looked at her. "You don't even know what I intend to ask ... oh, never mind, you probably do." Jack shrugged. "I might believe nothing he says, but believe everything that he is."

"Okay, and you are trying to be lucid, I take it."

"And you are worried because?" retorted Jack with just a hint of ice in his veins.

Charlie turned her hands up in exasperation.

"What are you doing, Jack; taking chances for, for, what? One misstep, Jack, just one misstep and you risk dragging down not only yourself but your family, your friends, the movement."

"Shit, Charlie, there is no movement, or haven't you been listening to me all these years? Oftentimes I wonder *what* it is we are doing, where we might go from here. It seems that there is so little room for us to grow into. I dunno, Charlie, sometimes a man needs to follow what he thinks is right even if it isn't. That is what I am doing now, Charlie, bringing Max down here. Foolish and expensive it may be, it feels right."

"Still, you're risking all on this fool that you've never met, who might well have been sent up for good cause?"

"No, there is more to this, there is something going on, a tie-in to us, there has to be. Max was pinched in Tucson, we are in Tucson. A young man named Paul might well die over this arrest. Daryl is coming, so there is something up with him. There is a tension in the air, I can feel it, and while I wouldn't say that this tension is related to Max, it seems all these points are coalescing now, and Max's arrest was the first point on the horizon."

"And you wonder what you should do."

"Yes, I do so wonder. I won't know whether to cut Max loose when he gets here and let him fend for himself, kill him where he sleeps for being a pedophile, if that is what he is, or go to the ends of the earth to try and save him."

Charlie didn't say anything for a moment, running her fingers through her hair; all folks have a behavior matched to a frame of mind, and Charlie's was running her fingers through her hair when she was thinking through something complicated.

"Okay, we'll wait and see. Maybe this Max guy is important. Maybe he had some reason to get pinched and poked. So I'm with you. When he gets here we will get some answers, or at least ask him some questions and make ourselves a well-informed decision as to his fate, or try to, at any rate."

Suddenly Jack grabbed her gently on both sides of her face and placed a soft kiss on her head. He gently pushed her back.

"Tusk, tusk, what do you think Mrs. Jack would think of that."

"Mrs. Jack would think it was just fine. Trust me, I married the right woman."

"Aw, you're just saying that because you don't want to admit your mistake."

"Mistake?" Jack frowned.

"Yeah, not waiting for me."

"That, Charlie of barely past the teenage years, would have been a long wait indeed."

"Hnuh," was the only response he got from her, then, "Hey, I'm almost thirty."

Max

Max ruffled the surrealistic photograph in his mind's eye; in the land of imagination he held it gently by the corner—he didn't want it smudged, or dirtied, or forgotten … the mind's eye is a finicky sense indeed, one in want of control. It had been a long time since he had seen the real photograph; Max didn't cry but he sure felt a swollen impulse to do so now.

So much lost, so much gone from the sensibilities of a near fifty-year-old man who hadn't always made the right choices; even when he had, things hadn't always worked out correctly either—yet there was something to be said for "incorrect" choices too. Somehow things worked out in the end, especially for those choices which were followed by a new beginning; or something like that; it was hard to keep track of what was mental musings and what was plain insanity.

The picture, real or imaginary, had been taken in San Diego fifteen years ago; Kate was seven and her mother was still alive—just the two of them had been in it, mother and daughter. Max particularly liked that picture; his two *"girls,"* as he liked to refer to them, had just come back from the beach, or a park, or somewhere fun, and in their moment of unmitigated joy Max picked up a camera and snapped a picture of heaven on earth, a picture he had grown to treasure above all others.

But the photograph was only a moment in time and time had moved on, as it does for all photographs, for all memories. How much had changed in the intervening years; Karen was dead and Kate alienated and alone.

It had been three weeks since his arrival at the prison camp and Max started wondering if he would ever grow used to it, not as in now, nor in a month or two, but in a year or maybe three or maybe fifteen. He thought of movies where hardened criminals grow stoic after years, decades in prison; stoic to where it seemed impossible for them to have committed the crimes of which they were convicted—over the years prison softened them and melancholy took the place of anger. Do the innocent grow stoic as well, or do they instead grow into the anger and violence that brought the guilty man here.

Is that what is to become of me, a stoic, melancholy old man, if I don't die tomorrow, or next week, or next year, or the year after the year after that?

He could already see that trait developing in the few weeks he had been here; he grew more at ease as the fear and trauma of his arrest diminished over time. He moved slower, slept better, he was almost thankful for his current surroundings. But Max was well aware that this sense of ease had very much do to with the circumstances of his imprisonment, and comparatively speaking, those circumstances were good, very good.

As a baker Max did little baking, and in truth he was a baker only for purposes of classification. *Bakers' assistant*, or shop worker, or some such designation would have been more appropriate, but he would not complain. Lifting ten kilo bags of flower throughout most of a twelve-hour day was fatiguing but not deadly; outside in the snow, logging, road building, that was deadly. It seemed weekly that at least one inmate fell. Who were these unfortunate fellows? He had developed a morbid fascination to know who it was that fell, in the anonymous cold, in his place. Empathy, that's what it was called, or so he thought; empathy—yeah, that sounded right—empathy was much better than dying.

True to his word, on their arrival at the Flagstaff transit center, the convict Larry did some fast talking and trading of some sort and the next thing Max knew he was marching to the right while another group of men were marched off to the left. To the right lay salvation, to the left death, or so he believed. Oddly, Larry was taken in with the group to the left; Max caught a rueful grin on Larry's face—to the left might lie death, but not for Larry, of that he was sure.

It was well past midnight and the room above the bakery where they slept was quiet, peaceful, almost contemplative. He sat on his bunk thinking as he smoked, thinking about Kate; she was actually all he really thought about—where she was, what she was doing ... he had the sense that none of it was good, even though he fervently hoped otherwise. But how could that be, what with him in here and that on the basis of her complaint. Regardless of what he had done to her, it was hard to believe that she would have turned on him like that. Someone was into her in a big way and that was scary; what was scarier still is she might not even realize it. As always, as ever, whether she would admit it or not, whether she would accept it or not, she needed his help.

But he was a far cry from being able to do much about it and he most certainly couldn't do much here; he would need to get out and soon—*that* was a given, though he couldn't see how just yet. He grounded out the half-smoked cigarette. It had been a long day, and it would be long one tomorrow and every day for … well, he didn't know how long for, there had been no termination point on his incarceration papers; he supposed that made the length of time indefinite—provided he lived. Perhaps they really never meant for him to get out, ever; or only when he was so old and feeble that he might as well be dead. Either, both, it made no matter; if he was killed escaping, the net result would be near enough to the same … Kate would never see her father again. What he feared most in life was that perhaps that was the way she wanted it.

Those who worked in food production ate better than the rest of the inmates; there was always a chance to sneak a bit to eat over and above the meager rations they were officially served—Larry had helped him in more ways than he knew, or perhaps he did know just how much he had helped the hapless *"man without a clue."* Those who worked outside mining, logging, and in construction fared much more poorly, and it was in those occupations with their own system of housing and rations, that most of the prison deaths occurred.

A peculiar thing happened several days later—it was the end of November, over six weeks since his arrest and he was now finishing his first month in the camp. Every morning for the past four weeks his day began and ended with the short walk across the grassy patch of land which was ensconced in the campus center to the bakery; despite the fact that the bakers lived above the bakery it was still necessary for them to first march across the parade ground to the lineup during roll call and then march back to the bakery to begin the day's work an hour before dawn. But today he was left standing on the grounds with two armed guards. Max couldn't help but think that they looked to be soldiers more so than guards. That was his first clue that something was wrong, the second was the shove to the back that landed him facedown, spread eagle, on the graveled parade ground; tasting blood in his mouth where his teeth had cut the soft tissue lining his cheek—it was all too familiar, the shove, the blood, the close-up view of the ground … it was not a portent of good things to come.

Indeed any thought of rising was swept away when a large boot planted itself firmly between his shoulder blades. Fortunately it was only meant as a restraint and not a telling blow; otherwise there was a good chance that his back would have been broken. It was so easy, took such little time, to go from the relative sanctuary amidst the harshness of hell to here.

"He is not who we thought him to be. Take him with the logging crew and see that he is quartered there."

That it was it; one short sentence to take whatever meager existence he had established and replace it with hell, and not just good ol'-fashioned hell either, but hell on earth and this part really scared him. It was to be hell in the woods.

It was hell too; logging in tumultuous winds and wet snow with temperatures bouncing below zero centigrade by day, to much lower at night, which they often worked into. They were ill clothed in padded jackets and felt boots, and pitifully fed; rampant was the talk of the food designated for the prisoners but destined for the kettles of the innumerable chiefs and guards. The first day's end found him a bruised and bloody wreck. He was not beaten; leastwise not by any guard or soldier—the trees and work saw to that. The felling was fast and clumsy; Max suffered a long bloody scratch that ran from just below his right eye to the bottom of his jaw, fortunately not deep—it had scabbed over by the time light had begun to fade from the day. The puncture wound in the back of his calf was deeper, though, if not so very wide; it seemed like the type of wound that could fester an infection. Max found himself morbidly thinking about whether there were sick days on this job.

It wasn't just the scratches and punctures either; a large log had rolled unexpectedly up against his ankle and it hurt to walk now—the pain in his muscles was extreme. The work was hard; hacking, chopping, hauling, cutting, lifting, stacking—all by hand …actually, hard didn't even begin to describe it. He was quartered with the real criminal element now, the murderers, thieves, the crazies, and the true child molesters. He fell asleep on a lower bunk that night and for the first time since his initial arrest, even during the nights following the beatings in prison, he didn't think of Kate before he fell asleep. His exhaustion and his fear were too complete.

It continued for the next six days. No one had beaten him yet, though the guards did not seem to flinch at smacking men as a motivational technique—Max had taken one such blow of a rifle butt to his shoulder—but that wasn't a beating in the real sense and the pain from the strike soon melded into the daily strain, comingled with the scratches and pokes from the ever-present trees. Nor had he been victimized by the criminal element, though he had seen it happen to others. Fortunate, he was in more ways than one to have been *transferred* into the work brigade; as a transfer he was of limited interest—of more poignant interest, the subject of beatings and abuse were the newly arrived prisoners, those with riches no matter how small still attached to them, or those who were as of yet virgins in the backside. As a transfer, Max was assumed to have neither possessions nor virginity. But such factors could only belay the inevitable for so long; eventually, interest or sheer malice would be turned his way, of this he held little doubt.

On the seventh day, as he sat on a large rock enjoying as best he could a heel of bread and a bowl of something that seemed like porridge, only thinner but with bits of meat, Max took a deep breath. It had been a week of hard labor, really hard, minimal diet, and living with murderers, rapists, thieves, and the general scum of the earth, and … he was not dead.

Bloodied, bruised, in shitty health, yes, but alive nonetheless. Once again he was reaching that stoic state of incarceration, of preserving in the face of all odds, gaining control in an environment beyond one's control; he could do this, he really could—maybe. He could be knifed by one of his newfound brothers, or a tree could bash his head in on the way down, but life itself would not kill him, or so he thought. He was quite thankful that he was nondescript and had no ambition other than *to survive*; the ambitious, the young, or the *cute* had problems beyond measure in this place.

Max's seventh night in the barracks seemed no different than the previous six; sought-after rest, if not peaceful sleep, kept the murmur in the barracks to a minimum. A wood-burning stove warded off the freeze of night, though the drafts from gaps in the hammered planked walls channeled in the stabbing cold at the slightest uptick in the wind.

Max woke readily to the prodding he had taken at first to be the start of a new day. He soon knew such was not the case; a soft but firm hand covered his mouth to stifle a cry of alarm that would have woken the barracks—while not easily disturbed by the slight rustle of one small person struggling against the pain of living, a shout would get them all up in an instant—whoever had woken him wanted very much to avoid that.

"Hush, do not speak."

The pressure of the hand lessened but did not cease; the woman's hand remained over his mouth. *Sweet hand*, he thought, even before wondering about the situation.

"You have been summoned to appear before our council. We do not believe that you are who you represent yourself as, Max Stein. In fact we have no clue about who you might be at all, but we mean to find out, and woe to you if you're playing us ill. Woe to you."

As quick as that she was gone, the woman whose hand was so sweet, but not her words. *He* knew who he was; he was Max Stein, convicted child molester, and, he thought dismally, he was about to lose his life.

Of course, the woman hadn't said when he would face this council. Nor had she specified who or what this council actually was. He didn't doubt for a moment that his life would change yet again. He had an image of being led down a dark alley at gunpoint to face a hooded row of his peers, fellow prisoners all; the condemned man's court of condemned men—if there were no mercy in the court of the living, what kind of mercy could possibly be found before the court of the dead.

A trial by one's peers, by one's fellow corpses.

No, there could be no mercy before such a court.

Max

"My name is Jack, and I am going to take you from here."

Max gave the man a steady look; "Jack," if that was truly his name, had picked him up at the train station—well, picked him out of a boxcar at the station. When Max had heard the lock rattle on the door of the boxcar he wasn't sure if his odd and very painful odyssey was coming to a safe end, or if he were about to embark on new and even deadlier journey as a *captured* escaped convict. He had been holding his breath as the first rays of the late-morning sun sprung through the opening door, grinding as it slowly opened. Even now, half an hour later, he wasn't certain that he had started breathing again.

"We own this wagon," Jack had said when he first plucked Max out of the boxcar he had been placed in yesterday. "We don't have to worry about losing control this way; there is no unsuspecting owner to fool, or schedules to be toyed with; such techniques almost always go wrong. So we own it and we use it as sees us fit; there is nothing half so safe as conducting illegal business from the confines of a perfectly legitimate enterprise—we schedule the boxcar as needed and choose our route and cargo with care."

"And now you send it back north for the next fugitive?"

Jack gave Max a sidelong glance, the clean-shaven thirty-five-year-old considering the rather bushy forty-seven-year-old next to him.

"I have said too much as it is; I am a trusting fellow at heart, yet I live my life as anything but trusting." Then in response to Max's raised eyebrows he continued. "Sometimes I forget to be paranoid, and you don't help, you know. I am sure that I wouldn't be the first to tell you that I feel at ease around you. I certainly am not the first person to think *that*—of that there is no doubt. I feel like I have known you half my life. That and the fact that I have been chasing you in one form or another for months."

"*Form?*"

"Ah, yes. You see at first I thought that I might have to kill you."

Jack winked at Max, who settled farther down into his seat; he felt that he had asked enough questions for now—of *that* there was no doubt.

The drive from the Tucson train depot to Jack's home in the desert was a far cry from the journey life had taken him on over the last couple of months; somehow the hour's drive seemed a most apropos way of ending the lengthy trip of this phase of his life. The informal council at the lumber camp reviewed his case and they decided to kill him, having determined that he was not politically set up but must have been sent up on the charge of child molestation and pedophilia. How they had eventually determined that Max was not a monster molester, that instead Max was to be freed, he would never know. Evidently, within hours of having been found guilty of perpetrating the most heinous of crimes of mankind's moral malaise, a lifesaving turnaround released him to Jack's operation; he was not to die.

Getting Max out of the prison was surprisingly easy—up to and including dispatch on the locomotive. His escape was simply a matter of being walked out a back gate, climbing into the back of a lorry for a short drive, then climbing into a boxcar, empty save for a small battery-operated space heater, a bag of odds and ends of food, and a hole in one corner through which he could relieve himself. There was also a rough though clean mattress and blanket stacked in a corner opposite from the latrine; all the comforts of home.

Get to Jack's house they did without either incident or much in the way of conversation. Max was unable to recall much about his actual arrival at Jack's home, aside from some mumbled greetings to Jack's wife, and an equally mumbled greeting to a group of seemingly endless friends, charges, and laborers; a lot of people seemed to be milling around what seemed to be a small, homely ranch … and they had the appearance of having been waiting for him, though just what it was he was supposed to do or have done to him wasn't clear. At least they hadn't turned out for his execution.

Jack's home was an Arizona Goldwater ranch, or of the motif, anyway; and the only thing that seemed to be more prominent in the sprawling one-story structure than the polished mesquite and white adobe was the people. *Goldwater* was the name that had come to dominate the architecture of what was considered a uniquely Arizona house: large, one story, lots of windows, wood trim, and adobe walls finished on the interior in a smooth plaster—*rustic elegance* is how Jack referred to it. The people, well, they were probably Goldwater motif as well, from what Max recalled from his history; jeans, boots, and hats were in abundance, and not just on the men, either.

Exhausted as he was, Max slept soundly for the first time since his arrest; without fear of *someone's standard issue kicking in the door*—odd, he remembered that line from some song his daughter used to listen to. But he was as ignorant as to who the musicians were, as he was in so much else about his daughter; so poignant were the missed opportunities with her that even if they came around again it would not be the same opportunity, for the two of them were hardly the same person.

Max slept for two days, dead to the world; he got up to take some water and to relieve himself a couple of times, once eating a slice of an orange and a piece of cheese that someone had left on the night table beside his bed.

While Max was sleeping off the morbidity of the last couple of months of his life, Charlie decided to rearrange hers by moving into Jack's ranch. Things were a bit chaotic in Jack's household for Charlie, but the free-spirited girl decided to live with it; life was becoming increasingly unstable in Tucson—mostly all of the out-of-town folks had left, winter residents for the most part, as well as many of the college students … it seemed like more people were on their way out every day. What exactly was going on was not clear; Internet connections had been subject to much interruption of late and the power in town was becoming erratic, going down for hours at a time on a fairly regular basis. Tucson and the other southwestern cities were becoming isolated bastions of anti-government sentiment as the United States took its seat at the global community of nations; this, after years of being ostracized for forging headstrong policies in her own self-interest. This newfound lack of self-interest was being reflected in a vastly reduced standard of living in the United States … and nowhere was this more pronounced than in the cities of the heartland and Southwest. With the inability to get regular and reliable information, people were worried; the exodus of those seemingly in the know, the wealthier winter residents and students of well-to-do parents, only added to the sense of unease.

"I have a bad feeling about this."

Charlie was sitting on the veranda after her first night on the ranch. The porch was replete with roughhewn oaken furniture, comfortable for sipping a mug of coffee to ward off the desert chill now accompanying the first rays of the newly arrived fall days; the air was quiet and still—a rosy hue pushing back the fading blues covering the desert floor.

"It has the feeling of a ghost town," she said, referring to the city. "Already down, hugely, from what the town once held years back, it *seems*, no, it *is* empty; like something out of some bad sci-fi book."

"I wouldn't know," said Jack, who had gotten up as one of his stable hands brought him a piebald gelding whose stoic gaze added to a sense of gentleness as the horses breath fogged in the morning air. "I never read much science fiction. But I agree, it is a concern."

"Concern my ass, Jack, you're going to go off riding."

"No, I mean it, *it* is concerning," he said, frowning, "or is it disconcerting? Hmmm. But don't upbraid me on riding, it is strictly a security thing," he said with a veiled smile. "How else do you expect me to keep an eye on my many acres, especially with the townsfolk leaving the city in droves. I wouldn't want them trespassing here."

"Oh yes, I forgot I was talking to the modern-day ranch hand."

"*Rancher*. No ranch hand am I. You want a ranch hand, see Josh, or Pepe, or Jorge. Even Bruce might do, but I don't think you're his type. Be back in an hour or so."

He tugged back on the reins, turning the animal around and with a soft tap of his heels to the stud's flanks, walked off, he loosened up on the horse and went off to see just how his five-hundred-odd acres were faring.

It was at about this time that Max woke to stay awake, leastwise as a normal human would. Jack's wife brought him a bowl of soup, chicken with homemade pasta and peppers. It was hot, both in temperature and spices, and it was filling. Ellen left him on the sunny south porch, he was alone and gratefully so—he still needed some time and a few smallish activities to feel fit for the human race again; one of those activities being a shower. Returning to his bedroom after eating he found a thick cotton towel, fresh from a warmer and just so to the touch. There was a hall bath which was unoccupied and ready for use. It was the first private shower he had since his arrest. He grimaced at the memory of his prison showers, infrequent and unpleasant for sure; at best they were a humiliating public event in a crowd of men—sometimes no more than a blast of a high-pressure hose, but never a private shower of indeterminate length, with hot water, and soap, and … well, it was *such* a pleasure as he never thought to have again.

Shampooed and showered he headed down to see the nature of this place and his newly found place in the human race, at least for the next few days, at any rate; after that—well, he would see, would he not?

Jack's ranch was not a working ranch in the traditional sense; the income of the place was based solely on the monies derived from the several thousand or so cases of wine that his acreage of grapes produced. It was not an extensive income, but then again, his living expenses were fairly meager. The ranch did produce an abundance of dairy, produce, fruit, and meat; pork and chicken—the *beef* part was not raised at his place. Once, Jack did have a cow. Gave good milk and even better meat, but that was not an *experience* he relished overall; try as he would he could not get so detached from the animal that slaughtering it was of no consequence. After that first sow, Jack had taken to housing his future meat at a neighbor's *traditional* working ranch. Jack didn't even bother to pick out the calves, he just knew that he owned a half dozen of them; a freezer full of meat he received six times a year, representing his share less expenses to the rancher. Jack and Ellen had many mouths to feed at any given time; guests, relatives, friends, ranch hands, or folks working on various projects, ranch related and otherwise. There had been as many as twenty living at Jack's at one time, doing various shades of the above; Jack treated them all like family while they were here, providing sit-down meals every evening and taking a couple of carafes, or *many* carafes, a night from the oaken casks in the cellars that held his full-bodied red; the perfect accompaniment to his rare beef—Jack was a griller extraordinaire.

With Jack on his tour of the "north forty" and Ellen and Charlie resting in their rooms, Max had little to do but wander around the dozen or so buildings that comprised the ranch, including lodgings for guests and ranch hands. In one building, a machine shop of sorts, were saws, presses, planers, and sanders; clean, well-used, and standing tall above older parts and devices lying about in the corners, broken and dead. It had a very functional feel to it and an oddly spiritual one as well; as if past pieces of dead machinery were gazing on the offspring that had taken on the task of keeping this simple and sprawling shop running. He sat for several minutes on a bale of hay enjoying the contrast between a clean, well-oiled tractor and its broken counterpart; a simile to his own life in the telling—today he felt like the shiny red tractor, but his gaze was continuously pulled to the broken, rusted one .... *I am the red tractor,* he told himself every few minutes. He wasn't completely sure he believed that in the end, but he did feel the better for the exercise.

After a time Max returned to join in the afternoon's activity for those who weren't out and about; sleeping—and a nap he took, though this time it was for relaxation or pleasure, not the desperate sweaty sleep of when he had first arrived. It wasn't until the sun was well west in the sky that all the residents at Jack's were up and about at the same time.

A well-rounded dinner was served to all hands present, which this night numbered twelve in all. It included beef with baked potatoes, crisp and hard on the outside from being cooked on the coals and soft on the inside, a fresh garden salad, all from produce grown locally on the ranch, and dessert of a thick, rich, and sweetened coffee.

Most of the diners had retired, leaving the three of them, Max, Jack, and Charlie together and alone for the first time. Jack's wife Ellen would not be joining them; indeed, she never joined in on the political side, or rarely, anyway, regardless of who it was. *One person in the relationship has to be satisfied with their lot in life,* she would say, and if it wasn't going to be Jack, then the task fell to her. A gracious host she was, and a tireless farmer, volunteering at the local school; between the two of them, Jack and Ellen had no children—she lived her life and she lived it well ... she loved Jack completely, but his political work, well, that was something that she just couldn't cotton to. Ellen went off to read, or to sleep, or to whatever it was she did when Jack turned toward politics and political action.

Ellen's noninvolvement in politics was a boon for Jack; it gave him at least one thing in his life that wasn't his work—his wife.

Off porch, the desert was quiet except for the chirping of crickets and the rustle of the occasional field mouse. The green and brown hues of the late desert day had gone to gray and the impenetrable shadows of evening. The conversation had been going on for about an hour, and it was not a simple one; Max feeling his way along the mental corridors of the barriers that Jack and Charlie had set up to keep him in place—Max had responded by immediately pushing at those barriers, against the invisible box around him. That the conversation was an inquiry about him was obvious to Max; he suspected that they didn't know what to do with him now that he was in Tucson—that they were not completely sure why they had broken him out of prison in the first place … his assumptions were not far off the mark. It didn't take great insight to come to that conclusion; Jack and Charlie, in spite of playing the role of sophisticated conspirators, wore their feelings, and their confusion, on their sleeves—and they obviously didn't know much about him, nor how to go about being the tough guys. All warmth and fuzziness aside, if there were any to start with, they feared just who he might be; what he might do, and where he might lead them—the latter most of all.

Max pushed at the barriers a bit harder.

"You still haven't told me why you got me out, or arranged to get me out, or maybe just authorized it, or whatever it is the two of you do in other people's lives. So it is not clear why you brought me here or what you want of me. One might think it is because you couldn't stand to see an innocent man slave away in prison, yet there are many innocent men there and you left them behind. Too, you won't let me on my way. In a very real way I feel a prisoner."

"You wouldn't last an hour in town," interrupted Jack, who was frowning. None of this was going well nor making any sense. Besides it was he who should be asking the questions.

Jack was beginning to think this was a mistake and that he should have left the doddering old fool to die. It hadn't been worth the cost or the risk to save young Paul; saving Max was a lot more expensive and a bigger danger—what had he been thinking of, bringing him here? He should have left him to die.

Max coughed to get their wandering attention. It was obvious that while his mind was on the conversation, theirs were not.

"Look, I need to get to my daughter, and quickly. She is in a lot of trouble right now. That, after all, is why I let you break me out of prison in the first place."

Jack chose to ignore that last incredulous statement on Max's part. "My patience wears thin. We have been at this for hours. You have said much, though almost nothing that I had expected to hear and little that makes sense. You profess gratitude at your rescue, your freedom, your avoidance of death, yet you really do not cooperate with us. You want us to help you on a quest that could tax our resources in the extreme, yet you offer us nothing in return."

"In my position, what would you do?"

"Stop it, Jack, give the man a chance. We are certainly foreign to him, aren't we?"

Charlie turned and smiled at Max, who gave her a level stare from a lean, bearded face well salted with gray. Jack fumed but he did so inwardly, he so disliked losing his temper in front of Charlie. Why *wasn't* Max cooperating more, *better*, if he had nothing to hide, with the truth on his side.

"You don't have any idea why you were popped, then? If indeed you are innocent; why would The Man go to such extremes to take you off the street if you're not, as you claim, politically active? C'mon, man, you can tell us, we are, after all, all on the same side."

Jack immediately felt pitiful using a line like that. There had to be a book on this stuff somewhere, *Interrogation 101: Getting What You Want Without Ripping Off the Other Guy's Fingernails.*

If for no other reason than to try a new approach, Max began a recitation of his life story, up to and including his arrest, imprisonment, and escape. It made, for the most part, droll entertainment, and he left some of the more *personal* facts out. It took him about half an hour.

When he finished, it was Charlie who took up the lead, and the tract she followed had Max all ears. She looked at him earnestly, trying to ascertain how much he was comprehending even as she was explaining it.

"Of course, child abuse, a child rape charge, those are charges that don't involve a trial or any type of defense, or leastwise only at the discretion of the prosecuting attorney. The thinking is that child sex crimes are so abhorrent, the victims so innocent, that a preponderance of evidence is enough to put the accused away and thereby spare the victim the further humiliation that would be required by a trial.

"The authorities also use this as a means to railroad those they want to get rid of; bring a political subversive up on child abuse charges and in a blink you have them off in tethers before they know what hit them. But you, Max, they really wanted to ensure you disappeared by not only slapping you with the child rape charge, but doing so particularly brutally and not so discreetly either. This was key. They wanted to make sure that *the right* people were looking more closely at you and would ascertain that you are not a politico in any sense of the word and not deserving of their protection. Not a very good situation for you.

"Basically they first made you disappear, completely and quietly and very politically, and then shoved it in the faces of those who cared about such, ah, activities. Indeed, I am sure that the intent was that you would be dead by now, killed by those who would have saved you had you been a politico falsely accused of raping your daughter."

"If he is telling the truth."

Charlie shot Jack an indignant look, she so hated being second-guessed, but acknowledged Jack's point.

"Right, if. But I'll tell you, Jack, nothing makes any sense otherwise, so I think we ought to go with what does—make sense, that is. The question then is *why?* Who are *you* that the government wanted to smack you down a dark hole, so deep that you'd never see the light of day again?"

"Oh, you make it sound so permanent, the part about the deep, dark hole," said Max with a slight sardonic grin, then a slight shrug of his shoulders. "Trust me, I am none too pleased with this myself. I am, or was, about as much of a nobody as a person could be."

"That certainly seems true," muttered Jack under his breath.

"What did you say?" piped up Charlie.

"Oh, it was … nothing."

Jack stroked his chin between his thumb and forefinger, looked over at Charlie to make sure she was done. He was in no hurry; they had been at this for hours, and as the stars cartwheeled overhead, his brain was beginning to soften around the edges and his thinking was losing its focus. But they needed to move this conversation somewhere. Suddenly an elusive thought coalesced in his mind.

"You know, you don't question anything that we are telling you. Usually those sent up for sex crimes, er, 1C, aren't given the time of day. Wham-o, the whole thing is done quickly and quietly. Why go through the bother of letting the victim know anything? It all happens administratively, without fanfare. But *you knew* this was happening to you, you knew about it before we told you. The question we can't answer is, how do you know all this?"

"Because I saw the indictment and the supporting complaint, and since you are going to ask, yes, I know who signed it, it is my daughter."

Jack shook his head in disbelief, not so much disbelief that Max's daughter would do such a thing, for he had no basis on which to evaluate the morals of two people he knew so little about, but in disbelief over this latest turn of events in Max's saga. Was there no event impossible in this man's life? But it was Charlie who threw investigative caution and good jurisprudence to the wind.

"Your daughter signed a complaint against you? Why would she do that?"

A note of uncertainty, where before there had been only a smug understanding of the facts, had crept into her voice. Only *true* abuse cases had an identifiably signed complaint against the accused; for politicos, the whole thing was done in the cover of darkness, often having forged or nonexistent complaints in their file jacket … but that would mean that Max *was* a child abuser? A pedophile?

"Yes, it was her signature on the sheet, and no, I don't know why it is there. I have never in my life done anything other than to love my daughter, in the sense that God intended a parent to love a child. But sign it she did all the same. Now you know why I need to get to her."

Or so he said.

Marie

The next day, at Max's urging and with Charlie's unexpected support, Jack left Ellen at the ranch, having spent only three nights in ten at home, and headed back to town Max and Charlie in tow; Charlie rode shotgun and Max sat in the backseat of a large Chevy truck, a relic of the purely gas and oil days. They had room for one more and the plan was to pick up Daryl, wherever it was he gone to ground; all Jack knew was that it was near downtown—then get Daryl to a safe house on the east side of town. Daryl had left his abode on the mountain to take some of the pressure off his wife, keeping the undesirables from sniffing too closely around his home; for reasons unknown the hunt for Daryl, after years of neglect, was on—the last thing Daryl wanted was to be sighted anywhere near his wife. So, after fifty years of marriage, Daryl was leaving his wife for the safety of his wife; but in doing so he was rolling the dice—parted was parted, and there was no guarantee that the parting would only be temporary.

Whatever Max thought about the prospect of seeing Daryl again, he kept to himself; had they been more than acquaintances—had they been friends … odd friends but friends nonetheless? The whole event had taken on a life of its own; Jack had forgotten that it was Daryl who had started Jack's involvement in Max's saga. Whatever was going on was bigger than any one of them now, and most likely bigger than all of them put together.

Using Jack's apartment as a safe house, Max and Daryl would provide cover for each other as lovers, one of Jack's better ideas … two gay men would attract little attention. Charlie thought the idea funny, though she was well aware of the need for such discretion; Jack didn't understand why it amused her and had no interest in pursuing her wily notions—for Charlie, it was the thought that Max and Daryl might not even like each other anymore … let alone want to pose as lovers.

What did concern Jack greatly was on the nights when he, Daryl, and perhaps Charlie crashed there, all the eggs would be in one basket, as it were.

But the impetus for their excursion back into town this day was not to situate Daryl in his new abode, important a task as that was; it was for Max to find his daughter—though he felt uneasy about his encounter with her. They had not parted on good terms, her insinuating that Max would never be more than a burden on her life, that he would never let her grow to be the woman she wanted—not that Kate really knew what that woman looked like … that Max would forever be judging her and trying to cloak her in his insane system of ethical values and protective morals. Max doubted that the three months since their parting would have eased her anger any; he knew her too well—the last time he had pushed her too hard, mayhap pushed her to the point of breaking, of breaking off whatever remained of a relationship between them.

Well, what of it?

A father could not idly stand by and allow his only child to fall into the clutches of a rat like Guy; he had let her know that and let Guy know that as well. Max knew he was interfering in the life of a grown woman; to do what a father should be doing outweighed the irreverent concern for social decorum between consenting adults—but perhaps it was only in his mind … regardless of which was correct, Kate undoubtedly had a much different take on the whole exchange.

Jack slowly drove down the side streets and alleys to where his flat was located, and then parked the truck in the garage; an old Chevy truck tooling around on the outskirts of town was one thing—driving down Main Street was another. They could ride in a less conspicuous car, but less conspicuous yet was walking, and even more so would be taking public transportation; safety in numbers and whatnot.

The three of them settled in for the balance of the afternoon and evening, before the desert chill moved in; a pot of coffee was brewed and a slow-moving conversation touched on what had been years ago and what might be in the years to come. Charlie listened to Max as he told stories of his life raising Kate, and both Max and Jack were taken in by Charlie's tales of growing up wealthy on the West Coast. Neither Jack nor Max mentioned their own parents, which Charlie thought odd but didn't comment on it; they might not be alive—over the last twenty years the death rate had soared in terms of violence and disease ... the flu from fifteen years ago taking almost one in thirty, while murder in cities of any size had tripled. Innocent bystanders and those caught in gangland crossfire and police crackdowns had contributed distinctly to increased casualties.

No, best not to ask what was not volunteered, thought Charlie.

In the morning Max would accompany Jack to Marie's so that they could get the latest take on the lay of the land. Charlie would catch up with them after they left Marie's; Charlie and Marie were not strongly taken to each other—perhaps Marie was a reminder to Charlie of what awaited her down the road ... old age, sarcasm, and the loneliness that comes with living alone longer than some people live. Besides, Charlie needed to get some stuff ready for Daryl, the type of food he liked, toiletries, etc. But she would definitely be accompanying the two when they went for Kate; based on the trouble Max had with her, all were in agreement that a female coconspirator would be most welcome to provide guidance to what might otherwise be two bungling middle-aged men traipsing around in a young woman's life.

Midmorning the following day, Jack and Max left a small grocery mart near the center of town, each with a bag in arm, and started walking to Marie's with potatoes, milk, eggs, fruit—fresh food and staples. Max thought to ask why they didn't just bring it in from the farm and then thought better of it; he didn't really care and the answer was sure to be cryptic at best—Jack was not one to suffer questions willingly ... those from Charlie and his wife being the exception.

Jack had divided up the groceries as evenly as possible, but the weight still grew into a burning sensation in his forearm; he should have taken the car, but in truth Charlie was the one who needed the car—she was the universal fallback position, and so situated as to get anyone out of trouble in a pinch ... without a car it would be hard for her to get anyone anywhere.

The downtown area was strangely quiet, very much as Charlie had said it would be; it was a situation that seemed to be evolving nightly. As to why this was occurring, the answers varied with each person asked; what was clear was that anyone who had a permit to live someplace else was going to that someplace else—and those who were leaving weren't talking. Jack actually hadn't a clue as to what was going on; he should have, true, but he didn't—this was another reason for paying Marie a visit. She would know.

They crossed a small patch of dirt that passed for a yard and fronted her house, stepped onto the porch, and rang the bell. Max was fidgeting, Jack was bored and hot. Always with Jack there was serious work to be done, serious work being done, but sometimes it was all so darn tedious and slow in producing the results he wanted; what he wanted very much right now was to be back at the ranch, with Ellen and him in bed, sipping the sweet young wine they bottled from the grapes that grew on the eastern edge of the Rincon Mountains. Someday he'd grow some luscious grapes and then lay in the truly superb wine that would follow. Vintner to the "secret well-heeled" he would be, and rich too, just like them. But for now he kicked softly with his toe at a knot in one of the planks of the porch.

Marie opened the inner door on the second knock from the saguaro knocker and immediately began rambling on about how it had started, how it wasn't supposed to happen like this, and some other words strung together, not making sense. Jack stepped back as she pushed the screen door and stepped onto the porch. She was livid, a wild old woman. She stumbled slightly and Max reached in to steady her before Jack moved; *that was good,* he thought, *nice reaction.*

Jack gathered his wits about him, which even so, did not provide a sense of where to go and he lashed out in his confusion.

"Marie, what the fuck are you talking about?" he yelled, bewildered. He had to strain to hear and be heard over the rumble that was coming from the next block over.

Marie straightened and leaned back on her heels, ready to do who knows what to who; literally—she was on the verge of violence, or so it seemed. To say there was something very wrong here was an understatement of the obvious; he had a very bad feeling about where all this was heading … a shudder shot up his back, ending in a tingling sensation of "*knowing*" at the top of his spine. He was not going to like this day and he would probably have a headache before it was all over.

Marie was shouting, Max was shouting too; Jack was only partially aware of what they were arguing about; the clank of machinery was the predominate sound—no, actually—he craned his neck looking back over his shoulder but couldn't see much … it sounded more like construction equipment.

Jack looked at Max who was swearing, Marie who had started sobbing, swayed in toward Max—someone died? The noise grew; Max was so wrapped up in what Marie was doing and Marie was just out of it—neither seemed to be aware of the incessant mechanical clanking, the clatter of tread over concrete … the roar of a diesel engine coming around the corner.

The clatter of the treads jiggled to a stop; time slowed.

The desert air pulsated expectantly like ripples of thick oil molting over a wide pond after a pebble was tossed into it; Jack could see but he could not move—the sound of silence.

The staccato crackling of gunfire sliced through space, and everything seemed to jump to life at once.

Amidst a shower of splinters a hail of metal ripped from the vacant building to their left, worked its way across Marie's house, ripping apart the wall behind Marie in an incandescent crescendo of lead and tracer bullets.

In the briefest of moments before death would tear through them, Jack threw his outstretched hands and his weight against Max and Marie, crashing all three to the floor as splinters and plaster rained down on them. Jack urged and shoved them back across the floor of the porch toward the shattered and smoldering doorway, the three of them teetering like crabs on the deck of a boat. They needed to get inside before another round tore through them, leaving *their* bodies a smoldering ruin.

Marie looked stunned as she unexpectedly sat up; Jack knew that was a mistake, but he was powerless to stop her—a gash above her left eye was his last memory of her face before it exploded in a burst of gunfire that blew her head off her shoulders, covering Max and Jack in viscera and gore. Too late, Jack's blow to her chest flattened her against the floor; a headless corpse was the price he paid for his delinquency. Jack reached out and smacked Max downward with a stunning blow, hard, on the side of the head lest he try something equally stupid.

Towering furniture looked on defiantly as the two men crawled over the debris-strewn wood floor; *keeping low*—then with a guttural *roar* the furniture blew up in a fury of batten and stuffing and the metal shards from large-caliber bullets.

Jack was dragging Max by the shoulder, the other man's jacket bunched in his fist like the scruff of a kitten's neck and almost as vulnerable; Max struggled to keep moving and keep his balance while being dragged close to the ground. A fourth volley careened above them, absolutely panicking Max, who thought to stop moving but didn't.

"What's going on?" he screamed.

"I dunno," was all that Jack could squeeze out between labored breaths before pushing a startled Max down a short flight of stairs to a landing inside the rear door of the house. The firing had stopped for the moment; reaching around Max, Jack twisted the knob, pushed open the door, and the two of them spilled out into the dirt and gravel, one on top of the other. Jack, who had never lost his grip on Max's jacket, immediately began pulling him across the short yard into a ditch behind the house; it was more of a wash, really, than a ditch, dry, full of gangly weeds and refuse. Another push had Max stumbling forward into the wash, hoping not to land on anything sharp.

They crawled through the brush, taking cuts on their hands and face, scrambling over abandoned shopping carts, rotting tires, rusty cans, and soiled diapers; thirty yards, forty, they moved. They could hear shouting behind them and intermittent gunfire punctuated by louder bursts from the large gun on the personnel carrier; they saw no one and the firing seemed to be directed away from where they scrambled, evidently unseen. There were helicopters in the area as well, but they seemed to be hovering more than searching, at least that is what Jack guessed by the steady drone of their engines. Fifty yards, then sixty; still no one, thankfully—they came to a culvert under a road, six inches of water pooled inside … splashing through the dark, scaring off the rats, the light penetrating only slightly at either end.

They exited the far side of the tunnel, bruised and bloody, spent but alive. Here the wash was cleaner but also wider, more open; more of a shallow fallow of scrub and sparse desert grasses than a wash—it would be a simple matter for death to find them here.

They slipped back into the mouth of the culvert , chests heaving, gasping for air. Max's face and hands were a mess, mottled with sweat and blood running freely from a dozen cuts. Jack slipped back out into the wash and, lifting his head slightly over the edge of the embankment, took in the surrounding scene. At this point the wash fed into a large open field bounded by buildings of all sizes and shapes about a quarter mile distant in every direction but west, where the field was bounded by a freeway. To the east, north, and south fires were glowing beneath plumes of smoke; sirens, the sound of small arms, and the occasional explosion reverberated through the alleyways and down the streets, but there was little activity to be seen. *What is going on?* he thought, but only for a moment, till the more pressing question of how to get out of there took hold. There seemed to be troops everywhere, or at least it seemed that way from the sounds if not the sights; this was bigger than the government hunting just him, or Marie, or Max. The image of Marie, her face spread out and plastered over the floor in front of him came to mind and was just as quickly pushed aside; *no time for that now,* he knew, even as he wanted to give in to mourning and vengeance for his elder, gentle friend.

Jack dropped back down into the bottom of the wash. Max was holding his own, crouching to the far bank, sweating profusely, breathing heavily, but unharmed aside from the scratches and shallow cuts.

"Come," he grunted, still out of breath, to Max, "I am somewhat familiar with this part of town. We can follow this wash to a drainpipe that runs under the highway. Once on the other side I think we will be safe behind the embankments and ramps and the like. There are a couple of service stations and a hotel there as well," he gasped and panted, "from the looks of it the fighting, or whatever is going on, hasn't spread there yet. Yes,"—almost as much to himself as to Max—"we should be able to lose ourselves in the hotel area. I'm not sure, but I don't think that they are particularly looking for us."

A wordless jerk of his head in the direction they were to go was all the response that he got from Max, and all he needed. They took off at a crouching run, hoping that the flat barren field at this end of the wash would allow them to make better time, offsetting the greater likelihood of them being seen.

Night was coming on and the gloaming moving into dark was eerily quiet after the day's tumultuous events. Once they had crossed beneath the western highway as planned, they lost themselves in the parking lots and roadside businesses. Working their way north about one mile they reached a west/east thoroughfare—only to see that the fighting, or police action, or whatever it was, was going on there as well. Seeking to avoid being seen, they slipped back south two blocks and paralleled the main road five miles easterly until they reached their apartment complex. It took extra-long on account of their having to hole up along the way; some minutes here, some there—at one time as long as half an hour when they unexpectedly came upon a large raid of some sort on a house in the older district. A personnel carrier was there as well and they saw the soldiers take away an entire family at gunpoint, with hands over their heads. Max pointed out a couple of bodies in the neighboring yards—all they could do was watch, shake their heads at each other in grim fatigue, and wait till it was clear to go on.

It was dead silent when they reached their complex. It had been hours since they had seen more than the occasional soul scurrying across the street or yard in the hushed darkness. Neither Charlie nor Daryl were to be found; Jack could only hope for the best from her—at least the truck was still parked beneath the overhang … driving that behemoth around tonight was a surer invitation to death than most anything else Jack could think of. With Charlie and Daryl gone and the truck still ensconced at home, well, they would have a chance, wherever they were and whatever they were up to.

Jack quietly closed the door to their flat, threw the dead bolt, and pushed a chair underneath the doorknob to at least slow down any attempt at forced entry. He then made sure that the window off the kitchen area was unlocked in the event they needed to make a rapid escape that way. His mind was racing hard along two parallel tracks at the same time: one searching for a point of reference to what he had seen today and what to do about it; soldiers, *not police*, out everywhere and killing people indiscriminately—and the second track, more of a goal, really, of planning a way to stay alive.

Being as they were alive as alive could be, for the moment, it was the first track that concerned him now. While convinced that neither he nor Marie were the target of the sweep, for it was bigger, much bigger in scope than what would be required for just the two of them, it was too much to be mere happenstance that one of the hammers fell on Marie's house; while not specifically looking for Jack or Marie, the authorities must have had some inkling, through an informant, perhaps, that people of interest were in that house. Yeah, that must have been it; that part of the city is a bastion of Socialists—Marie would have been comfortable among them, but not one of them … a phone call to the authorities identifying one who might be different turned out to be a phone call of death.

Then there was Max; head slumped down onto his chest, snoring softly—a soft, contented snore, almost like that of a cat purring.

Dream on, old man. I'd take a place in your dream versus my place in this nightmare. Any day of the week.

Kate

Kate didn't go to work again today; she hadn't gone yesterday either—there probably was no longer any work to go to ... she'd spent most of the last two days in bed with the covers pulled up over her head.

She didn't know what bothered her most, the body laying curbside, just outside her door, or the incessant machinegun fire which had died to a trickle. There were still sporadic bursts to be heard, and the thought that some of those she knew were perhaps part of the dead, weighed heavily on her; that Guy had most certainly known in advance of the day's atrocities weighed even more—he had to have known, his remark that last time he had seen her in her office ... *"not everyone will be coming with us."* His foreknowledge of these horrific events and his coveted interest in her was an extremely repulsive and quite probably dangerous combination.

Kate stayed in her home, in her room, and in her bed for the better part of three days. On the third day he came for her. Kate hadn't known for sure that he would, but in a prescient way she had been expecting his call; for good or for ill, his arrival signaled the end of at least one nightmare even if it were the forbearance of another. She didn't fully understand the nature or degree of his interest in her. Why he did, she could not say; perhaps he had never had another woman before stupid enough not to say no to him after the first date.

When he came he was not alone; he had a pair of thugs with him—two tall, brutish fellows, dark hair, and thick-jowled, with hard, mean-looking hands. Evidently he no longer cared whether she wished to be with him or not; somehow Kate knew that resistance would embarrass him and she would pay dearly for that embarrassment later.

They waited patiently, chatting about stupid stuff as she got her purse; there was no mention of her packing her clothes, or of any of her belongings or trappings of her past life; Kate's life was about to change dramatically, and the fate of a nightstand vase or a blouse seemed pretty immaterial in comparison to what awaited her and what had befallen many of the people who lived in this town—she only hoped that her father was not one of the slain or maimed.

Kate pulled her sunglasses down over her eyes, bloodshot from lack of sleep. She tied her hair back, and stepped out the door, grateful that the body of yesterday had been removed—she slipped sideways into the back of the government sedan, sitting between Guy and an armed guard … a driver and another guard in the passenger seat. All in all it seemed more like an arrest than the start of a new life and frankly she was scared; she wished her father hadn't run off at this particular time, if indeed that was why he had been missing these past few weeks—of course it would have been impossible for him to have known that these events were to occur, obviously, or that she would end up in the clutches of a madman and most probably a sadist of some sort. Her father had warned her about Guy and had threatened him in her presence more than once … it was one of the unfortunate reasons she had distanced herself from him. Truth be told, she had enjoyed his absences—as nosy a busybody as he was— but this was different; for the first time she was facing the future without … without, what? It was not as if he had held her hand through life, nor did she fancy his knowing the ins and outs of her days, but she was about to step off into the great unknown and no one knew she was leaving. Her father would return, the city he had grown up with was in a shambles, and his Kate would be gone. It could very well kill him, sad sap that he was.

She looked over her shoulder as the car lurched away, while thinking that she should have taken a minute to leave a note, and then she looked to her left and the scowl on Guy's face left little doubt that as to what he would have done had she tried. Kate settled down lower in her seat, conscious of her frail femininity among these large brutal men as she never had been before.

Throughout the day she said little, and Guy paid her even less attention; indeed he virtually ignored her other than to instruct others in her disposition. There were a lot of arrangements to be settled in a relocation such as the one he had in mind; in his mind he was coming to own her—she knew it, he knew it, and he knew that she knew it, and that was the most unsettling part of it all … they both understood that Kate's passive acceptance of the events as they unfolded around her was basically acquiescing to his dominance over her.

God, she wished very much for her father to stomp this creep; she could feel the swelling pressure build in her chest and behind her eyes as if she was on the verge of crying, giving herself over to the immense sadness that accompanies the sense of impending doom. She choked back her tears as the car arrived at the airport without fanfare, Kate soon to be little more than luggage with a seat; the sun shone brightly as they crossed the tarmac but an icy cold had gripped her heart. When Guy left her in their compartment of the private luxury jet to go off and bandy about the plane and have a drink with his fellow assholes who were to be flying with them, Kate finally let herself go, and cried … the tears filling the emptiness that had become her life. Later still, after Guy had rolled off of her and fell asleep for the remainder of the flight, Kate lay in the half-darkness; it never got totally dark on board the jet, what with light leaking in from all sorts of sources—it occurred to Kate that she didn't even know where they were headed and she hadn't thought to ask, or if she had, she hadn't the nerve to do so … like the prisoner she was and as a prisoner she was behaving. This would not do.

Kate decided that while she definitely disliked Guy, she didn't hate him, at least not completely, leastwise not at the moment; it was the first major decision that she made in what was becoming her new life—everyone would have a new life after December the 11th, that much was for sure. On that day, someone, or *some ones*, threw all the chips into the air; chips that had been lying idle, some rotting, some basking, some scheming, *some loving*. The chips were now landing; some were landing well, some not so well, and some were coming down in damn awful positions. Of course, some of the chips had simply been removed from the board … broken, burned, or ground into dust.

As to *her* landing, Kate's chip probably hadn't done too badly, at least on first blush, which is why she didn't completely hate Guy. She had been abducted, but she had not been imprisoned; she had been taken to be a concubine of sorts, for a somewhat handsome young man, a young man whose star was rising, or at least it appeared to be rising based on the authority he had over those in uniform. Her situation, whilst personally deplorable, did show promise; she would not go hungry—perhaps she could rise to a role of power in her own right.

But she was not going to do so by being Guy's little doll whom he diddled as he wanted and shown as a trophy on cue; that was not what her life would become.

But she could not challenge him, at least not in public. For one, she had no idea what it was that she was getting into; Guy could be going anywhere to become anything—information … she needed information and she needed it now. A time would come when she could act, and act she would, but until then she had to stay alive.

To say things had turned topsy-turvy in the last week would be to understate the obvious; and the obvious is that, for reasons beyond her understanding, Tucson had been turned into a police state of sorts, or, more accurately, a militarized detention center. In her previous life she had known Guy as a supervisor with whom she flirted and date-talked. In this life he seemed positively dangerous; she could of course have taken a decidedly different start to her new life if she'd denied him when he'd first come to her today, but the look in his eyes—she was not certain that she would have lived out the day had she balked at going with him … a show of strength on her part could have well gotten her killed. She had to remember that being strong could be more dangerous than appearing weak. But weakness, giving in, had hidden dangers of its own; how does one stop, where does one stop, giving in? It seemed like yesterday she was simply flittering through it like an aimless butterfly without a care in the world, and now it seemed that her survival was rooted in every action she took, or failed to take, as the case may be.

Personal bodyguards, private jets—this for a man who just days ago was a nobody … things had apparently changed outside of Tucson as much as in, perhaps more so. If Kate was going to take her place in some newfound royalty she was going to do so as something other than a love slave; she needed to make her own contacts, she needed to find the information to plot her course—and there was no time like the present … as her sultan slept she would plot. But Kate needed to be careful; a door could easily be opened at thirty thousand feet, and all noble aspirations aside, she would die as easily as the next breath if she should be shoved through it.

Kate cleaned herself up first; she'd had sex enough that the fluids that went with it were not unpleasant, indeed she rather enjoyed them from time to time, but this time it was different. In a way she supposed that she had been raped. After all, Guy had not asked her consent and he had physically forced himself on her *unresisting* though *unwilling* body. If that did not constitute rape, then what would? In truth, Kate had all but decided halfway through the act to use sexual intimacy with Guy as a tool, *a weapon*, for getting what it was she wanted (whatever that might be); surely, one of the criteria for rape was that the victim had to feel victimized, rather than victimizing? And what of the part that enjoyed it, even if only a little bit; it was, after all, Guy who had taken her—having pursued him for months, not all of her hated him in spite of what he may have done to her. Maybe she had enjoyed it some, well, a little, anyway. She wasn't at all sure that she regretted it happening.

She put the thought out of her mind permanently; it would not do to dwell on it going forward—what happened had happened, she was either assaulted or not. Besides, justice delayed was not justice denied; yet justice delayed could easily turn toward vengeance, which she had neither the time nor the inclination to invest her energy in. So be it, she needed to be hard as nails. Guy's retribution could wait; he wasn't going anywhere she wouldn't be going.

She opened a suitcase that stood next to the bed; funny, she didn't remember taking it—or even packing it, for that matter—but evidently someone had arranged it. Kate looked over the clothes; an assortment of skirts, blouses, slacks—a dress or two, even, though none of it hers ... all bought in advance, which begged the question of how much in advance. How long had her fate been moving along a line of which she had no foreknowledge?

Going forward. These clothes were either prison garb, or the tools she had at her disposal.

Kate slipped into a modest pair of underwear, thought about a bra and discarded the idea; her attire in this new life needed to be premeditated and a slightly racy appearance wouldn't hurt—it was a bunch of males around her age or slightly older who had the information she wanted. There was a tad of a chill to the plane, so she settled on a pair of jeans and a light sweater. She brushed her hair free in the private bath that adjoined their quarters and, barefoot, she set out on the carpeted floor.

The plane was long and narrow, as planes were; utility and private rooms ran along the right side of the plane while small oval windows on the left peered out into a jet-black night sky. Kate stopped at one and looked through it toward the earth below, but either they were too high or there was nothing below casting a light. It was as dark below the plane as it was above; for all she knew they might have left earth far behind—not that it would have distressed her ... she wasn't at all sure this new life was something she wanted to live through.

There were voices coming from the far end of the hall, toward the front of the plane, so she took off that way, the carpet a comfort to her feet. Her short jaunt ended in an open room behind the cockpit, a room that spanned the width of the plane; seated around a cheap veneer coffee table that was hosting a bottle of whisky—scattered, too, were several glasses with varying amounts of the malt-colored beverage. There were peanuts and shells of peanuts scattered on the floor and table, around which a half dozen men in an unfamiliar uniform lounged in repose.

Thirty thousand feet, barefoot in a room full of armed men, concubine to a man of some unknown power, Kate took her first steps in her new life. She took a deep breath and prayed it wasn't her last.

The men were pleasant and accommodating; it was not difficult for a young woman with a good figure and short dark hair to invoke that response in men. A drink was fetched, some type of scotch mixed with a sweet lemon-lime soda. To Washington, DC, they were going, set to arrive in about four hours. Most of them knew Guy and had worked for him for several months, though in what capacity Kate couldn't even begin to guess, for she had met none of them before, and commanding men seemed to be one of the less likely things that Guy might successfully do. But here it is, the six of them working for Guy; and before that? Several of them had been on assignment for the governor of New Mexico, prior to the dissolution of that state, of course, which along with south Texas, was returned to Mexico in exchange for six billion barrels of oil, or almost the annual consumption of the United States. Not a bad deal, really, as the land was virtually worthless, with few, if any, people residing in the transferred lands. Most of New Mexico had been abandoned years ago, along with its indigenous people. When had this government started caring a whit about Indians and a bunch of poor half-breed Mexicans, anyway. South Texas was much the same; with the local decline in oil production, the United States government sought to use the land as a chip in some bargain arrangement with the Mexican government. The question really was, why did Mexico want the land back, anyway? One theory bandied about was that it was pride alone; they had outlasted the United States and earned back what had been taken from them by force almost two hundred years ago. What was to the United States' worthless land was to the Mexican government national pride, so the Social Democrats got tangible oil in exchange for dirt; if anything could be said about the Social Democrats, it was that they had a good ability to focus on the bottom line—damn the torpedoes, full speed ahead … never look back, never learn.

What these men had been doing up till now was not what Kate was out and about for; she had begun to get an idea as to where this was going.

"Who is Guy's father?"

"Assistant director of the State Department."

That took Kate back a minute; this was no small-time operation she had landed herself in.

"Oh, he must be highly placed."

"Hard telling, miss, he's new to the job."

"How new?"

That brought a few soft chuckles, though from anything humorous or from alcohol Kate couldn't tell.

"Took the post about a month ago. Guy's father had a hand in the crackdown. It was nationwide, you know. Moving his son up was one of the bennies allotted to him. Everything is much more centralized now and everyone who had a hand in it got something in return, and I guess Guy's posting was one of the things the old man got for his services. Anyway, he did his thing and now we do ours.

It wasn't just Tucson, you know, all the smaller 'flyover' cities got hit … all were clamped down on, but they left the big coastals alone. I guess they have always been quite loyal."

"So Guy is?" she asked them.

That answer seemed to come more slowly and she noticed that the room had lost a bit of its jovial atmosphere. "Oh, he's to be an assistant of some sort, I am sure, for his dad or someone else."

Kate nodded. He was a nobody, it would appear, but a nobody of a somebody, which made him a somebody after all; *but maybe not initially*—he was somewhat vulnerable now, as these men offhandedly showed. He was their *assignment;* that was much different than being his men. He would be new in town and looking to establish a name for himself. Well, Kate could help him with that, perhaps help him to a bigger name than he had his sights on, and in the process make a name for herself, a bigger name perhaps than his.

Such it was when Guy awoke about an hour before landing. He went out where she was still talking with his *men* and made a grab for Kate to take her back to their room. Kate tactfully avoided his grasp. This was a risk; she saw a flare of anger appear in his eyes—but when she took his hand and coyly led him toward the door to their room, his scowl turned to a grin, but that didn't lessen his roughness with her behind the closed door. He *could* be rough too, that was something that Kate hadn't really considered in her new plans; she had no intention of being beaten; of that she was sure. Not that Guy had done so, yet. But in her heart she knew that she would hurt him if he did, and kill him if he beat her bad. Kill … the idea seemed at once foreign and comfortable to her.

Where was she coming from with these ideas? Surely a woman had a right to defend herself. As she lay in the darkness next to Guy, Kate chewed on her lower lip; not for the first time and certainly not the last, she felt a moment's indecision, a regret.

Where was the little girl of just a few years gone by?

Where was her father?

Jack

The streets were still with the late-morning air; a crisp net of winter stars had given way to a high-spirited, brisk desert morning. But such a sunny day was not to be the case today; a bank of dark, fast-moving clouds was drifting in over the mountains to the west— this time of year such clouds were usually the portent of rain ... of storms lurking just beyond sight and awareness. The day held the promise of deteriorating conditions. Jack, Max, and Charlie drove slowly through the streets, in the older electric car they used in town, moving slowly, steadily down Speedway. They saw police, soldiers, actually, at most corners but no one made a move to approach them; it was as if after the violence of the last couple of days, everything needed to get wound up again, like a windup toy that had run its course, waiting for the tension to mount again before moving on. It was quiet, the traveling easy, and everything was going fine until they showed up at Kate's house, when it all fell apart.

Max's hand grazed along the edge of a saucer beneath a tea cup; it was a pretty little thing–porcelain, with brightly raised green vines topped with little red flowers intertwining on the cup and handle. It was the type of trinket that Kate would buy and keep around the house, to be used for sure. It was also one of many things that she would have taken with her had she had the time to pack, leastwise the way she would want to pack for herself.

Kate's house was definitely disheveled; it was not the messiness of a young person who lived alone, but the violent messiness of a house that had been twisted about—it almost did not seem as if someone had been taken forcefully from the premises ... but the evidence was there, such as that tea cup with the green vines sitting unpacked on the kitchen table.

Max's unease grew and was borne out when Kate's neighbor, an older woman, came over to see what they were about. Her presence was a tense moment at first, though she was probably unaware of it; the trio had been caught unprepared and hadn't expected to have to speak to anyone, explain themselves to anyone. Quickly they played off each other, through glances and slight nods, putting together a routine; Charlie was a friend of Kate—Max was Charlie's divorced father, and Jack was Max's younger partner … everything needed to be as inauspicious as possible. Satisfied that there was no funny business going on, the old woman recounted how the young girl had been taken away the day before, in a government car, in the company of uniformed men and another man in plain clothes. It had been three days after the shooting; as to where she had gone, the old woman hadn't a clue. There was an uncomfortable silence with each side waiting for more details that weren't forthcoming. Sensing that they should leave first, Charlie thanked her and made to move on, Max slipping a picture in a pocket of his sport coat and the cup and saucer in the other; the picture for him and cup for Kate when they found her—he only hoped that she would be coming back to all of this soon.

Jack was pensive as they slowly drove down the street heading toward the university's main gate; Charlie beside him scratched slowly at her left cheek with her index finger, lost in thought. Max was in the back, shocked, wide eyed; the three of them slowly going nowhere fast.

"Sorry, Max, not the best news we could have hoped for."

The words sounded empty, but something needed to be said to fill the silence before it engulfed them all in worry and guilt. Jack, over the last several days, had started looking on Max with a degree of respect, not something Jack was known to grant people in such a short period of time. Now he sought to reassure the man. For his part, Max was, well, *Max*; he was on a mission to first find his daughter and, second, to get a new life together that included her and some semblance to normality in it. He found Jack's concern irrelevant but touching; empathy might make dealing with the moment easier—but no less painful.

"The part about the man in plain clothes sounds a bit ominous. Any idea who it could have been?"

Max frowned slightly in wistful uncertainty. "If it was someone she knew, it could have been anyone. I hadn't seen much of Kate this past year, and know even less of her acquaintances. It could have been someone from work, I don't know."

"We need to find her or find someone who knows where she is," stated Jack flatly.

"Or find someone who can find her," Charlie added.

Max said nothing, but looked out the rear passenger window. The car turned left through the campus gates; a moment stretched on, to two—then three. Charlie and Jack said something softly in the front, and the car proceeded slowly into the campus, the graveled asphalt crunching beneath the tires; they were heading in the general direction of the library—still, Max remained silent.

"That is a beautiful house. Does she own it or was she just renting?" asked Charlie.

Max squinted as if having to remember where he was and that he had just been addressed.

"Own ... she owned it. Bought it about two years ago. I think."

"Nice place."

"Yes, but not so expensive, at least not now, not as compared to before. I think that it had stood empty for several years prior to her purchasing it ... you know, everyone moving to the big cities. Where are we going?"

Charlie leaned back, over the front seat, closer to Max.

"To where Kate works. Perhaps it will yield us some clues as to her whereabouts."

"You seem to know a lot about her, about someone you never met. Someone you were unaware of until just a few days ago."

"We have our ways; we can do that—we're not exactly who you think we are." Charlie gave Max a rueful grin. "Knowing things is our job, though most of us still have day jobs. If we were *really good* at what we did at night we wouldn't need our day jobs. Did you know Jack is a moonshiner by trade?"

Jack tsked and shook his head. "Vintner, how many times must I …?"

"The two or so years that Kate worked at the university's planning department ... I never once set foot in there, she wouldn't have it. To call on her in public was something she just couldn't abide."

"Really? Why?"

"Let's just say that I had a penchant for interfering."

"I bet you did," Charlie said with a smile.

They decided that only Charlie would go in; Max was way too hot an item, and there would no good way to account for Jack's presence. Besides, there was no telling what the authorities had on him. He used to think it all probably amounted to nothing, or very little; but he wasn't so sure, not now, not since Marie had been killed—it would not do to make a spectacle of himself where he had no business being in the first place … they could very well rake him in at first sight.

Yes, they needed to find Kate, but Jack needed to get back to the ranch too, *and soon*; that was a life that he couldn't let get away.

His thoughts drifted back to young Paul, what seemed to be a lifetime ago. Perhaps knowing what he did now, he should have been more diligent in helping him; perhaps not—it could well have cost Jack his life. Helping Max had its own risks, to be sure; if caught, *this* would cost him his life—but here he hadn't given danger a moment's consideration. What was the difference? Had it to do with himself or with the two men on whom he had made the different decisions. Was it that Max was intriguing and Paul just a lost soul?

Jack smoked a cigarette while they waited; Max bummed one and they sat in the car, the windows down for a bit of air.

"I didn't know that you smoked."

"I don't, really," said Max, "it's not kosher."

"Huh?"

"Never mind. I *don't* smoke, not really, anyhow, only I do when I am with someone who is, sometimes, like now."

Jack gave him a quizzical look. *A real straight-thinking guy.*

"I have been meaning to ask you, if you don't mind. But there has been so much to cover that I, well, didn't, you know." Jack paused, then went on. "You were, I take it, beaten?"

Max winced. He tried to think about his short, endless interrogation as little as possible, and he had talked to no one about it; there had been no one to tell. Certainly not his fellow inmates at the logging camp, and since then, well, he had not been inclined, period. Max ofttimes wondered what he would do if he came face to face with his interrogator again, which could well happen; his emotions ranging from ordinary rage to a vision of the bastard quaking in his shoes and soiling himself in fright. Physical abuse was probably something that never left a person, like the streak of a permanent marker it was always there, just a memory cue away.

At first Jack didn't think that Max would answer; at first Max didn't think so either. They both took a drag on their cigarettes and stared out the window.

"It was bad," he said in a soft voice. "When I first got there they beat me for about three days straight. Never said a word, not really, just beat the piss out of me. Day, night, it made no difference. They particularly liked to wait till I had fallen asleep and then beat me awake with club, boot, and fist. That was the worse, really, the *fear* of going to sleep. I tried so hard ..."

Max got this faraway look in his eyes, almost as if he were working out his horror in the overcast skies that was threatening rain for the first time since his release.

"I tried so *hard* not to sleep, but that, too, was hard. You see, being beaten is among all else, exhausting. I tried so hard not to feel hurt, not to feel helpless, not to bleed, not to cry out ... and I failed at them all. I lost on all counts, and for that,"—Max's faraway look firmed to a hard glint—"for that I would probably kill them if I had the chance. Though violence is not natural to me."

Jack was silent for first a moment, then two.

"You didn't lose on all counts, Max, you kept your spirit. Revenge is not something a broken man aspires to. You know," Jack said, flicking his cigarette out the window, "revenge is a relative thing; the intensity of vengeance is relative to the intensity of the bad which precipitates the vengeance. I mean, vengeance against brutality is a noble thing. It is therapeutic because it is a step back from being a victim. Evil must pay the price for being evil, and the price evil pays is particularly high when it causes vengeance to be precipitated by the innocent.

"However, I prefer the word 'retribution.' For one, it doesn't carry the negative connotation that vengeance often does; guilt or innocence of the individual oftentimes gets lost even in well-justified revenge, or vengeance. Some upstanding and forward-thinking people can't abide by the word 'vengeance,' even when it is justified, and protest against it vigorously. Retribution on the other hand, well, they just don't know quite what to make of that word. Retribution is conceptually tied in with justice, which makes it difficult to be outright shunned. Retribution is what happens when the innocent exact a toll on evil. And that is a good thing. A very good thing."

Max hadn't much to say to that; he was completely unsure how he felt about the idea of vengeance; what was simple to him was his own case—he would kill anyone who harmed his daughter, preferably preemptively, and that wasn't vengeance, or retribution … it was survival.

They sat in silence and waited, Jack reaching into his shirt pocket to pull out another cigarette, offering one to Max, who waved it off. Charlie returned about ten minutes later, wearing a frown that was starting to become commonplace on her, a bit too commonplace on her for Jack's liking; at twenty-nine, life should be more smiles than frowns. Charlie opened the door and sidled into the front seat.

She started in before either of the men in the car could ask her a question. "Well, it wasn't what I thought it would be. That is a scary place."

"Scary?" asked Max with a touch of disbelief. "What could be scary about a planning department?"

Even as he said that, he instinctively realized that living under a scary government made anything having to do with it scary, sometimes scary to the extreme; that made Max feel really bad again, instead of just plain bad. He wanted to jump up and do something, do something in the *past*. Why hadn't he known what kind of life his daughter had led? How could he be so ignorant and judgmental as to be shut out of her life?

Charlie took a nearly finished butt from Jack and pulled a long drag, the smoke trailing through her nose.

"Well, there was just one guy, and he had these really shifty eyes. He was kind of checking me out, which is so commonplace that it isn't necessarily bad, but it was, at least the way *he* was doing it. That gaze, the room, the *isolation,* made me feel … well, vulnerable, like there was a good chance that I might end up being shut up forever in his office. Let's just say that I had my eye on a big pair of scissors sitting on his desk."

"Alright already," Jack broke in, and Charlie stiffened perceptibly. "We all know that you're a tiger in a pussycat's gown, and woe be to any man who messes with you, but what was it that you found out about, Kate?"

"I am getting to that," Charlie said, and none too gently either, "but it was a creepy place and I need to tell you that. It seems there is a fella who worked here till recently, a guy named Guy, who was bragging that he was going to Washington, DC, 'cause his father was getting a big promotion. This guy Guy, sheesh, that's a mouthful. Anyway, *Guy* said that he was going to work for his father and live it

104

up and he was taking Kate with him. What with Mr. Shifty Eyes in there and what he said about this Guy fellow dragging off your daughter to be his, well, you know … *I'm really sorry,* but this doesn't sound all that good."

Charlie reached out and placed her hand over Max's to help him hold on to … what, life? Breaking this news about his daughter was something that Charlie had not been looking forward to, with all Max had been through and his evidently being a real caring father; telling him some bugger had taken his daughter as his sex toy was one of the worst things she had to do in a long time. Being active in the Movement put her in some really awkward positions from time to time, but the feelings of those who managed, through no entanglement of their own, to get wrapped up in the shit coming down from on high was something she thought that she'd never grow accustomed to.

Max sat stone-faced and quiet; eventually he replied. "Kate needs my help, I have been too slow, taking it too easy, being too careful, and now she is anywhere between here and the capital."

"No, not really. Mister Shifty Eyes said that they were flying on a government jet to Washington, and that was yesterday, so we do know where they are, they're there."

"Shit. What am I going to do now. I know my daughter, she'll get herself in a bind, maybe even killed. This fella Guy is going to push her too far and she will kill him if he does, and God help her then."

"God help me," he appeared to mutter under his breath afterward.

"I hope so, *er,* that God helps her, I mean, but if we can get to her first, then *we* can help her and perhaps leave God out of the picture, or at least give him a helping hand."

"Wow, that's really good, Charlie," interjected Jack with a sardonic grin.

"Oh, shut up, Jack."

He gave her a short, sharp nod and laid off.

"That's great, Charlie, but just how do you propose to get us there to help my daughter?"

Jack stared out the front of the windshield; it had started raining ever so slightly—he started thinking out loud.

"Well, we can't fly, you need to get a permit to fly, and we are not going to get those, especially not here in Tucson." Jack hesitated. *Why was it especially not here?*

Max shot him a grim look, bordering on adversarial, which really wasn't fair; it wasn't Jack's fault that Max's life was becoming a complete mess. Bearers of bad news, especially bearers of really bad news, were often the targets of baleful glares from the recipients of that bad news.

"Flying is out, so we will need another way. We could take the train but that entails its own risks, like already being locked in a box. We could drive, but we would need to take a gas car to make any kind of mileage at all, and that would involve being stopped repeatedly for cause. No one drives gas cars anymore without being stopped and questioned about it, and no one drives the type of clunker I have stashed on the ranch."

"Why don't we just walk," broke in Max sullenly from the backseat. "Shit. *I'm going for a walk.*"

He opened the back door and strode off a dozen steps and stood there, hands on his hips, the drizzle a bit stronger now. The sound of footsteps behind him was expected and not unwelcome, but it surprised him some that it was Charlie who came up behind him.

"We'll take the train, Max. We'll get there, don't you worry."

With that, she put her head on his shoulder, giving him a firm hug. It was, aside from the irregular hug from his daughter, the first innocent expression of compassion he'd had in the fifteen years since his wife had died. It was all he could do not to look down to her and kiss her slender lips. Her face was plain, but her dark hair, he liked; the warmth between their bodies was unmistakable—it could have been no more than two people being next to each other on a cold, rainy day, yet ….

It was late December and it was raining. There were risks in taking the train, that was true, and what did she mean by "we"? There were plenty of unknowns on this path, and danger, too; real danger abounded in this land and time—he had the scars to prove it. Who were these people he was now with? Violent, righteous, *moral?* They were helping him, *him,* Max Stein, but why? A thousand other questions ran through his mind as he stood there on cracked and blackened asphalt in a parking lot between the football field and the facilities building. He was afraid, and angry; he was worried, excited, and tired all rolled up into one, and here, in the middle of nowhere, was another person willing, no *wanting*, to share his fear, to be a part of his agony. She was willing to do this outside of whatever daily motivation drove these people—outside of her own torments and needs. He put his arm around her shoulders and held the slim, vulnerable person next to him, sensing, oddly enough, that her vulnerability was greater than his own, which was massive.

He spoke, without looking at her directly, his grip on her arm unintentionally firming.

"Thank you."

Washington, DC

She ran her hand over the wooden railing; well-appointed, stained, and varnished—intricately carved it bordered the stairs that led up to their bedroom. *Bedrooms* actually; she had to keep that in mind—she now had her own.

Kate still had to be available for Guy when he wanted to get off; she had to keep their flat up, cook, clean, and keep his clothes ready—though only lord knew what for, as all he seemed to do was hang around his father and the self-important diplomatic crowd. Guy did absolutely nothing aside from drive her life and hang around his father; then there were Guy's friends—they were creepier than he was, but he wouldn't bring them to the flat … Kate had seen to that.

They had an arrangement of sorts, an arrangement that worked; a room of her own and no creepy friends in the home—that in exchange for her nightly sexual favors, or daily, or daily and nightly. Kate had successfully negotiated their life together, such as it was, into a business arrangement; for her body and the chores she did, she'd bought herself some leverage in her life. Even before their arrival in Washington, DC, Kate knew that she had to battle Guy where she could, but she could only battle him to the extent that she understood him; their current agreement was a testament to her understanding of him at a previous point in time. Soon, today actually, she was going into battle again; this time a hardened warrior of sorts. Kate wanted more than clothes, shoes, tasty food, good wine, and the chance to accompany Guy on his social outings; Kate wanted out.

Not out of servitude to Guy, that would never do. He had no reason to let her go; he didn't humiliate her in public, didn't beat her, never offered her to his friends—but there was no doubt that he owned her, or at least viewed her as his possession. If she pushed him too far, displeased him too much or too often, he could, and would, dispose of her; she didn't doubt this for a second. Even if he just turned her out, credit less, friendless, without family, in a city unknown to her, Kate might not last a night, and a week could truly be hell. Running away from Guy could be a fate worse than death; he would hunt her down and punish her, severely—of that she also had no doubt. Kate knew her place, knew her role, yet slowly, surely she worked to push the limits of her existence. Her own room, no creepy guys was a start; today she was going to push for a little freedom.

Kate wanted out.

She wanted to go outside.

In the two months they had been here, Kate had not left the confines of the flat once; well, she had—part of being Guy's life meant hanging on his arm and fawning over him—or to give such an appearance at the functions and parties that he took her to … rarely enough, which was another thing she wanted to change. Kate definitely needed to meet more people so she could build a new and different life for herself; a life of confidence, albeit with help—help from other people … friends.

Today she was going to get a measure of freedom for herself or Guy would get a measure of displeasure. Not too much, for sure, not enough to change the nature of their arrangement, but enough that he might be spending his nights alone, even if she might put out for him during the day; admit it he would, or not, but her companionship was a part of his life—she was, thankfully, more than someone he just fucked … he at least talked to her about his life, which, stupid as it was, at least that kept her from going crazy. He could on occasion be funny too, though she tried hard not to let him know it; anything to keep him from thinking that he was winning her over; that was something she would never do. But in her maneuvers Kate needed to be careful; there was little to keep him from beating her if she took this displeasure thing too far; she would start sweet—Guy definitely responded well to her charms, almost foolishly so.

She had prepared chicken in tomato sauce; a bit of rosemary, sage, and some pasta. She wasn't much of cook, her father had always told her that, but she was trying; lord knows there was little else for her to do around this flat; immense and well apportioned as it was, she still was virtually always alone. Kate often thought of her father, where he was, what he was thinking—he had always been so predictable—if he was still alive. The crackdown that had preceded her departure had been brutal and many had died, of that she had little doubt, though she knew this only from deduction; the sound of gunfire echoing across the living room of her small one-bedroom house, and echo it did, seemed to have come from all around. Kate had not gone out of her house that day nor the two days that had followed, until Guy came to take her away; but that much gunfire—many must have died, of that she had little doubt.

There was no reason to believe her father would have been involved in anything that might have been suppressed that day, in anything that could had have gotten him killed directly; indeed he didn't even seem to be in town at the time. Kate hadn't seen him during her last month there, even though she dropped by his house twice within that time; he appeared to be gone. Probably on one of those trips he had been taking, camping, she thought it was, which he seemed to do much more of now that Kate would have so little to do with him. But it was his own fault; he just meddled in her affairs too much, always worrying about her, which was cute in one sense while totally annoying in another. She had rarely sought him out or let him come see her. But something had been different that last month; he had never gone away for so long without giving her some notice that he was leaving. True, if it was but a day or two, or even a week, he would casually go on his way without a word, but always, if it had been a couple of weeks or more, he would say *something*. He could have been in town all that time, but for him to go that long without trying to contact her, well, that had never happened. That is why she had gone to his house after not seeing him for almost three weeks; not finding him at home then or several days later when she had dropped by a second time, she now hoped that he was gone when the crackdown came—when men fire blindly, one need not have done anything at all to catch a bullet.

Capable or not, she cooked for Guy and herself. It was good that Guy worked for the government; even better that he was, rather, *that his father was*, so highly placed—decent food was very hard to come by in the city, or so it seemed from the bits of conversations she overheard and news snatches that she caught when Guy watched the television. It was hard to know what was real, though, cooped up in their flat for days, for so many days at a time. She supposed that she could watch the television news herself, keep up on what was presented as real about the world, but she hadn't really the interest and doubted that it would be true.

Kate could smell the liquor on him when he walked through the door: scotch, bourbon, whatever—that was not good …he would want to have her immediately, whether she willed it or not, and since she never willed it, what difference did it actually make? Well, to start with, it didn't fit in her plan.

She could feel Guy's hardness as it pressed into her groin when he hugged her to him; demanding though not abusive, his embraces were more of lust and innocence than power and brutality—he actually believed that Kate had grown to enjoy his company and the arrangement they had. He was so very, very wrong, though there was little she could do about it. Never the strongest of individuals, the thought of herself alone on the streets of Washington, DC, hunted, perhaps, and not only by Guy, was more than she could bear to think about. No, as her father once said, *given time a better option will present itself.*

When they finished, and Guy had spent himself in her for perhaps the hundredth time, Kate got up from the bed. She said not a word during the whole process; she let him take her as he would, allowing his desires to guide her actions, but never a word did she speak, nothing did she initiate; how he could find it enticing she had no idea—that he saw their relationship as one of latent affection astounded her.

Kate first cleaned herself up and then set about to put the dinner on the table. The chicken had gone a bit dry during the time it had taken to pleasure Guy, but no matter; Kate put a splash of wine over the meat, covered it with more tomato sauce, and put the entire dinner on the large mahogany table—just so, with a couple of glasses of wine, and sat down to wait. Her preference would have been to start eating at once, but Guy liked to play at being husband and wife; if she had started before he got down, well, that would not have been very wife-like—so she waited. At one time this abode must have been the home of someone very wealthy, maybe even happy; no doubt it had changed hands many time since then—there must be an abundance of homes of the formerly wealthy capitalists for this one to work its way into Guy's hands. Kate ran her finger over the rim of her glass, waiting for Guy; the Social Democrats, or was it the Socialists, no wait, maybe it was the Progressive Party now—oh well, whatever they called themselves, they excelled in using the accomplishments from or of the past, but created little in their own turn. There was something perplexing about this, though just what it was Kate could not put a finger on it.

Guy entered the room, sat down, and put his napkin in his lap; a sort of totem to begin the meal. They ate in silence for a while before he began talking, always about himself, as if he knew that she couldn't possibly have anything worth saying.

"Today we met with the ministers from IsPal. Seems that they have some technology that they want to transfer to us in exchange for additional offshore manufacturing capacity."

Kate always had a latent interest in anything having to do with IsPal, the new Mideast, some said world power broker, grown from what had originally been Israel and Palestine. Maybe she could run away there; Guy's reach couldn't be that long and it was a place that she had always wanted to visit. Guy kept talking, but Kate found her thoughts wandering back to when she was a child, before her mother died; father had been at times a fairly religious man and would take her with him to services at the synagogue he attended two or three times a month. The melodies and words stuck with her to this day, but that was about it in terms of the religious experience. Suddenly she realized that Guy was talking, and contrary to her normal frame of mind, she wanted to hear what he was saying.

"The technology they want to offer us has no military advantage … as usual, they seem reluctant to transfer any technology that has any military application to it. Their *Ray Cannon*, the one that can track and shoot down planes twelve miles distant with 100 percent accuracy, is something that we—*my father*, thought Kate—again tried to get them to offer to us. Indeed, we told them that we were willing to exchange a year's worth of manufacturing at any industrial cluster for simply a look at the plans."

"And they said?"

"Well …." Guy paused.

He was actually fairly intelligent, if unambitious, the life of pampered luxury, but he could be ignorant as well; telling her things which obviously shouldn't be spoken of outside of the offices of the State Department, yet he did so all the time. Only sometimes, like right now, she could tell he would get a sense that perhaps he should not be saying what he was about to say. But Guy could not resist impressing this woman he thought of as his wife.

"Well … I wouldn't say they laughed at us, but they did brush the offer aside, almost as if they didn't hear us make it."

Kate nodded, and they both ate for a moment and drank some wine, another advantage of living in the diplomatic world … fine wines, this one from Italy, last night's from France, and the night before was a California varietal. If the common folks could see how they lived right at this moment, they might have second ideas about the wisdom of having handed so much authority and control to the government, which meant the Socialist Party, or were they the Social Democrats. Again she sighed, confused.

"Everything fine?"

Kate gulped a quick mouthful of wine to hide her expression and steady her nerves. Had she detected a *"honey"* or *"dear"* dangling at the end of his question? She gulped another mouthful—it was scary how he kept moving their relationship along. *Though perceived as unfair, the capitalist system had provided a much more* balanced *distribution of wealth and standard of living, even if it might do so from ignoble purposes.* Kate was jolted; where had that thought come from? She brushed her shoulder-length hair back over her right ear. *I should really braid this.* She must be losing her mind; previous musings roared back and odd thoughts kept poking at her as if to ground her and wall her off from the sentiments of a madman.

She gulped another quick mouthful of wine as if to hide her discomfort over her discomfort; she really was going mad—she needed to get on with her game … and get out of her mind.

"What technology did they offer to transfer?"

"Oh … enhancements on the water desalination technology they transferred to us two years ago. Seems that they have developed a means to increase output—of water, that is—from the same level of input, *without* the need for additional power or collateral resources. We obviously did not understand the technology, but took the plans to be reviewed by our science team. If it pans out, it would be worth the additional capacity they are seeking, though again, it is not a military application, so our excitement level was not high."

No, most certainly not, of what benefit to the State are benefits to the common man? Again! Where had *that* thought come from? Though she was a PoliSci major Kate had never been known to hold a political point of view; but that seemed to be changing as well—maybe it came from being confined for these so many weeks … maybe it was due to a case of nerves from what she was about to ask.

"I've been thinking that perhaps it would be good, for us, that is, if I were able to spend some time out of our flat on my own." She stopped. Originally she had penned a whole speech in her mind to work through to get to this point, but she couldn't help it and always played in a bold and adventurous way; it was what she wanted and she had come too far to cover her aspirations with a complex cloak of conspiracy, even if it was a conspiracy of one.

Guy's reaction was part what she expected and part unexpected. He had been drinking from his glass of wine when she broached the topic; that had been intentional, though she wasn't sure what advantage she might accrue from that other than to catch him more off guard, though it was debatable that such would actually be to her advantage. He studied her suspiciously over the rim of his glass. He was thinking, *What is her motive here,* as she knew he would, but his reply came from a totally unexpected point.

"What will you give me for this additional freedom?"

That pretty much floored Kate. All this time, what with a room of her own and keeping his friends at bay, she thought that she had been playing *him,* stealthfully getting, incrementally, what she wanted in her life; evidently he had been playing her as well. The scary thought was that perhaps it was only she who was being played; from start to finish, her every move, her every effort at gaining a bit of independence was being guided and exploited by Guy.

No. He was smart but not that smart, yet he obviously understood the rules of the game they were playing. Kate had to keep that in mind.

"Being outside, my body tone will improve, a bit of exercise, you know, firm my thighs, tighten my butt," she said with a coy smile.

"If it is exercise that you are offering me, I can bring you gym equipment. What you are asking me for is something more, much more; what I am wanting in return is something more than a more *toned* you."

This was not good. While it was one thing to be a kept woman, even when one was kept against their will, it was another thing altogether to trade physical favors Guy was looking for, for certain benefits to her life. Did trading sex for some freedom of movement make her any less a whore than the woman who traded her sexual favors for money? Well, did she have a choice in the matter?

"More?" Kate choked softly.

"More."

Why was this so hard? How was it different than what she did now for room and board? But this was not how to *win* at this game; in order to *win*, one had to trade that of the lesser value for that of the greater, while not appearing to be doing so—and she intended to win.

"More, then," Kate cooed, much calmer than she felt. She made her way over to where Guy sat. "*More*, you say, so very much *more*."

She felt confident, but not good; how could she ever feel good with what had happened to her, what was happening to her, with what she was becoming—but she knew what she was doing and she could do it well. Best to pay early, by playing to Guy's immediate and short-term fascination and avoid a bigger bill down the road; the price would only go up from here if she had to ask a second time. Kate kneeled in front of Guy and opened his robe. Guy put his head back and began breathing deeply and then soon began moaning. After they had finished in the dining room, Kate led him by the hand into the bedroom for round two; if nothing else, three months with Guy had educated her to all his sexual lusts and perversions—and tonight she played to all of them. It wasn't long till Guy lay on the bed drained and exhausted, with an immense feeling of satisfaction.

"Damn, Kate, that was the best yet. You were holding out on me. Imagine, all that for the chance to move about a bit on your own. I can only imagine what you would have done if I had offered you your freedom." Then his eyes narrowed. "I am not offering you your freedom, though, do not be mistaken about that." His voice moved from amiable to harsh. "You are still mine, and you live and die by my word. Do not live to regret this day that I give you your request, for if you betray me you will pay with more than your life, I promise you."

Kate looked at the man whose bed she lay in. This was a Guy she hadn't seen before; all pretense of affection and illusion of a relationship was gone from Guy's steely eyes; it was as hard a look as anyone had ever given her, which was appropriate—no one had ever threatened her life before and Kate was not one to miss nor forget so blatant a threat.

Kate dressed; she marveled at the feeling her newfound freedom brought her. The gloom of last night, the way in which she had debased herself, the means by which Guy had threatened her, were but the bad vestiges of an evil dream. It was a new dawn, a new day; Kate had what she wanted now, what she needed, and she did not need to ask for anything more. It was just as well, for Guy's parting remarks to her this morning were ominous; there was no limit on the toll he would exact from her with her next request.

Kate was half-dressed before she realized what she was doing; looking in the mirror she saw a vibrant young woman dressing to go out on the town; a button-down sweater that accentuated her toned figure, a smart pair of dress slacks, stylish leather shoes, her hair down—this would not do at all. She was still a pretend wife to a temperamental and likely vicious man, and it would not do to go out looking young, attractive, and … well, like she wanted to meet someone. Ha! At this point she would like to meet anyone who didn't know her, or at least wasn't Guy. To have one normal day in her life at this point would mean more to her than all the fancy wines and polished banisters she could get her hands on. Her life was not right, that was a big for sure, but to go out looking like she wanted to get something else out of life would not do, leastwise not on her first foray out on this December morn.

With a bit of a huff and a tsk to herself she changed into a pair of jeans, a light sweatshirt, a pair of tennis shoes, her hair in a ponytail—there, now she looked the part of a wife, which was all the more likely to keep her out of trouble. She grabbed the keys and stuffed them into her pocket and headed out the door; for the very first time *alone* and on her own, and down the steps to the street below.

The day had some bluster to it, a late-winter day without the snow, though it had rained the night before; while dew covered everything and everything was wet, two degrees Celsius kept it all from freezing. Today, the world seemed almost magical, clean, the air fresh and brisk, the morning quiet. The *happy couple* lived on a side street equidistant from the White House and the Washington Monument, and Kate headed toward the latter. A fifteen-minute walk brought her to the base of the monument, where she sat in the sun admiring its grandeur. The tall white spire pressing against the gray morning clouds flushed red where the sun made an effort to pierce the veil; the absolute greenest of greens of the grass that circled the monument flowed off to the east and west like some vast river. She was glad that she could see it as an adult, instead of the child she had been the last time she and her family had toured Washington; to see it before it was torn down—leastwise, that was the talk … years of American dominance on the stage of world affairs was bringing membership into the League of Nations with a price, nation America must turn her back on her imperial past. The monuments, the American pride, had to go; even her currency was at risk … there was talk that the United States, soon to be called the American Confederation of States, would be taking up the World Dollar as its currency.

None of this made sense to Kate; if she could understand the wonders and affluence that America had brought the world, then certainly the rest of the world could see it too—so why tear it all down?

But that was a moment in time for the politicians of the future. Right now, here, today, there was so much wonderful American history in this town; it was hard fathoming why she had not pushed to be on her own before—indeed she found it hard to fathom why it was that Guy showed no interest in taking in these sights, with her on his arm … it might actually have endeared her a little, a very little, to be sure, but nonetheless some, to him.

She ran down the grassy hill, the monument at her back, feeling the exhilaration of being out on her own; her shoes off, she stepped through the grass, crossing the occasional asphalt walkway, and made her way along the right side of a long, shallow pool, the Reflecting Pool—and soon wandered into the Vietnam War Memorial. Kate spent some time contemplating a war now years gone, virtually all of the veterans dead. There were still POW/MIA medallions attached to the wall but they were long-tarnished things that probably had been put there thirty and forty years ago, back when there were still some who talked in terms of finding America's missing boys, or old men, as the final result of that conflict. But no more; the missing were all dead, and those searching for them had died as well. Kate remembered reading that attendance at the memorial had fallen to new lows with each succeeding year as the veterans, the families of veterans, and those in general who had lived through the war died off. She ran her hand over several names of men long dead and wondered who they were and how they had died, if they had died alone or in the company of friends; she drew a strange sense of power from the touch.

She marched up the hill fronting the memorial, to a statue honoring a group of nurses tending a dying soldier. The clouds had reformed and it started to lightly drizzle, sobering her mood, yet somehow appropriate as the rain formed tears on the faces of the female statues comforting the dying man—it was as if they were crying over their fallen comrade, over the loss of a man, the loss of Man. She looked back over her shoulder at the wall sequestered in the low hillock and then back to the larger-than-life statues in front of her confronting death. Yes, there was much wonderful history in this town. Kate put her feet together and like a minaret, pushed herself up on her toes and did a pirouette. It was exhilarating.

Through a small grove of trees and across a short expanse of forested lawn she spied a set of overly large figures cast in roughened metal, soldiers all, laboring through an overgrown meadow. It was the Korean War Memorial, a tribute to a war even more distant in time and public consciousness; yet after generations the immortal figures still spread out on patrol, every morning, every day, looking both purposeful and forlorn—such sacrifice, such a sense of self-worth ... all adding to the strength she felt building in her. She was right to have demanded her freedom of Guy; her world was turning and for the better—whatever the price she had paid, the payback to her was coming in tenfold.

From the Korean War Memorial she made her way to the Lincoln Memorial; squat and pillared it stood in opposition to the stark and towering pinnacle of the Washington Monument standing directly across the Reflecting Pool about a mile distant. Lincoln and *his* monument were a quixotic moment in time so different than today.

Lincoln had been a bold man, living in a bold time, a decisive time. Many of the books on Lincoln had disappeared as of late, and his strong, moral, and male leadership was no longer as pronounced in the histories, from what she could tell; it was part of the standardized push to level, or as Kate liked to say, *neuter* history—in this case attributing much and more of Black emancipation to the Blacks themselves ... only the older textbooks and books of literature disputed this new view and reinforced the strength of Lincoln, but it scared her more than she could say that history, a recorded and documented history, could be so casually rewritten.

Kate wandered through the cavernous pantheon in which a figure of Lincoln sat towering above her; a marble figure, in a marble chair. Along the walls and in kiosks throughout the monument were glass-covered display cases; ensconced in them was the history of Lincoln and this time, original documents dating back almost two hundred years. It occurred to Kate that these were more than just monuments to a man, but testaments to what had transpired. When these were gone, who would know what transpired of her country's history?

Electronic media was intransient and even in times of good intentions was liable to be inaccessible; formats change and the format that was readily legible today could become inaccessible tomorrow if storage failed to keep up with technology—who determined what literature or which documents got rolled over and at what cost? Who was tasked with making sure that some mundane yet critical piece of history was not overlooked? America was becoming more neutered every day; soon, perhaps, only those with an active and persistent interest in history might know the truth—and how many folks would make such an effort in a society where satiation of immediate needs was paramount?

A ten-minute brisk walk from the Lincoln Monument amongst the hillocks and trees along the river brought her to the Roosevelt Monument; more an open-air exhibit than a monument, really, winding near a quarter mile, replete with historical waypoints of Roosevelt's life, times, and policies chiseled into granite that flowed around the grounds at varying heights—at ground level and rising up twelve feet … bronze statues and statues thematically placed around waypoints of history. Roosevelt's reign began a history wherein once the Conservatives slipped behind, they never regained their ground … a slow descent into obscurity was all that the future held for them.

Pressured by the expanding entitlements of an ever-burgeoning welfare state, the public, *the electorate*, did not care to understand the policies that were putting the country in an increasingly precarious domestic situation and a global competitive disadvantage; once the economy began to lag it was too late to return to any type of rational economic planning—straw dogs were set up as the sources of the country's ills … knocking them down presented the perception that democracy was still functioning, even if the country was not.

Lured by the prospect of harsh and poor-paying jobs, and inexpensive housing cheaply built with toilets at the end of the hall, people began to leave middle America for the coast; the populations of Los Angeles, New York, Houston, Seattle, Miami, Boston, and the like careened off the map, while cities like Phoenix, Dallas, and Denver, once economic giants in their own right, lost almost a quarter of their populations over a five-year period. Staid and conservative middle America had always been a stumbling block for the Social Democrats on their road to power; the electoral college vote, relocating out of the conservative heartland, now added to their growing grip on power … value, wealth, and middle America went the way of the dodo bird and the Studebaker.

Boston to New York became a single city jokingly referred to as New Boston; Baltimore, including Washington, DC, down to the Atlanta area became Capital City—spanning near four hundred miles from north to south. On the West Coast, San Diego finally met LA, and San Francisco would have incorporated Portland into Seattle but for the intrusion of the towering cliffs along the north coast.

America the free, America the proud, limping along on the Socialist model wherein small groups of people saw their standard of living rise, while the majority of Americans experienced an equal, uniform, and steady decline in their standard of living. As America wallowed, for the most part in despair, international centers of political power and economics rose; Europe, with its antiquated infrastructure and scraggy socialistic policies, was not one of those centers, and neither was Asia with its staggering population loads. Rather it was the African nations, rich in natural resources and vibrant young cultures; IsPal, the newly formed union of what had once been Israel and Palestine, became one of the leaders on the global stage. In a very few years IsPal had become an economic and political powerhouse, dominating the Middle East in patent applications and capital acquisition, on the strength of being the sole democratic and free market nation in the region.

Leaving Roosevelt and his memorial in the past Kate followed the asphalt path along the lakeside walk, a lovely narrow trail shrouded by trees, with the soft lapping of water ever so close—it was a true Virginia gem in a city of mega proportions, with its massive structures and boundless citizens. Despite a cold, overcast day, there were ducks trailing in packs around the lake which ran about a half mile in length and about half that again in width.

It was an impressive and beautiful thing, the way the country honored its past. Statues and monuments to major individuals and events stood tall for the citizens to see. What would come of them? Destruction of America's rogue and robust past was the price to be paid for joining the international community of nations; in this day and age it seemed unlikely that any of those memorialized *would* have been heroes, or that any of the heroic achievements would have been achieved.

At the end of the sparse and somewhat hidden lake sat the Jefferson Memorial; conspicuous in its subdued architecture—far from grand in contrast with the Lincoln, Washington, and Roosevelt Monuments, it was a small, quiet rotunda which was difficult to find and once found, quiet to enjoy ... it seemed to feed off its location, the lake gently lapping at its granite stepped shores with seeded and coned pine trees surrounding it. The Jefferson Memorial, as was the man himself, the very face of contemplation and reflection.

Her troubles began shortly after she left the Jefferson Memorial and started making her way back to the Mall.

It was late afternoon and a homeless girl not much older than Kate was sleeping on a bench along one of the asphalt paths leading back home. The girl's hair was an unwashed tangle of mismatched lengths, her clothing was soiled and patched, or just plain faded and worn; she had an unpleasant smell to her—a smell of not having washed for days upon weeks. Kate certainly didn't know this vagrant woman, nor did she have any particular sentiment toward her, but the sight of her brought home to Kate how precarious her own life could be and was. She hated Guy, that was a given; inside, she couldn't deny it—she knew that eventually she would get away from him one way or another. But she didn't want it to be in such a way that resulted in her ending up like that, sprawled out in the middle of a park sleeping on a bench with all her worldly belongings in a shopping bag underneath the bench that made up her bed.

Kate hurried on. The sight of the homeless woman unnerved her more than she could say; it would have been enough to spoil her first outing on the town, but then something happened that really sent chills down her back—Kate realized that she was being followed.

A man wearing jeans and a heavy flannel shirt had been sitting on the steps at the Jefferson Memorial; he had a foreign look, maybe Middle Eastern, and he made some attempt to hide an interest in her but left the same time she had. Kate dismissed his interest as male gawking and their simultaneous departure as coincidental, but since that time he had been taking the same route as she was, albeit in front of her, but he had been pacing her; what really set Kate's hair on edge was the fact that he had stopped for exactly as long as she had while looking at the homeless woman.

Kate quickened her steps and passed the man; he made no notion of recognition, which in and of itself didn't mean much. As she passed him he stopped, feigning interest, perhaps legitimate, in a plaque commemorating the life of some patriot from years gone by; there were many such plaques set among the eves of the forested park, in honor and remembrance of people of significance and events from the past.

She slowed some, glanced behind, and saw he made no move to follow her. Perhaps it had been nothing after all. She breathed a sigh of relief, but her relief was short lived.

She had gone no more than a dozen paces when from a grassy knoll on her right, a knot of six or seven young men started moving toward her. This she didn't like one bit. The homeless girl was nothing, the man following her was threatening but not in a violent sort of way; but this—Kate found it hard to believe that something bad could happen to her in broad daylight, in a public place ... but she wouldn't say for sure that it couldn't.

Kate looked over her shoulder; the man that had been following her earlier was gone, but this other group of men was moving quickly toward her. The Mall, while not empty, wasn't exactly crawling with visitors; she had no one to appeal to for help, leastwise not in the six heartbeats or so it would take for this group of men to reach her.

She took this moment to panic, breaking into a run toward home.

But not on the path; Kate veered through stands of trees and brush, hoping to lose her pursuers in the denser, forested parts of the park—but it wasn't working and they were gaining on her, no more than perhaps forty yards back. So she cut back toward the path hoping that maybe speed instead would prove to be her advantage.

Kate could see the main boulevard that ran along the park's northern edge; maybe she could find a policeman or someone to help her.

She looked over her shoulder.

She wasn't going to make it to the street—the two fastest pursuers were now only twenty yards behind her and gaining rapidly. Kate reached into herself for all she had, for more speed, her legs pumping furiously, her calves burning, but she barely felt the pain. Fifteen yards now, in a moment they would be on her and there was no telling what would ensue. It was so unfair that something so fast could be taking this long; if only *thinking* of someplace else would get her out of this.

The roar of an engine startled her and almost caused her to trip; she did stumble. Keeping her balance, but barely, she glanced around as she flailed backward in her steps. A man, no, actually *the* man in the flannel shirt who originally had been following her, was running a motorcycle between her and her pursuers. The two in front threatened him, lengths of pipe and pieces of chain apparently appearing out of nowhere; Kate kept running.

The man turned the motorcycle hard, goosing the accelerator as he did so; clods of earth flew out in the bike's wake—again he cut through the path of pursuit. Kate was pulling away, but now she saw that the man on the bike might be himself in danger as the pursuit began to rapidly surround him; he pulled a handgun from along the side of the gas tank and pointed it at the lead man who tripped, stumbled, and went down, tangling up his compatriot with him. Kate made her break across the street and up a side street to an alley heading back in the direction of her flat. Her last glance over her shoulder showed that the gang of men had stopped where the two had gone down.

The man and the bike were nowhere to be seen.

Kate had a good sense of direction; heading alongside the park but keeping a block north of it she came upon the security cordon along the southern facade of the White House. Finally she stopped running; she felt safe. There was security everywhere. Trying to look like a young woman finishing a morning jog, she slowed, breathing heavily, and headed south toward the Washington Monument. From there she cut back uphill and two blocks to her flat, pushing the key into the lock and giving the handle a firm twist.

Stepping inside she shut it with a strong push, throwing the dead bolt, and shutting out the world.

Her prison had become her sanctuary; she broke down and cried.

Tucson

Go, they did not; there were no hours spent preparing for a journey to Washington, DC, no covert plans to locate and rescue Kate; it was a journey that Max realized he would never make—his thoughts of going to Kate, like so much else that had been part of America, died in the days that followed The Crackdown ... as violent December afternoon had come to be called.

It would not have even been possible for Max to have been brought to Tucson, *covertly* or otherwise now; if he hadn't come when he did, he would never have made it all. It certainly was no longer possible for him to leave—it was no longer possible for anyone to leave. Reports were coming in of repressions all across the Southwest; what had seemingly started in Tucson had in actuality been a simultaneous operation; military law had been declared in what remained of the heartland cities of any significant population.

In an odd nod toward legality, or perhaps to avoid the pretense of complete illegality, an explanation was crafted to cover the crackdown and address the little-known, or perhaps little-remembered, prohibition on the use of military force within the geographical borders of the United States; the military was not acting *against* American citizens but rather it was *protecting* Americans living in the isolated cities of the country's interior—protecting them from threats emanating from terrorist agents in neighboring cities.

It seemed that disaffected elements in Albuquerque were going to march on Tucson.

People will manage; they will live, interact, plan, and simply enjoy life together. As it became increasingly evident that Max wouldn't, or couldn't, go after his daughter, he and Charlie began spending more time together, if for no other reason than Charlie was bored and Jack had moved on to other things; having no idea what to do with Max, he had left him on his own—or at least to entertain himself.

Max was a wanted man; in this life of irregularities he could not hope to lead a regular life, whatever that might be, even if he knew how. Jack saw progressively less of Max, which he didn't mind that much, and less of Charlie too, which bothered him more than he would admit; Jack had a fond affection for Charlie—somewhere between a romance that could never be and a daughter he would never have. But today found Jack seeking Max out; today Jack finally had some answers to the many pieces of Max's puzzle.

He knew well where the two of them were living, and Charlie answered on the second knock.

"Hello, Charlie."

"Jack! Whoa, I haven't seen you in so many days." Charlie planted a nice wet kiss on Jack's lips, who didn't push away, at least not right away, but did so rather quickly when he felt a well-remembered squeeze to his buttocks; she could be a rambunctious young woman.

"What can I say? It seems that Max keeps you too busy for me," he said, disentangling himself from her embrace.

"Indeed he does," she said with a sly smile.

Max appeared at the door, recently showered, toweling off his well-toned upper body above a pair of well-worn slacks. He'd trimmed his beard and wore his hair a bit shorter, making him seem, well, almost respectable. Honestly, *what* she saw in him; that wasn't completely fair, though. The man was as forthright and honest as one could be, and handsome too, beneath all that fur.

"Hey, Jack," came his proffered greeting.

Max didn't look forty-seven at all. Jack frowned; maybe he was making it up, his age, that is—but why would someone lie about their age … upward?

"Good to see you too, Max, clothed, or at least partially so, at least."

Max's manner was easygoing, but Jack had never been quite comfortable around him; even now, when he knew Max's secret, or, rather, the secret about Max, he still couldn't get over his discomfort—knowing Max's secret just affirmed in his mind that the man was trouble, whether he willed it or not. At the same time it was hard not to like the fella.

"How are you doing?" he enquired.

"Much better than this harlot is telling you, I am sure."

His towel lightly snapped at Charlie, who giggled.

They suit each other, Jack thought. *Charlie makes Max feel younger,* that had to be it, Max's youthful appearance, rather than him lying about his age—and Max makes Charlie absolutely childish … *at times, but not all times.* Jack couldn't and didn't even try to forget the two men she had killed last month; granted it had been self-defense, but she could have walked away—another might have.

"And you?"

"Huh," came Jack's reply, as if caught out of thought, or at least out of the thought of the conversation at hand. "Good as can be expected," he said rather stiffly.

It didn't take much for the reality in which they lived to rear its ugly head in an equally ugly reminder.

"Right. Thanks for the food."

"You're getting it? Good, though I suppose I would have heard, had it been otherwise."

"Yes, but we escapees can't exactly register for food cards, now, can we? You broke me out, now you have to feed me. Just kidding. I am yours and in repayment I serve the opposition, or the resistance, whatever you call it; I suppose were I a mere mortal and not an immortal, I would be in the resistance anyway."

That remark brought a guffaw from Charlie, which in turn brought a smile to Max's lips, and then, reluctantly, to Jack's; Charlie was very special—Jack understood why Max, *and he*, loved her.

"But surely you didn't come all these seventeen blocks to check on our well-being."

"Of course not. Ah, actually I mean yes, what I meant … I …"

"Don't, Jack. It is okay, really. Life is shit and we all have a lot of shit to do."

Christ, Max was even starting to talk like her. Then Max continued, all seriousness.

"Jack, what have you come to tell me? It's not about Kate, is it? It is not bad news."

"No, not bad news. I mean yes it is, but not bad about her. Look, I haven't found her and I don't know anything more about her or her whereabouts than do you … that she is in Washington somewhere"—he waved off to the east—and left the *probably with a sadistic bastard* unsaid. "It's more about you and it isn't necessarily bad news—it's more, well, more just *is.*

"Being lucid, eh?"

Jack smiled. If he remembered rightly, he had used that term once to describe Max when they had first met. He chuckled slightly, then tightened up.

"Max, I know why you were arrested."

Silence.

"Maybe we'd better go inside."

Jack noticed that their banter hadn't gotten them through the front door; instinctively he looked over his shoulder and thought of another morning on a porch, half expecting someone to take a shot at him; it was all written into that one day, and everything that had happened since, the life they were all leading today.

God, how he hated Socialists.

Jack shook his head; his thoughts were wandering again, which usually spelled disaster, leastwise it did in the type of conversation he was about to get himself into.

Inside the house was cozy. Sparse, with gently used furniture and a wholesome smell of simple foods, a little tobacco, and natural cleanliness, a smell that reminded him of home, not of his parents' home, but of his grandparents', back when success was the same for everyone, and everyone wanted success; success without qualifications—his grandparents' success had been a home with a front porch and trees in the yard … who could argue with that? Now they did; *what was the environmental cost of that house with the porch? What was the impact on the environment of getting to work?* Of *having a job? Of living? Breathing?* It was a good distraction for the Socialists, possible only because people tended to eat what was spoon-fed to them—have a little environmental propaganda, a little racism, a little class warfare with your welfare check and government subsidies.

Today a family was looked upon as being selfish, 'specially if there was more than one child in the family; the Socialists, had shepherded the American dream into the arena of international condemnation—the previously good, strong, and independent America was now a bitter reproach from foreigners who owed almost everything of value to the Americans of yesterday, from the barbarous regimes of the National Socialist dictatorship of Nazi Germany, the ultra-repressive regimes of Africa, or the communist dictatorships of Russia and China, the world owed America.

For elimination of viral infections, feeding the world, electric lights, and running water, the world owed America.

But not anymore; today's leaders of the United States allowed America's exceptionalism to be turned on its head and become a liability; the big, strong shoulders that built American railroads were now seen as the shoulders that carried the arms that crushed, not Nazism, but indigenous populations' aspirations to power; the genius that produced electricity and had saved countless lives through refrigeration was now seen as a madness that gave rise to global warming, the fact that global warming has been demonstrated to be a natural shift in ecosystems notwithstanding. All that was bad and wrong in the world was to be laid at America's doorstep; now loved by the European Liberals, the American elite were willing to do what it took for acceptance into a world dominated by the stagnate societies of Socialist Europe and sacrifice the freest, most prosperous, and racially inclusive country in the world.

One can only believe that American leaders are grievous to be American.

God, how he hated Socialists.

Jack paused on entering the room; it was the first time he had actually entered their flat—the room was filled by the natural light from the late-afternoon sun. Charlie was quiet, somber, a rare state for her, though becoming more frequent each time he saw her. *This world sucks,* he thought, *and it will be the end of the once innocent like her.*

God, how he hated Socialists.

Charlie quietly took Max's hand as they sat on the couch; she was confident there was only one type of news coming from her old friend—bad or worse. Jack wasted little time and got down to business.

"Well, where to begin?"

Silence.

"Okay, that was silly."

Pausing and taking a deep breath as if to assuage his guilt for having to be the bearer of this news, he continued.

"Max you were arrested not because of anything you did, or because of anything you knew, nor anything you might do. You really were, politically speaking, a nobody. Just as you claimed. Just as we always expected. You were arrested to get you out of the picture."

He paused a moment to invite a question, but other than an impatient look, none was forthcoming; they were not going to make this easy on him, so he continued.

"This thug, Guy, whom we all have grown to love to hate, had you arrested so that he could, how can I say this simply … oh yeah, as I had been planning, so that he could make off with your daughter."

This time he hurried on, not inviting questions; this was going to get a whole lot messier before it got better.

"At the time when he had you arrested, I don't believe that taking her to Washington was what he actually had planned. That came later … I think. After all, why take you out of the picture if he were taking your daughter out of the picture. Unless, of course, he just is the mean son of a bitch we all think he is. Sorry. What was part of the plan was to get you out of the way forever, if possible.

"That was why he set you up, or *had* you set up, on a political charge. A political charge was the fastest, easiest, and safest way to have you disappear, permanently and quickly. People hauled off for political reasons aren't actually charged with political offenses. That would only serve to legitimize and energize whatever opposition remains in this country, which would never do. People who the government wanted to make disappear for political reasons were almost always charged with sexual offenses, usually rape or child abuse. The processing of charges under these crimes is expedited through the military courts, such as they are. The victims of which are not required to testify in open court, for 'their protection,' but since the crimes are all falsified anyway, there are no victims, but just the same the sentences are lengthy and punitive. All this is designed to support a government's desires for certain people to disappear quickly, completely, and forever.

"I don't know how often this technique is used to settle a personal score, but I do believe it is fairly atypical. While the administrative process behind this type of judicial abuse is swift, there is a good deal of oversight inherent in the program to make sure that it isn't abused. There couldn't be so many sexual predators so as to seem fantastic, or dispiriting. So, targets for this expediency are thoroughly reviewed and vetted. Only the most powerful could bypass this review and have the target sent straight to that northern mortuary. Guy, through his father, had this power, though it is unclear that his father knew that Guy was using this power for his personal ends. Guy only needed to drop his family name to the right people and obedience was pretty much guaranteed; it would have

130

worked too, only he hadn't counted on me, or people like me. I don't necessarily mean altruistic, self-sacrificing people—of which I am not—but people who watch out for things that don't sound right and can't keep their noses out of other people's business."

Jack paused and smiled sardonically. Max and Kate just sat there not saying anything. Jack knew that this was really an earful for them, with both of them sitting quietly at one and the same time. The chill in the room was discernible and for some reason he couldn't shake the feeling that his recitation of these events somehow made him culpable to their having occurred; it was one more scheme that had ensnared a little man—all ideology aside, a schemer shared the trait of scheming with all other schemers of this chosen profession.

"It all began to unravel when Paul came to me."

That gave him pause for a second; there were *so many* victims of what was transpiring now and over the last several months.

"When Paul told me you had been arrested, I agreed to check into to it, briefly. Little did I know, heck, even suspect what I would uncover and what it would lead to. In a way you are like the butterfly in the Gobi Desert. The butterfly that flaps its wings, raising a puff of dust, making a bull sneeze and causing the herd to stampede, which in turn raises a dust cloud, which, as it drifts over the Pacific Ocean and collects moisture, becomes a cloud, causing it to rain in San Francisco." He paused and frowned. "Or what used to be San Francisco. Anyway, that is you, or something like that."

He frowned again. *Talk about getting way off on a tangent ....*

"So you were arrested, beaten, and sent off to slave the remainder of your pitiful life away. Only you didn't. Your arrest, my response, and other people's involvement, set into motion a chain of events culminating in Marie's death, marshal law, and even this,"—his hand swept in a circular gesture—"this mess."

"No, no," Jack said, and waved a hand of negation as Max and Charlie attempted to offer a protest, "it is not your fault, don't get me wrong. You're as much a victim in this as anyone, maybe even more so, for you've been battered about since the start. Only, who could have foreseen ..." His voice trailed off. Max's fault, no, it was not— but what if he had died in that shitty little spot of forest, in the snow ... would the rest of the world have known? Would it have cared? Or would it have been better off?

No. The hell that rained down on them all was sprouted from other people's nightmares, designed for the waking world, regardless who happened to be on hand.

"Guy did you no favors. No real surprise there. From his report, or the report he concocted about you, you were the leader of a band of terrorists, and as such it took very little to get you classified unofficially as a 1C, and officially have the necessary sexual deviant charges concocted against you. With all that in place it was relatively a minor matter to get you sent off to Flagstaff to slave away and die in a matter of months. Of course his scheme first subjected you to a full beating just to ensure that you would die quicker upon reaching the Netherlands. Or perhaps even before.

"But there was one thing that Guy hadn't accounted for, the fact that us politicos watch out over our brethren, *real and imaginary.* That's the real reason why, as a suspected politico, you got such a gentle posting in Flagstaff, at least at first. It was not through the efforts of a crazy, skinny convict. It was the local political mechanism working as it should. The main thing here was to keep you in sound body and mind long enough for us to figure out just what you were, so that you didn't spend *that* much time on general labor, where you would most certainly have died, which we cannot let a politico do."

If Max felt surprise that Jack knew about the little arrangement he had made on the train on the way up here, he didn't show it.

"Only, in your case your political *credentials* didn't pan out, never were intended to, since you really weren't a politico at all, but only being framed as a politico by a two-bit thug. Once you were out of sight he didn't care whether you were worked to death as a politico or murdered for being a child rapist. In the labor camp, when your political credentials didn't pan out, you were treated as the child molester you were charged as. Fortunately, I got suspicious.

"Not wanting to risk a good man's death, coupled with a touch of hometown camaraderie, I took a chance that something wasn't right, at least less right than usual, and had you plucked out. Once we had you here, we then cleared up the situation, at least enough not to have you killed."

"Hooey for me. It happened none too soon," Max said sarcastically.

"Plucking you out or clearing up the situation?"

"Oh, plucking me out. I had no doubt that once you got to know me you wouldn't kill me. But that was then, and this is now. Basically I am screwed; I have lost my daughter and the little pittance that I had here of a life."

"Going forward, yes. You can never go back to who you were, anonymity is lost for you. Of course, like everything else it is actually not all bad," Jack said with a slight sardonic smile.

"Oh? And *what* part of being framed, nearly killed, and on the run while my daughter is kidnapped by a psychopath, *is just not all that bad?*"

"Why, just this, of course." Jack almost beamed. "Guy made many, many, mistakes along the way. He was a slob and he was an amateur, all of this enabling an incompetent buffoon such as you to be alive today."

"So?" he said, ignoring the jab.

"*So?* So just this. This incompetent buffoon, alive and well in this very room, has a power all his own. If this buffoon's daughter"— Jack smiled broadly as he got into Max's face—"has a fraction of the tenaciousness of her old man, then there is one mean bastard in this world who we have all grown to love to hate, that will undoubtedly get what's coming to him."

For a moment, Max said naught; he sat there thoughtfully stroking his beard, taking in just what Jack was saying.

"Right. Jack, a favor. I can't get to Kate stealthfully, you haven't the contacts needed to get me there. Even if I could travel openly, which I can't, I would never be allowed to get to her, to get near her, to even leave Tucson. No one is. But perhaps there is a way to get someone here."

"Max, my old friend of many months." Jack clapped him on the shoulder and for the first time actually felt comfortable with the man. "I am already on it. Trust me, I want very much to have your daughter here—we need all the buffoons and buffoons' daughters we can get our hands on."

Silence.

Max looked up, looked at Jack with a level gaze. "Thank you."

Jack gave him a sharp nod as the last light of day faded from the room. Like a cat, Charlie uncurled from the couch on which she had been sitting. Coming up on the two men she put an arm around each of their necks, smiled, and kissed both on the cheek.

"Let's eat," said Max, "our treat."

Max smiled at Jack, and Jack returned the smile. The rules were always changing, the game began anew each day; whatever awaited them tomorrow would be better met than it would have been today—true, there was no lack of things that could go wrong ... but today had gone just fine.

Washington, DC

1

It wasn't long after the incident on the Mall that she and Guy attended a gathering honoring the appointment of a man to whom Guy's father was more than mildly beholden to, his father's immediate supervisor, the Secretary of State. Guy's father was the director of the Ambassador Corps and one of the inner circle of the government's ruling elite; a circle comprised of no more than a couple of hundred in number. That made Guy one of the elite, by familial association; Kate too, in her own way, was part of the elite, though how she fit in wasn't at all clear to her.

She had tried to put that day on the Mall behind her, had tried not to think about it overly much. True, she did still leave their flat, every day; she had paid too high a price not to take what she had paid for—but it had become a purchase without much joy. She had slid into Guy's fantasy, at least, becoming the housewife he portended her to be; she went shopping—for clothes, for food … it made no matter, she did the things that all the true housewives in the capital did. Socialism had brought women on par with men, or at least women who had chosen to become men—or was it that Socialist men and women had chosen to become the elites that ruled the land regardless of gender … asexual elites, a new race of people, not quite human.

The evening's affair was gowns and tuxes, Mediterranean décor of wood and red velvet, champagne in fluted glasses. A government car picked them up curbside at their flat. Guy beaming, Kate by his side; she alone knew the horrible scoundrel that he was—the man must never have had a mother … of that, Kate was sure.

The event grew stale; Kate wandered off a bit to escape the boredom and to extricate herself from the devil incarnate. *Stop that,* she scolded herself, not because it wasn't true, but because developing a burning hatred for the man she had to lie next to this night and perhaps many, many more to come, would get her nowhere.

Kate chanced to meet a rather ordinary-looking man at the beverage counter who smiled at her and raised his glass in salute, drained it, smiled at her, and left the bar. Kate watched him go for a moment, thinking, until a moment later she was interrupted when another man sidled up alongside her.

"Another delightful capital function, my dear, don't you think?"

Kate eyed him more closely; yes, she recognized him now, but not at first. Kate had only been to Guy's office a handful of times and she had done her best to be nondescript on each visit. But she did recognize this man even if she didn't know his name. He was one of the older fellas in Guy's office.

"What?"

"Another delightful capital function, don't you think?"

What a loser line, thought Kate. *Stop it,* she had to tell herself, *not everything is a come-on even in this, the great city of come-ons.* "I wouldn't know, I don't come to these events often."

"I am not surprised. If I were Guy, I might just keep you locked away myself."

"Locked away?"

"Yeah, isn't that the way of it? The way I heard tell, you are, excuse me, were, a prize from his former life. That plus, well, we never see you; we figured Guy knows a good thing when he's found one."

Kate gave him a cool look. "I'm sorry, this *caged* woman didn't quite catch your name."

That was her guarded answer, risqué though it might be; what was this man up to? His comments were lewd or rude, but incendiary for sure; could Guy have put him up to this to see how she would respond?

"Ralph, call me Ralph. Did you know there was once a book that began with the line 'Call me Ishmael'?"

"No, but I don't read much."

"Shame. I could lend you a couple of books. One on bondage might appeal to you."

Was he making a joke here, at her expense? If there was such a thing as a shit-eating grin, then Ralph had it, had it by far; Kate took in his smile, his white teeth, his thin, trim build.

136

"Ehm," she said in as sultry voice as she could manage, leastwise she thought it sultry, "might be I will need to take up a new hobby."

Ralph almost choked on his drink. Evidently he was not expecting *that* response. Ralph stuttered some and managed to get out a question as to how he would get her the books. Kate simply said that there would come a time, and then begged off to find Guy, which was *expected* because as his good bed trophy, that is exactly what she should have been doing. She left Ralph choking on his dumb humor and even dumber come-on. Maybe she should tell Guy to see what he would do to Ralph, or to see if Ralph were a plant; if not, give Guy a chance to carry through on his repeated threat to bloody and maim anyone for the sake of his slighted pride and honor—well, pride, definitely, as Guy had no honor and plenty of the former.

But finding Guy was exactly what she did not do, she just couldn't bring herself to do so.

Instead Kate went downstairs a level, to where a second bar was located; she heard tell that it was less pretentious, where the drinks were stronger, and no one counted how many you had or who you talked to, at least she didn't think they did. They wouldn't be counting their prestigious titles down here either, as *they* were on the floor above. Kate got the sense that most of the folks attending the party out of obligation ended up down here; which was probably fine for the actual invitees—fawning wasn't a particularly honorable activity, and those doing the fawning and those being fawned over would just as soon have their own little party, out of sight of those who were "no *fawn*."

Kate laughed at her little attempt at humor.

What Kate really needed was a glass of wine, enough already with the champagne; well, that and to be as far away from the idiotic male component in her life as possible—imagine Guy referring to her as a winnings of sort. She took the proffered glass of wine from the lower-floor bartender *and* a long swallow, feeling the warmth radiating through her chest.

She took another, smaller sip, tasting it for the first time.

"What wine is this?"

"It is a pinot noir, from California, and very good vintage to boot."

Kate didn't know what to say to that; she could spell *vintage* but beyond that, had little need for the word—wine was good or bad, and this wine was good. She took a long look at her surroundings; this pinnacle of culture, at least material culture—there was no denying that those whose job it was to make sure that no individual did *too* well—certainly did well as a group.

There might not be many millionaires working for the government, but the entitlements they afforded themselves certainly allowed them to live as such; their government affiliation provided a lifestyle that would have been the envy of the corporate boardroom, what had once been the pinnacle of American materialism—there was, however, a difference. Those once vibrant, now vanquished, behemoth corporations produced things of value; products, many good, though not all, providing at the same time a standard of living excellent for many and essentially good for the rest. True, some folks back then could not own a new car and a large-screen LCD at the same time, but almost everyone could afford one or the other and, over time, both.

The current government provided an excellent standard of living for a much smaller bunch of worthless shits who produced nothing but big egos—and the rest of the country was suffering.

Kate looked around in alarm; she really shouldn't think this way—someone might hear.

"Well, I am not familiar with this wine, but it is quite tasty."

The man she addressed, more of a boy, really, might only be a bar-back, but she was desperate for a conversation that didn't involve Guy, his work, or his penis.

"This is nothing compared to the vintages that I have access to."

Kate turned to see a man who looked a tad familiar, though she didn't recall seeing him in Guy's office; probably just a common look—there were many men from the Middle East in Washington.

"Do I know you?"

It was a leading question inviting any one of a number of unpredictable responses; in this town such a leading question could prove to be quite dangerous. The man flashed her an honest smile.

"It is a small world we move through, Kate Stein, in spite of the seemingly large numbers of people around us. But in answer to your question, yes … er, no. I mean no, you don't know me, but I do know you. I chance to work with Guy on occasion, and know of you through him."

More trophy claims, though she did not speak that thought aloud.

"It seems that many folks, most of them male, seem to know me without the reverse pleasure being true."

"Pah, would that our good man Guy knew of your talk."

His smile held and his gaze was steady, but there something dangerous in those eyes. Kate was beginning to wish very much that she had not taken the opportunity to get out of the house tonight—next time she just might let Guy make his attendance on his own.

"I didn't catch your name."

"Oh, Jared, Jared Weiss. I am an ambassador of the IsPal delegation."

Whoa, this was big, or rather, this was a big man, that much Kate knew. There was no relationship more strategic than the one which the United States shared with the IsPal nation.

"Really, the IsPal ambassador, I mean the ambassador to IsPal? You're like, what, one of the ten most important people in the government?"

He laughed and scoffed at the remark, though in good humor, his white teeth flashing in the mouth on a slightly bearded chin. The balance of his face, handsome, actually, was framed in short black hair with a slight wave to it, which might have been a curl if it had been longer.

"No, not really, not that important at all. There are actually a dozen or so IsPal ambassadors, and I am one of the assistant ambassadors of culture. An important post, to be sure, but not so important as the ambassador of culture to IsPal, and he is not as important as the political ambassador, or the near kings, in America's eyes, the ambassador of security or the ambassador of science and technology. But I do enjoy certain, ah, privileges of power."

Kate frowned. She decided to chance something. "Does IsPal really not trust us?"

"Whoa, that is a direct question for such an informal meeting. Even more, a direct question from someone who shouldn't even know to ask the question. My, my, just what has Guy been filling your head with?"

She looked at him and put her hands on her hips. Jared chuckled quietly; such a tactless act of defiance directed at one who was nothing if not tactful. However it was obvious that Kate was not going to back down or even flinch at the insinuation that this line of questioning could get her in trouble. He laughed out loud, which was something she had not expected.

"You are an inquisitive one. Before you grow too concerned, nothing of our conversation will ever reach the ears of your, *nooo*, it is not husband, but … well, whatever Guy is to you. What we discuss remains between us."

Kate gave him a disdainful, smirking look. "What makes you think that we have anything to discuss?"

"What, with the questions you ask? How could there not be something for us to discuss. Besides I know things … things about you. Too, I have saved your life at least once now, and will save it again, of that I am sure."

Boy, was that cocky, and just what did he mean by that last remark? Kate gave Jared a searching look; his frame *looked* the same—though she had little to nothing else to go on.

"You're the one on the motorcycle. In the park, the other day."

"The very same." He pulled a pair of sunglasses out of his breast pocket, put them on, and held his finger beneath his nose, simulating a mustache rather than the two-day growth he was sporting. *It was him.*

"Why?" Instant embarrassment on her part; was all that she could blurt out?

He shrugged. "Why what? Why did I save you? That is easy. I would have done the same for anyone in that situation."

A vision of him pointing the large pistol in her pursuer's face floated to her mind.

"The real question you want to know is why was I following you."

Games.

"Okay, why?"

"If I told you that, you would have to commit to more than you are capable of, at least right now, or at least more than you *should* be willing to right now. But the time will come, Kate, the time will definitely come. You think you are a player, but you are an infant, really. Oh, don't say it." He put up a hand to forestall whatever objection she had. "You cannot play this game without risk, without

140

danger, and angering Guy is not the real danger, not, ah, the major danger.

"You cannot play the game without at some point committing to this or that. And that is when the danger really starts, regardless of what you commit to, for everyone that you did not commit to will be your enemy. Yes, in this town, that is the way it is. *'Enemy or friend; with us or against us; the enemy of my enemy is my friend; you today, me tomorrow.'* All truly spoken here and with good reason. But keep in mind that I am watching you, watching out for you."

"Maybe, maybe not."

He might have saved her, true, but that was then, that was a onetime thing and did not equate to him establishing a presence in her life.

"Maybe I don't want to be watched. Did you ever consider that, Jared?"

"Easy enough said, but will she keep singing the same tune once the dice roll?"

He spoke to her in the third person, which was unsettling and irritating in the same breath. Jared held her chin softly in his hand for a moment and looked into her eyes.

For a moment she did not resist. *I owe him, a little*, she thought.

He let his hand down, took a mixed drink of some sort, and started to walk away.

"Jared."

He paused but did not look back.

"Thank you."

Now he did turn; there was a firmness in his eyes that brooked no argument—indeed she knew his next words rang true even before he said them.

"No, Kate, it is I who will be thanking you before this is over."

Then he did walk away. Kate stood afterward, looking thoughtfully at the man now trailing away from her.

Up one floor, and Kate slid her arm into Guy's, and he turned and smiled at her; a trophy, his prize. She hated him all the more for that, yet she was still dependent on him as ever.

This was a very dangerous city, both on the street and in the citadels of power. The danger from the former was physical: rape, robbery, *murder*. The danger from the latter was more subtle yet no less dangerous, and in its own way could be equally violent, though the rapist, thief, or murderer was more likely to be known to her here among the well-to-do than the anonymous attacker who would brutalize her on the street. Either way, the only thing between her and danger was Guy.

Maybe not; maybe Guy was not the only thing standing between her and oblivion.

She slid her hand from his arm; Guy didn't even notice.

Washington, DC

2

The corridor in which she sat was old and it was warm; it had that feel one finds in high quality design and construction, but only if the construction is of wood—the lower half of the hall was paneled in cherry, with white, thin-set plaster covering the walls above. The baseboard, chair rail, and crown molding were trimmed in cherry as well; lathed benches and trestled lamp stands in a style once referred to as Americana lined the hall—comforting colors ... an idyllic country manse sitting room of days gone by.

Following the directions slipped to her discreetly if not clumsily, Kate exited the underground tram at the Capitol Building and walked along a white-tiled corridor, up the stairs and turned left at the end of the hall, left again, up, then down several more flights of stairs, packaged in a series of left and right turns. She still had the directions in her hand but wasn't sure she could reverse the process and find her way out. Standing in the trimmed-out hallway she saw that the directions indicated that she had made it; she took a seat on one of several benches in the corridor which had that stately feel of quality, and waited—what exactly she waited for she couldn't rightly say.

"Take control of your life" was all the note had said; well, that and the directions that had brought her here. The note had been slipped to her in the most unimaginative means possible, taped on the front of their townhouse door. Guy would never have seen it; not with him leaving early in the morning and not returning till dinner. True, there were days when Kate barely got out of bed, so she could have missed it, but those days were becoming fewer and farther in between; especially since the ambassador's party where she had met Jared— there was something about him that inspired her ... something about that evening that had washed away the lethargy of her life and the ominous events that had surrounded her first outing to the mall. He had saved her, of that there was no doubt; then he had bantered with her and put the spark of adventure back into her when she thought it had been snuffed out—she traveled farther and more often ...

though not to the Mall, staying only on the most public of paths and going to the most well-known places and events.

That the note she now held in her hand had to do with Jared she also had no doubt. This was his doing, of that she was sure; if she hadn't been sure, and she was only sure by instinct at that, she would never have come. Of course the possibility existed that it was a trap of some sort, but the phrase *"Take control of your life"* was a bit of an intellectual stretch for Guy, who so unthinkingly dominated her life; he was petty and cruel, calculating, yes, but creative, thinking outside of his own little fantastic schemes for power, he was not; but still, that gave Kate a reason to take pause—Guy could have done something like this because it seemed so likely that he couldn't.

Kate frowned. This line of reasoning would not work.

There *was* an element of risk here, more than she had considered going in. Too late now to do anything about it, she was either going to be satisfied with her decision to come or not; nothing she could do now would change where she was; she could leave, of course, but she had been here and that forever changed her status from passive to preemptive, if that was the right word to use. What she needed to do from here on was make decisions she would be satisfied with, and not just relating to today, either.

Her wait was not long; a man with short, curly dark hair, wearing a pair of black pants and a denim jacket, strode down the corridor, the first person she had seen since she had stepped off the tram. He took no notice of her and passed her by, moving on about thirty paces and stopped in front of a door as if deep in thought.

This is odd, thought Kate, *perhaps he is not the one.*

Still, not having looked at her, he returned and sat on the bench at the opposite end from her.

This was *really* odd; Kate was about in the middle of nowhere as she could get, and here was a man sitting in the middle of nowhere beside her—and he could do just about as he pleased right at the moment … he was either her contact or her rapist. It was inconceivable that anyone else would have taken a seat on this bench.

He wasted no time on introductions.

"Call me Jambi, a friend of Jared. I am to take you to him from here. We will go to the surface and take a land cruiser. I must warn you that I will blindfold you before we arrive."

He still had not once looked at her directly, at any rate; indeed, it seemed that he hardly acknowledged her presence at all.

The same could not be said for Kate; she gave him a steady look.

A secret agent, she thought, *espionage. I am a participant in espionage.*

She shrugged her shoulders and nodded in the affirmative. *There,* she thought, *if he truly is not acknowledging me, then he will never see my acquiescence.*

With barely a glance in her direction he got up and continued down the hallway. He did not like her, she thought, though lord knows what she could have possibly done to put him in such a frame of mind, as she had never, to her knowledge, met the man before.

Kate thought she should have felt more, following a grim stranger down an isolated hallway; if she thought that she should feel fear, she did not—good, bad, or indifferent, she was growing bored with what happened to her. On the other hand, the fact that she was making decisions, initiating actions in her life, was of such significance unto itself that the ramifications of her decisions were of secondary importance … at least she hoped so.

Kate stiffened her step and her resolve; she had been locked in Guy's life for too long.

At the end of the hall, Jambi led her down several flights of stairs, to a door that opened onto the street level. There was a land cruiser waiting for them, with no driver; in the East they did not refer to them as cars, as Kate had quickly discovered, but as land cruisers so as to differentiate them from rail cruisers, high-speed little shuttle-bugs dashing along established routes, the primary mode of transportation in the capital—which made land cruisers so discreet … hardly anyone was out and about the streets in them, and they were private, without navigating or communication devices, and no eyes in the compartment other than those of the occupants. Jambi held the door for her, then took the driver's seat, pulling out to the middle of the street, under a maze of long-abandoned overpasses. It was quiet this time of morning on a Saturday—Guy was golfing with his bigwig peers, so the timing had been perfect … Jared must have known.

It was overcast as Jambi guided the quiet electronic vehicle on the semi-deserted streets; Jambi drove calmly, casually, he seemed at ease—there was no conversation between them, there seemed no point … they were both apparently of a type that rarely did anything for no point. The quiet of the engine, the hum of the wheels running over the road were timeless. After about ten minutes, Jambi reached into his jacket pocket and retrieved a black strip of material and handed it to Kate.

"Already?"

"Yes, why wait? Now is good."

Kate gave him a long look, as if trying to decipher for the last time if she were making a mistake, and then tied the blindfold over her eyes, catching a bit of hair as she knotted the back; she would have to remember to take it off slowly.

They continued for several more minutes and then accelerated; they must have turned onto one of the concrete highways that traversed the city—used so infrequently now. So many miles of roadway with so few cars—it was quiet and empty, but most of all it was creepy, especially on an overcast day like today … on days like this it looked like the end of the world.

What were they to do with millions of miles of concrete?

Of course, with the blind on Kate was not seeing that now; Kate wasn't seeing much of anything at the moment. She felt a gradual turn to her right, then a slowing, then a sharper turn. Leaving the expressway, no doubt, a thought confirmed when the vehicle came to a stop. From there it was a mixture of short bursts of acceleration followed by short, regular stops; local streets, it must be. In all, they had been traveling about another ten minutes when she noticed a muffling of sound and a sharp slowing. *An underground garage,* thought Kate, which was borne out when the vehicle came to a stop and her companion told her that she could remove her blind. It *was* an underground garage; dark, empty, the oil stains on the floor still sharp after all the years since gas cars had faded from the scene. Overhead were conduits and naked bulbs of about forty watts throwing the enclosure into weak relief.

Without comment they got out and headed to a door a short distance to the right. Behind the door was a staircase; up two flights, through a utility door and down a narrow confine, exiting mid-hall, a left turn and forward about fifteen paces to the first door on their left.

Standing at the back of a small, unfurnished room, lit by the natural light coming through a window that was only half curtained by a thin, gossamer material, was Jared, his back to her, his left hand

146

holding a curtain back slightly whilst he looked down into what was presumably a street or courtyard of some sort; Kate was not given the privilege of the view out the window.

"You came. Good," Jared said, dropping the curtain and turning to face her.

"Did you expect me to do otherwise?"

She feigned interest in a piece of fuzz on her skirt. *Was a simple hello too much these days?* The skirt was burgundy, just shy of ankle length, and linen; ideal for an early spring outing and it accentuated her figure. She had worn it specifically for this encounter, though to what end she could not say. Men held no interest for her whatsoever, and Jared's manner was so cocky that for that reason alone she intended to keep her distance.

"I live a Spartan existence with a mean, stupid little man. What did you expect me to do, given a chance at diversion?"

"Yes, we must all bear witness to our fate," he intoned with either weighty or feigned exasperation, she couldn't say which at the moment.

"Your man will perhaps not be little so soon."

The way he tied that statement to her offhand remark unnerved her. Was there nothing he did not know, nothing that was not sacrilegious?

He took a step toward her, rubbing the back of his neck, his face fair to look upon. He had a shadow of a day's growth of beard.

Kate had nothing to say so she stood watching Jared, using the silence to her advantage; *he* had brought her here, he had done so for a purpose, and she would let him get to the point, which would probably come sooner rather than later if she kept her mouth shut. Jared smiled at her as if he knew just what she was thinking and gave a slight incline of his head.

First tilt, Kate.

"Jambi, would you bring in a couple of chairs and a table."

Jambi nodded and left to comply.

"I didn't know for sure that you would be coming, so I left a hasty exit open until you arrived; phones, all of them, are not to be trusted—neither are public places. No one but Jambi and I know of this place, and so long as we keep it empty, I mean truly empty,"—he motioned around with his hands at the empty room—"there is no chance that it will be bugged or that a bug can be hidden herein.

"Before you ask, Jambi does not work for me, any more than I work for him, sort of. He will help me get you settled and then take leave. He is Palestinian by birth and I am a third-generation American of Jewish descent; we are both on loan from the state department to the IsPal government, which is our employer. He is actually my superior, but we both have our areas of specialty; when he says duck, we duck—a very big responsibility having our lives in his hands … I wouldn't do it for anything. And, yes, we are the one, that same delegation so highly spoken of by your hus—I mean Guy, sorry. I know, he doesn't speak highly at all of the IsPal delegation, it was a joke; again, sorry. Though I must say that Guy's dissatisfaction is no small part a result of our efforts."

Jared looked at Kate and felt like an ass. He had managed to make her quite uncomfortable with all his aimless and cynical babbling.

"Certainly you have more *'whys'* and questions than there are ants in an anthill; I will answer as many as I can in the time you think you have."

He stopped and they stood in awkward silence, waiting. Jambi returned with two folding chairs and a table, set them up, and left. Jared pulled out a bottle of alcohol from his briefcase, retrieving two metal cups, and poured them each a small drink.

"Scotch, a little to warm the soul. We talk of things both dire and cold today. Sit, drink."

Kate noticed his accent for the first time. "You might be third-generation American, but you're not from Washington, are you?"

"Ha, most are not and neither am I. My mother moved here with the rest."

"The rest," Kate interrupted with a frown. "We didn't come, though."

She said the last after a short pause, as if she were deciding whether or not to pipe up that information. Then, all at once, as if her last statement needed explanation, indeed as if her whole life needed explanation.

"When I was born, or shortly thereafter, the exodus from middle America started. We stayed when the first people left for the coasts, and we were still there when the last left. Now they say some are coming back, but I never saw it, leastwise not many, not while I lived *there*."

"You live here now."

"Is that a statement or a question."

"What do you think? What kind of question would it be? *I* live here, Washington is my home. Not always, but it is now. You asked where I was from, if I was from Washington. I said no, but I have lived most of my life here. But I lived in IsPal for a while, in Jerusalem. I picked up my accent there. I lived there for fourteen years, from the time I was twelve till I was twenty-six. I came back about five years ago for this."

"Twelve, huh. You had a Bar Mitzvah there?"

He laughed. "Yes. Odd, isn't it. Almost seems like from another time. I hardly ever hear an American use that term. Were you? Bat Mitzvah, I mean."

"No, but I could have. It all depended on how my dad woke up on any given day. Some days he'd wake up and the very thing we had been doing for years we never did again. Sometimes he'd wake up and even though we hadn't ever done a thing before, we did it every day going forward, as if we had always done it."

"For example?"

"Hmmm. … For a while we'd go out to eat every Thursday night, a burger, it had to be a burger at this one particular place. I am not sure it was an obsession with him, though I was sixteen at the time and I never missed a Thursday burger. But it was no matter. After a year or a year and a half, we one day stopped going, never even talked about it. It sounds weird, I know, but wasn't. It was just the two of us, you see, and that made everything a big deal, or nothing at all.

"On morning he woke up, and after having attended services every Saturday morning as far as I can remember, he just stopped going, never talked about religion again. I think something happened for that one; it was about two years after my mom died—and he was like that back then, always changing who we were, what we did. I was ten then, and then I was twelve and I didn't care who we were supposed to be and the less we did, the better."

But had she really believed that when she was that young? Hadn't that come when she was older, say, sixteen or seventeen?

"So it was no Bat Mitzvah, even though we had talked about it some and, well, I didn't care."

"You were twelve," Jared finished for her.

"Yeah."

Jared gave Kate a long look, a friendly look. He took a sip of the scotch and, nodding, motioned her to take one as well. She left hers untouched.

"Okay, what's up? I mean, you save me from those thugs on your,"—she looked questioningly at Jared—"ah … some motorcycle. You saved me on your motorcycle, and—shit, I could use a cigarette. You don't smoke, do you?"

"No, it is bad for you."

"Yeah. Well, *why* did you save me? How is it that you were in a position to save me? Why approach me at the party? Why, why … *why are you so interested in me?*"

He laughed again.

"Well, we can sorely misread people, can't we? I mean I, I can sorely misread people. Perhaps I should back up some. I was so involved in what I wanted to talk to you about that I forgot your point of view, which I am not just going to be able to sweep under the sofa while I do my thing. Will I?

"Huh?"

"Kate." He tried a smile, which fell short; scratching his lower lip with the tip of his thumb, he turned his hand and stroked his chin before continuing. "Kate. What I am about to tell you could get you in really serious trouble if you do not turn me in, a fact which is not lost on me; we both have a lot to lose if I tell you what I am thinking of telling you."

He traced an imaginary circle on the table, focusing his thoughts.

She replied, "If you're having trouble, how about one of these." She took the bottle and topped his glass off. "You seemed to think it was a good idea just a moment ago."

"Yes, but times do change, and I am not so sure now."

Kate wasn't exactly sure that he was referring to the drink.

"Ah drat, if you will, bottoms up." Jared tossed his down in a single swallow.

Kate decided to slowly nurse hers. Scotch wasn't something she ever had much luck with.

A quiet silence followed, both unsure where the conversation would go, could go.

"Kate." "Jared," they began at the same time. Jared "doffed a hat" in Kate's direction for her to continue, but she declined.

"You brought me, all cloak and dagger, you go first."

"Yes …" Jared began slowly, "let's get started."

When Kate stepped off the returning tram from the Senate Building some thee hours later, she had a lot to think about, not the least of which was making sure that she returned home before Guy.

Everything that Jared was offering was just that, an offer. An attractive offer, to be sure, but only an offer nonetheless. Kate still had to live with Guy, actually get even closer to him to accomplish what Jared had asked of her; what Jared wanted was no inconvenience to her, really, she'd gladly given it—it wasn't helping Jared that interested her, but helping herself.

This crazy domineering relationship with Guy, she could do; it had become sort of a personal challenge for her. The sex part wasn't hard, she sort of enjoyed it in a self-loathing kind of way; Kate frowned at that, but it was no use dwelling there.

The personal challenge had always been to beat Guy at his own game, to be the one who came out on top of this little unmatched union in the end. By playing Jared's game she gained not only an ally with an understanding of how these games are played, an understanding she desperately needed to win, but other resources, connections; Jared might be master of his domain, more so than most men were, but there were many domains out there, and Jared's was not first amongst them. There was no guaranteeing that she would not become hostile toward Jared before this was through.

True, it would not be like going after Guy; that, after all, was personal.

Washington, DC

3

A cat, that is what this flat needs, she thought while sitting on the couch as she rubbed her left calf.

Kate had been out walking, as was her wont these days, every day. It was the best way for her to build herself up: her stamina, mental and physical, her focus—all to improve without seeming to improve. Guy was as suspicious as he was cruel, and for her to work out in his presence, or have evidence of her working out around the house, could be deadly; he was just that kind of man.

Too, the gyms were out as well; there was talk aplenty there and none of it was of the slightest benefit to her; even if she were eavesdropping, which she wasn't, the level of intellect and the misinformation of the women at the spas was phenomenal … Kate might as well have cast bones to seek the truth.

It had been three months since her first covert meeting with Jared, and it had come as no surprise to either of them that they had begun a physical relationship as well as a conspiratorial one. All the parts had been there; people only avoided getting physically intimate in the movies when everything was in place, like it was between the two of them. They were both relatively young and attractive, single, with little or no family, lots of time on their hands, and the ability to schedule their time as they pleased—they were already meeting furtively in out-of-the-way adrenaline-laced places that were confining … one would either have to be gay or married not to portent to some level of intimacy at their meetings, at least on occasion.

Jared was addictive to her, in her, and she hoped she was having the same effect on him, though with Jared it was hard to tell; had he a passion beyond his *cause*? At times she wondered whether he had a true emotion in his body. Well, he did, really; he had a lot of compassion, even some tenderness—but compassion is not love, and

Kate ofttimes wondered whether he could really love anything but his cause and perhaps himself ... and yet that too was part of it all. Sometimes, what is needed for good to succeed is the sacrifice of all that which was not associated with the cause, or the sacrifice of all that which does not sustain the bearer of the cause. But, oh, what a narrow line to be walked that requires.

On the other hand, *she* could love Jared, but she wouldn't; the fact that it was all business with him annoyed her more than she could say. Jared was always scheming, always working on an angle for his cause; this level of intensity would assuredly lead him astray, into dark passages she did not want to travel—yet she knew that all that would be required for her to love him *would be for him to desire her love.*

Though she became part of the cause, and how could she not, Kate was not at all certain of what she had become a part of, or what the goal of Jared's cause was. What was the *master event* that Jared and Jambi pursued, the event that when it occurred the two of them would look on it and say to each other in a solemn way, *We were successful.* Kate was not fully convinced there was a *master event* beyond whatever it was which Jared and Jambi desired to accomplish on a given day, or a given set of days—there appeared to be no founding principles or manifesto ... she had met no other conspirators as of yet.

Three months or so since her first covert meeting with Jared, and the best she could tell was that she had grown the conspiracy to three.

Kate and Jared met each other on the grassy Mall later that same afternoon. The sun had been edging toward the horizon for the past hour or two. He had his helmet with him—he had taken his bike, meaning it was unlikely that this meeting would progress beyond where they sat on the small rise leading up to the George Washington Monument. The shadow of the monument was flowering on the hill above them; it was Washington who chopped down a cherry tree and had to tell the truth—an odd attribute to a towering artifact that had watched over the conspiratorial meetings of two hundred years of history.

Washington was first in a long line of presidents in the United States, which soon was to be but one republic of the *North American Union.*

Could it really be?

Had European sophistry actually reversed the strength and the ambition that had brought the world space travel, the cure of many a disease, the defeat of first its own slavery and then the international scourge of national Socialism and Communism?

Was the world to condemn the very people who had given the world so much, saved so many lives?

Apparently so, but only with the help of America's leaders who were undermining that supremacy in hopes of achieving that supremacy.

The Socialist Party truly was schizophrenic.

*This was one of Jared's a*gendas: the North American Union—well, stopping it, that is, this North American Union thing. As to how he would effect *this* was not at all clear to Kate; it was his passion on this issue which made her *almost* love him—Kate dearly loved what the United States was, an ideal passed on to her by her father which she was now coming to appreciate … the *ideal* and *her father.*

It was logistically prohibitive to regularly utilize the secret room that Jared kept, the room where they had first met. Here they could be aloof but not secretive; secretive would arouse the suspicion of anyone who might be watching private lives unfolding in this very public park. But it wouldn't do to be recognized either; hence, a man and a woman sitting on the quiet side of the hill; sunglasses for him, a silk bonnet for her, and he would betray the truth to her for his cause—how could there be love in that?

I am a fool, she thought, *for getting involved in the likes of him.*

Jared had a way of knowing things about her and her life that he shouldn't know, that no one should know; and not just her life alone. While she was happier now that she was with Jared, that was but a small part of her world. What he knew, and how he came to know it, was unnerving; even though she had been in the big city for months, so much of her was more comfortable in the Tucson minor-league way—today found her in a life that could take years, perhaps a lifetime, to get used to, in which to feel truly at home … somehow she felt that she only had days. If that long.

They sat silently for a time; a heron from a nearby inlet or bay flew in close, circled once, and then took its leave. The monument's shadow lengthened some and then lengthened some more.

"Don't fret, Kate, I know you're angry. When we get what we want, or a part of what we want, it magnifies that which is lacking in our lives. In a way this is good, for we are ever chasing goals, striving for the next thing that we want in our lives. Perhaps for you it is control; it would be for me, ah, that is if I were you ... I mean."

Kate gave him a sour look; he should talk about control, he was *Mister Control.* Then she laughed. Jared was at his funniest when he tried to reason his way out of some obscure point of logic he had reasoned himself into. That was his saving grace; he was his own harshest critic—he was hard on himself and sometimes that hardness manifested itself in truly gracious, or should she say, graceless ways.

Kate laughed some more and pushed his head down into the grass. It was a good thing to do, it made her feel like a girl again, a plain, young, ordinary girl; she just wanted to date someone and have a day job. Jared laughed as well and came up, wrapping his leg around her waist and pulling her in for a quick kiss; she let herself go for a moment, leaned in, and whispered his name.

He kissed her again on the neck, then lower on her neck; and then she pushed him away, though not urgently and not without some hidden remorse.

Better to be part of his life than any other right now. She took solace in that.

Kate stroked his cheek with the back of her hand; they moved apart some.

"What is it that you think you know about my life, Jared? You have taught me how to observe, see what is hidden, *see* what is *meant* to be seen even though it will bear little in the way of truth. But do you know what it was like for me growing up in my family, without my mother who I lost when I was ten, leaving me with a father who didn't know the first thing about how to raise a girl? In reality, you know little to nothing about me, my wants, my desires."

Jared looked on but didn't say anything; there seemed little enough for him to answer to—she could get up this minute and walk away from the whole thing and the worst part about it was it would be in keeping with her character ... which despite thinking he knew so much about her, he knew little about.

"Fine, what we want is yours to decide, Kate." He sought to take it down a notch. "You are not beholden to us for anything. If I had to choose your course, I would have you do what you do so well, observe, understand, report. The rest will come later, the action that is. Right now the most important thing is whatever you decide to do, you are ready to do it, and that you do it well when the time comes—when you decide what to do, that is.

"Having you with us is a windfall. I know that this is hard for you, but if someone were to tell me six months ago that my lover would move among the highest levels of the government elite, I would have, well, I would have believed it possible, but I surely hadn't expected this."

Kate surprised him by punching him in the chest with the flat of her hand and actually with some force.

"You can be an ass, do you know that? What do you know? A windfall? I have been raped, battered, emotionally, at least, and used in a terrible way by a man whose sperm you wouldn't even consider being in *your* body. And you call this a windfall?"

She was glaring, no doubt about it, glaringly mad, and it was to him that the anger was directed; she was fuming angry at him.

"Ahm, ah well, Kate."

"No, don't say anything. You have already said it. A windfall. Well, perhaps I am, and in the sense you meant it, and you know I am willing to play my part, to a point. But don't ever mistake that this is something light and easy for me, for it is not. I will turn on you as easy as I turn on Guy, if you even come close to debasing me in such a fashion."

"Ah, right. Been put in my place, I have."

"No you haven't. I was being easy on you."

Kate was right and he knew it, but all the same there was work to be done. He needed to test the waters, so after another minute of silence he continued, more softly and with less frivolity, to be sure.

"You move among the truly high-ranking people, attend parties that I would never be invited to, parties for those of power, of money. For now, the best you can do is watch, learn. We've some time, we will figure out how to best make use of your, ah, position. But keep in mind you do have influence. Influence over the course of events, a wide range of events, actually, you know, directly, with Guy. And indirectly. A chance remark at a party to a specific individual, a coy observation to a well-heeled bureaucrat. Use that influence. At first it may not be much; a word here, a word there to move a conversation, or someone, down a path. Of ah, altruism, yeah, let's say altruism. Decisions *will* come your way, eventually. There will be events, big events, surrounding you that you will have input in. You must force your involvement as deeply as you dare. But not right away. Patience, that is key."

With a short piece of twig in his hand Jared sat tracing a random repetitive pattern on his trousers. For a moment he didn't say anything and it didn't seem that he would. Then he became wistful, as if he were speaking on something he'd rather not talk of, likening it to telling a new adult that the world is not all spring and summer, but the coarseness of fall and the dead of winter too.

"Our current leaders are growing very comfortable with shooting people, and they are no longer bothering to be discreet about it. It is not a lot yet, the shooting. Probably in the hundreds, and they are not doing it in the capital nor the coastals, again, not yet; it is mostly in the heartland, out where those who didn't cotton up to the new regime and had thought to weather out the storm. But the storm has not passed and those people are about to pay a heavy toll for their intransigence; they are many of the ones being shot. They have been hanging around long enough. At least, as far as the government is concerned."

He looked up at Kate, eyes snapping into focus, as if he just remembered that he was talking to her.

"Our country is not developing equally, as I am sure you know. The coastals have always been dominated by a rash of everything at half the quality it should be and in half the amount that is needed. But it is all there, the underpinnings of a standard of living and a level of freedom which the people are hoping to get back. I wouldn't say that it couldn't happen, this rise in the standard of living and refound freedoms, but I would bet against it, all the same. Even if the previous standard of living returns, the freedoms that existed in the past will be slower to return. At best, we will have prosperous Socialism, and I don't even think we will get that.

"Not only is the country not developing equally, but the distinction is about to get quite harsh. All my sources,"—*So, there are others, thought Kate*—"say the same thing. The government's sort-of secret experiments in forced labor have gone, ah, unfortunately well. With a recipe of production for mining, logging, farming and some manufacturing built on forced labor with perhaps two dozen isolated heartland cities totaling about four million folks, what do you suppose our leaders are going to bake from this recipe?"

Jared stopped and frowned; there was no answer forthcoming from Kate—she didn't answer because she didn't want to answer … Kate could see that he had more on his mind and letting him have his lead was the best way to draw him out. He didn't disappoint.

"The heartland cities, including your alma mater, Tucson, are about to become one giant slave labor enterprise. And that will be no small accomplishment." He held up his hand to forestall questions. "It will be a significant accomplishment not because of the difficulty of the task, but because of what the State will reap from the accomplishment.

"Tucson … copper and smelting ores. The same can be said for most of the Southwest cities, at least the ones which still have a population of any significance. The North and Northwest, lumber by the trainload. The South Central, oil. And the Southeast, fish by the boatful.

"These labor cities, labor camps, are about to drive the economy of the country through the roof. Or at least the potential is there for it. They want to become stronger and they will. There is little we can do to stop them at this juncture. I know what I have to do, what Jambi has to do, what the other men and women we work with have to do and will do. But you, you watch, you learn; weaken them where you can. Stronger for them is worse for us and every glitch in their plans, no matter how small, will slow them down to some extent."

This was truly an eerie moment in Kate's life. The clouds had come in during the afternoon, and a slight breeze had picked up, warmish. The Mall was quiet, like it almost never was. Before her, she had an image of Apollo, of a Greek god come down from the clouds, made flesh, laying out Armageddon before her. It was just words, but it was too much, too poignant, too revealing; it was one of those moments after which a person's life will never be the same—it was too much new vocabulary in her head … she didn't know what to make of it.

"I'm going for a walk," she said, standing and brushing the grass from her pants.

He hurried to his feet as well; uninvited yet hardly thinking he would not be welcome, he started off with her, matching her stride. They strolled amongst the low-hanging boughs of the nearby trees, moving back a bit deeper into the small wood. They kissed passionately, quickly; pressed against each other in unsatiated urgency. Kate put her head back and Jared ran his tongue lightly up her neck, giving her a soft little nibble on her ear; again they embraced, kissed—Jared gently push Kate back, looking into eyes that looked back into his. Jared smiled, and Kate feared that this might be the moment when Jared asked her to love him, to declare her love for him. She always feared that, even as she craved her urgency for him.

But it didn't happen. Jared promised to meet her Monday afternoon as was their custom; Kate would have preferred, and she believed that Jared would have as well, a twice-weekly rendezvous—but it wasn't safe, even at once a week, so why ask?

Time to part. Jared frowned as he kicked the motorcycle into high gear and headed down the freeway, back to the State Department building which housed his office. Unexpectedly, as he was preparing to depart, Kate had asked him to check on her father; she knew nothing of him during her stay here—neither had she heard from him in the month before she left ... too long, six months easily. Honor her request he could, for he had at his disposal the means for finding this information.

Kate wouldn't like the answer, of that he was sure; not only was Max Kate's father, which was bad enough, knowing what Guy was capable of—but Tucson was about the worse place in the world to be right now, though the people living there knew it not, at least not yet ... her maintaining ties of any sort to her past bode only ill for anything good. But he had agreed to do it, so do it he would; yet his frown only deepened as he drove back to his public life and the men of a higher power under whom he served, or so it appeared.

Days passed and Kate did a damn good job of filling Jared in on just what she was hearing at all the social gatherings she and Guy attended; social gatherings where Kate no longer wandered around hoping not to be seen—she enjoyed being at the pinnacle, a little Tucson girl in gowns and stones, with flutes of champagne in hand ... it was elegance bar none in a country that officially disdained elegance. It was a hot life, of that there could no denying; it was heady, walking barefoot in the grass around the stateliest of mansions as the sun was coming up. She found herself hating Guy a little less; playing husband and wife was becoming less difficult for her. She had to hand it to him on one count; he kept the two of them from engaging in the orgiastic behavior Kate knew was going on behind the closed doors all around her. But that still didn't prevent Guy's peers, male and female, from hitting on her—even if Guy would have none of it. Kate was adept at fending off advances in such a way that didn't completely dissuade an inclination at another attempt by her pursuer; twenty-four, with a pretty face, generated a lot of pursuers—soon enough she had the reputation as a flirt … unobtainable but pursuable, which suited her just fine; it was good way to get people to open up, to tell her things they wouldn't otherwise say. Kate smiled. If only her father could see her now; he would be certain that some mistake must have been made for her to be moving in such circles—she frowned … a mistake had been made and it was known as kidnapping. That was what had happened to her those many months ago when she had been afraid, not brave; timid, not reckless—closeted, not ambitious … and hopefully, as she wistfully remembered it, altruistic.

Days passed and Kate was gracious on Guy's arm and Guy beamed. Kate passed on to Jared invaluable information—information which she supposed might at some time be used … to kill.

"I found the answer to the question that you asked."

Kate's tongue rolled back into her throat and for a moment she could not breathe; she had only ever really asked Jared one question—she didn't know the answer but she knew well what the answer pertained to … a moment passed, then another.

"Well, are you to tell me or do I need to ask?"

"Hmmph. No, you don't need to ask, but I am hesitant to tell you."

"No, you are not, not really, or you wouldn't have brought it up in the first place."

"You asked."

"Yes, but that was days ago, and I haven't asked since then. To tell you the truth, I didn't think that you would be able to find out or, for that matter, be willing to try."

A pause.

"Well?" she said in exasperation.

In a hushed voice, Jared recounted most of what had happened to her father since the night he had been taken into custody, taken into custody unaware to anyone but a poor slob named Peter. But

Jared didn't have the whole story; Jared, despite his resources, couldn't say why it had happened, other than the arrest order had been countersigned by Guy, *which Jared did not tell Kate*. His knowledge of what had happened ended with Max's arrival in the logging camp and his forthwith transfer from the bakery to general work.

"He disappeared after that."

"Disappeared?"

In all she had considered, she had not truly considered that ill had befallen her father; actually, she had, but never to this extent—now, the worst of possible scenarios was being borne out … after all that had befallen him, her father was *missing*?

"Disappeared?" Kate said again.

"Yes. One day he was in the camp, the next he was gone. There is no accessible information regarding what happened to him. My contacts are only so strong in that deep, dark, place, and can garner only to a point. The best they can do is track him to that one morning when he was no longer with his work gang. You have to understand, Kate, that this was a punitive labor camp, one of the government's first experiments in forced labor and very brutal in nature. It was successful and it is in operation still."

Jared paused. Frowning to himself, he continued, but almost as if he were working this part out loud. "Disappeared, missing, if you will, is not necessarily bad. There are 'cells' operating in the camp—I think it likely that he was freed."

"You mean escaped?"

"With his life? Yes. But I don't believe it was an escape in the traditional sense. Rather, I think that he was essentially taken out of the camp. There had to be significant outside help, if I understand your father correctly."

"You mean to say that he is incapable of escaping on his own?" A note of hostility had crept into her voice.

This is not going well, thought Jared. *She is losing focus.* "Look, Kate. The gov takes men like your dad when they want, where they want. They deal with his type all day long—honest, moral, hardworking folks of the wrong political persuasion. It is not that he couldn't come up with a plan, I am sure he could. Likewise I am sure that he has the courage, the motivation, to try any plan that he thinks will work, and that's what I am talking about. He could plan and he could try, but he wouldn't succeed. *The Man* is a step, *miles*, ahead of men

161

like your father; they have been oppressing men like him for years. He would have needed help."

Kate was sitting on the edge of the bed, crying softly. Jared made to put his arm around her to comfort her, but she pushed him away and walked over and squatted with her back against the wall. Sometime during the conversation she had dressed, though she didn't remember doing so or when; it sort of just happened.

She shook her head and cleared the tears from her eyes; she decided to be confrontational. "My father was not a part of any *wrong political persuasion*. He would not have, could not have, been taken. Besides, even if he had, there is no one who would have helped him. He had no one to turn to for something like that."

Jared felt for her: sorrow, pity, compassion. But she had made it clear that providing such comfort was not the role for him now.

"Perhaps, as you say. But mistakes are made. Maybe they made one in this situation, or maybe he had political leanings that you were unaware of. You yourself have stated that you saw less of him as the months grew into years. People do change, especially when there are changes in their lives. Such as a daughter leaving the nest."

Kate would have hit him if he had been closer. It irked her, and Jared saw that, but things needed to be said, for her perception was just plain wrong.

"Also, Kate, help comes from the most unexpected places." He smiled. "After all, I showed up for you."

He lifted his hands in feign deflection of any object she might chose to throw at him; though lovers, as her savior his success had yet to be judged.

"If they have been oppressing men like my father for years, how is it that I didn't know it? How is it that no one I knew ever spoke about it?"

Jared looked at her quizzically; either she really didn't know, coming from that humble, small-town mind of hers, or she was being difficult—most likely a bit of both … he decided to play along.

"It is the scale, Kate. The scale has been small, at least until very recently. Things are changing. They are moving rapidly, faster than I can keep up with."

She gave him a steady look.

"No," he answered to her unasked question, "I don't know what is going on, and that is not good. Something is up, that is for sure, but I and my team are too locked up in foreign policy, which is too bad as it is domestic policy which really concerns us now. No, don't get me wrong, there is important work to do in the arena of foreign policy. Things in this country are so fucked up right now with the Social Democrats in power, that we cannot dig ourselves out of this hole on our own. We need help from just about anywhere. Foreign policy is important, it is what Jambi and I do, and not solely out of choice. We are in the State Department, after all.

"Yet we suffer from a lack of involvement on the domestic level. This wasn't a problem before. The operations of the different departments were fairly transparent to one another prior to just recently, at least to those at my, our, level of government. What I mean is that we in the State Department could see what was happening in domestic affairs, there was transparency. We all understood the big picture and we all benefited from that knowledge and understanding, and hence so, in theory, would the people. Eventually, someday, maybe.

"But that too is changing, actually has changed, and we were caught by surprise. Personally, I think the government suspected that there were folks like us who were using every crack they could find to muddle the government's plans. So a lack of transparency was instituted to make it more difficult for people to get the bigger picture, at least that was the effect on us. Since then, we had no one in the domestic area, it was closed to us, and we had no way to see in. You have fixed that for us."

Kate was only half listening to Jared; her thoughts had drifted back to her father. Torture? Interrogation? Prison transports; he hadn't been the same man after her mother died—he had never had the same passion for life after that … what she feared most was that he might not have the *motivation* to survive.

"But you think he is alive?"

"Your father? Yes, I do. Primarily because there is no word on his having died. Disappeared is just that, you're gone, you're forgotten, and you're not talked about. But if he had been killed or had died, someone would know and someone would talk, someone always does. It would at the very least be documented in, a, ahm, secretive fashion, which means anyone with the wherewithal could find out. In this case, silence is our friend.

"I don't have a clue where he might be. Maybe back in Tucson, maybe halfway around the world, or maybe in a cave not five miles from the camp. But the important thing is, he's alive> I don't know how I know it but I do."

She nodded to herself in a reassuring manner; she felt the same because, well, she felt his presence and she felt sure that if he weren't alive, then she would feel a void in her heart where she now felt his presence. The news was not good, but it did lighten her spirit.

Jared, on the other hand, grew more sober. Battle was coming, of that he was certain; as to what form that battle would take, where it would be fought, and by whom—well, Jared could not rightly say.

From where he stood now, it appeared that the fighting, whether in word or deed, would be widespread, would be undertaken on his side by troops not under his command, undertaken by troops, *people*, he didn't even know; but one thing he did know were his charges, his assets. Kate, who of all his charges was the most unpredictable, volatile, strong-willed, reactive—and she was willful, *that* he couldn't allow himself to forget … not even for a minute. Kate was a big gun; she had firepower well in excess of what she should have in the scheme of things—but that is exactly how resources, people, panned out. She was a big gun, and could cause a lot of damage both for and against them; Jared could not afford to allow her to become a loose cannon—this thing with her father needed to be managed carefully. Though unsure why, Jared knew that Max, or the ghost of Max, had a large role to play in the coming struggle, even if he never showed up for the fight.

Twilight

A small dust cloud swirled away, starting out low to the ground, and rising on an updraft of air. A second one followed and almost immediately behind it, and then a third. A moment later three cracks in sharp succession echoed along the canyon walls, followed almost immediately by three more puffs of dust.

Jack wiped the perspiration from his eyes which stung from the salt.

"Next," he hollered, though not unkindly.

There were seventeen today, women, men, children, all wanting to fire a gun, all thinking that it would be good to fire a gun. Jack looked up at the mountains in the distance, with the choppers crossing above the foothills, too distant to make out the roar of the engines. But they were there as sure as were the troops camped on the outskirts of town; an *overreaction*, that how the crackdown of some six months ago was being referred to, an overreaction by the government to a rumored uprising by militant groups in Tucson—apologies had been issued, civilian and military leaders reassigned, and a military presence was now regularly seen just outside of town to keep those seeking to start an insurrection at bay … though just why an insurrection would begin in Tucson was never clearly stated. It seemed an awful long march to Washington, DC, from here.

The economy in the West had come to a standstill, people for the most part were receiving rations of water, food, and electrical power; those with money or coin or items of value were trading up for better food or candles and matches, or just about anything to take their lives up a step from what was provided.

Jack had not been back to the ranch for about two weeks now, though he kept in touch with his wife every day by an old citizens band radio. They were not routed through the Net, and untraceable if the conversations were kept to a minimum. It wasn't that he didn't want to be there; he did very much. It was just too risky to go out there now, except at great need. While the idea of a small hometown fortress holding the evil government at bay was very romantic, all it would take was one two-ton shell fired from three kilometers out to flatten the entire valley and what good would that do anyone. No, the next time out there might need to be his last, and that was as depressing as could be. He had always thought of leaving it to a couple of long-term hired hands and a little to Charlie, if the time ever came to pass it on. Now it seemed more likely that *they* would all pass on and away from what he had spent a lifetime investing in.

Remember, he kept preaching to his would-be Minutemen, *it was just to get away, not to have a standup, shootout.* Jack drew out another thirty or so rounds and passed them among the half-dozen shooters. He knew this was silly but appropriate nonetheless; his small group would not win out in a blankety-blank shootout, but it might help one or two make their way down a dark alley at night.

What this event needed was a little of Charlie's sanctimonious ribbing; shielding his eyes from the afternoon sun, as if that were going to allow him to see what wasn't there to be seen—Jack saw nothing ... she wasn't coming. He sighed.

The passion of their lovemaking was hot and sweaty; appropriate for the season—winter was long gone, spring was nearly done ... in Tucson that meant temperatures approaching the hundreds. It was, for all intents and purposes, a hot time in the city.

"... Back of my neck getting dirty and gritty/ Been down, isn't it a pity ...."

That *was* an *old* song, by the Lovin' Spoonful; it had been one that Max's *parents* had listened to. How had it managed to get on the radio this morning?

Charlie slipped off of Max and rolled over onto the bed beside him, her breasts covered in a sheen of sweat; all of it excited Max more than he could say—talk of contradictions! Not enough to eat, people getting shot at, some even killed, and rock and roll was playing on the radio. He was in love, or close to it; close as he thought he could come with Charlie—Charlie, who seemed to love everything so hard that she just bulled over life ... Charlie, who seemed to love everything so hard that it was hard to say just what she loved. It was confusing; it was exciting—and it was dangerous ... these *were* very dangerous times.

As with most intimate relationships, theirs was complex and extended well beyond their physical passion for one another. If Max didn't actually love Charlie, he loved things about her; she was funny, she was confused—though she wouldn't admit to *that*—and energetic. Charlie saw herself as a wise and worldly being and Max as a relative novice when it came to life; that was fine and easy for him to go with—even if it was off the mark … Max had been dealing with disasters and disappointments before Charlie was born. Charlie's misguided innocence mattered not a whit to him, in fact it was one facet of her personality that really endeared her to Max; she was going somewhere, she really was, though nobody, including Charlie, had a clue as to where that somewhere was. At twenty-nine, Charlie had plans, goals, *broad goals*. At forty-seven, Max wanted but two things: one, to enjoy life, albeit in what was fast becoming the hellhole where he now found himself, and, two, to get his daughter back, though not necessarily in that order.

Max held Charlie tight, his hand on the small of her back pulling her close; Charlie pressed against his chest, her fingers tracing his belly—she wanted more, which curiously was what Max wanted. Pulling her closer he rolled her onto her back and slipped easily into her, their bodies for a while joined as one.

Max left the bed, still naked and unlikely to dress; Charlie was sleeping, which, in addition to laughing, fighting, and fucking, was another talent that Charlie excelled at, which suited Max just fine—he liked her asleep … Max liked, *needed*, time alone, time that was quiet. He walked to the entrance hallway and stood just off to the side of the window that looked out on the street in front of their house; he didn't want to be a naked spectacle should anyone chance to glance in the front window of their house.

Max looked beyond, at the mountains in the distance; questions, *happenings*, were swirling in his mind. He wondered most of all if he would ever see his daughter again, as it was unlikely that he would see her soon. He wondered too, or more exactly worried about events closer to home; there were more and more military types in and around the city and the tension was always palatable … food rationing, compulsory labor, it was all so unbearable. Illegal expropriations from food warehouses and distribution stations were becoming more frequent and more violent; compulsory labor was on the rise even as the whole system was showing the strains of rapid disintegration—there simply were not enough military personnel to enforce the labor laws while at the same time protect the food from gangs that seemed to multiply with each passing day.

It was all going nowhere good and this bothered Max mightily; he could see no way out other than all of them leaving and being wanderers in the desert; modern-day Hebrews, a thought which made him laugh quietly, but then the image of a herd of deer being hunted down by a pack of wolves came to mind—he never spoke this aloud and tried not to think about it, especially when he was around Charlie, which was just about all the time ... how could one's thoughts stray down such dark paths when he was with one who loved life so much. Besides, he could very, *very* easily be wrong; he usually was—everything would probably work out just fine ... enjoying life was an accomplishment enough for now.

Then, like water, his thoughts suddenly caught a downward current, cascading over a precipice and swirling around to Kate again; he couldn't help but wonder, daily, if not hourly, where his little girl was and if she was a little girl any longer—*he knew* that she had ceased to see herself as such some time ago, but Max knew better ... she was, and would always be, his little girl, which is as it should be. Which meant that he had to get to her, or her with him; with two thousand miles of hostile territory between them, and no way to get there but on foot and find her in a city of a million and more—he needed a plan, a new plan, and he needed one soon.

Charlie woke around midafternoon. She came out from the back of the house in a loose-fitting white robe, her slender feet poking beneath, her thatch of hair between her legs outlined. Max was dressed by now. He had walked up the street a few houses in each direction. It was a quiet afternoon and since neither of them was working, indeed, few in this neighborhood were yet employed in the compulsory brigades at the mines, farms, or cotton fields, they had time to do something out of the ordinary, but what? The government was going after the traditional labor set first, the old hands at manual labor, which in Tucson meant the poorer whites and most of the Mexican families. Stereotyped or not, accurate or not, it was felt that these groups would be the easiest to corral into the newly formed labor brigades, so the authorities had started with them, cordoning off blocks of the town at a time and bringing in trucks to haul the men, and some women, out to the jobsite. The take on it was the pay wasn't bad, though the pay was not in money but in groceries and expanded use of the now temperamental electrical grid, for such things as air-conditioning and refrigeration. It was not that the rest of the populace didn't have these; they did, but they seemed to have less and on a less secure basis. It was a tight act the government was trying to run, providing those who worked with material goods so they didn't get scared off or revolt, while providing less to those not yet in the labor collectives so as to begin building their desire for entry into the co-ops. Max felt he had a pretty good idea where this was going; once everyone was in the collective, the hammer would come down and they'd all be worked to death, sure as shit. Socialist modus operandi writ large.

Jack had gone back to his ranch either to get or see Ellen; Max wasn't sure and Charlie wouldn't talk about it—of late she didn't talk much about anything serious, any of the "real stuff," as she referred to it … at least she didn't want to talk about it with Max. With Max she wanted to, well, fuck; that and talk about odd stuff—anything but the horrors developing around them. At times their relationship seemed as much about escapism as love; certainly the escapism worked. As to what came later? Her reluctance to talk about the reality around them was a warning flag for Max, one he chose to ignore, at his peril; as did she, evidently.

The setting sun cast an orange glow on the day and the weather had cooled to the eighties; right now seemed the ideal time to take a walk.

They decided to a chance a walk in an isolated part of town when few people were about and even fewer military types were on the street; there was a corner shop where one could get a cup of coffee and maybe a pastry or two—though the proprietor was uncertain how long he could remain open … his chances boosted by catering to the military folks in the morning. Twenty minutes they lingered there on chocolate, sweets, and caffeine, and then moved on.

It was most unusual, taking in an afternoon as lovers of old would; though now it all seemed so foreign—no one enjoyed life any more, leastwise publicly.

As the yellow sun slid across the sky, emboldening to red as if to ward off the coming twilight, they stopped at another establishment that had also managed to remain open, at least for the nonce. It was a pizza parlor, or perhaps pizza shack would be a more apt description; it was old and dark but clean, and the food was good—the proprietor wouldn't take their money even if Max and Charlie had had any. He bought his ingredients on the black market, but that would soon come to an end; the government was printing new money, none of which was going to the cities of the heartland—the new money was to be the only accepted currency and as he'd have none, he'd have nothing to pay for what he bought and the business would consequently come to an end. He wouldn't do too badly, though, as a cook with kitchen management experience he'd fly pretty high in the new scheme of things. Those less fortunate in their previous experience would have coupons for rations; rations of food, rations of fuel, rations of clothing, and soon, unbeknownst to them, rations of housing. In the heartland where Socialism had been most virulently opposed, retribution was coming; it was coming swiftly and harsh and it was going to be the end of life as people had known it for hundreds of years.

The proprietor had made a big purchase of the ingredients needed for homebrewed beer while his money was still good, so he was able to serve them the first drafts they'd had in many a day. Alcohol had been outlawed shortly after the New Year, and was a law that was for the most part rigidly enforced.

They were the only ones in the joint; the world seemed strangely quiet—a palatable sense of doom hung in the air.

"Honestly, if things continue as they are, I do not know what I am going to do in a month. In a month not only will I have nothing to sell to customers who cannot pay, but I will have nothing for my family to eat, either. I who made a living making food, will be reduced to the level of swine eating from the swill."

"You make it sound so bad."

The proprietor gave Charlie a level glance.

"I have two daughters not much younger than you; it is bad. Lord alone knows what they might resort to for food. Fortunately, this white apron and a goodly amount of bullshit will get me into most any kitchen in the city. I was speaking more in general, for those who will not have the good fortune I will in a month's time."

That comment curdled Charlie a bit and a sour look passed her face. What would any of them be doing in a month's time. Today the sun shone bright, albeit setting now; how long the calm would last was not a meteorological speculation.

The proprietor walked off, and they finished what they wanted of their dinner.

"I think we should get going."

The man's departure, muttering under his breath, had seemed a dismissal of sorts, or at least a good time for them to take their own leave. They had been out now for about five hours and it was passing sundown; the two of them felt the ragged edge that only sleep could soften. Max murmured or hummed quietly to himself, rising to help Charlie up from her seat.

"I will never get over you, Max, you are so old-fashioned. Do you know that before I met you, it had been years since a man held a door for me, let alone helped me out of my chair."

"Just so long as you don't stop at old."

"Huh?"

"You know, the *old* in 'old-fashioned.' "

"And what if you are?"

"What?"

"Old."

"Not likely."

Max smiled and kissed her hair. Outside in the gathering twilight the street was quiet, the town, oh so quiet. There were now no more than one hundred thousand people living in the Tucson area, and until recently most had worked for a governmental entity such as the university or the local government; the balance had provided the infrastructure for the government employees in the form of eating establishments, cleaners, doctors—in short, it had been a self-sustaining economy where public money was raised, spent on goods and services by the government, circulated around in the infrastructure for a while, then raised again in the form of taxes and fees to start the process of government expenditures all over again. With the institutions that sustained this circle leaving, the economy was coming to an end. There would no longer be government expenditures; money would not flow in—the newly printed money was for the rest of the country only. There was no trade with the rest of the country, and no one was allowed to enter or leave; Tucson was a closed city, like most of the other cities in America's heartland. With astonishing rapidity, those institutions that made a community a community were dissolving before the eyes of their beholders.

Still, it was a delightful evening and they were in no hurry to navigate home, so they took a route that led through what had once been a neighborhood of happy households, now abandoned like the empty shells of long-dead snails in a once-vibrant neighborhood; the

Socialists had come to power with no time or desire to understand the common man—everything had to be fixed right away … move them to the Coastal areas or move them into a labor battalion, but by god they'd move or they'd die.

It *was* quiet, eerily so; all was as it should be when but a tenth of the population of a once vibrant city remained. Max and Charlie made their way home hesitantly; though there was nothing to suggest it, a strange sense of anticipation or foreboding filled the air.

The night was dark; it was quiet and warm—the buzz from the few flies scurrying about the streetlamps amplified the otherwise silence of the night. A vehicle approached them at a high rate of speed, preceded by a winding sound; clearly an electronic vehicle. Max looked at Charlie in alarm. They had no weapons between them, which was probably just as well; a shootout on the street would be very poor form and a losing proposition to boot—packing guns would most certainly get them arrested … or killed. They braced themselves for what was coming next; it could literally be anything. Tinted windows made it impossible to see into the car until it had pulled alongside them.

The window came down. "Get in, now."

The voice was his, of course, but by then Max and Charlie could clearly see Daryl and Jack sitting in the front; Jack was driving and Daryl was holding a shotgun across his knees—an odd sight that quickly became a frightening one when she got a look at the expression on Jack's face … it was an expression that so alarmed Charlie that for a moment she didn't move.

It was Max who finally got a hold of her, none too gently, pushed her head down so that she wouldn't smack it, and got her into the back of the car. The tension in the vehicle was palatable, thick. Something had happened, something large, very large. These two giants in their own right never looked so vulnerable.

Jack pulled away at a fast clip; it was only then that they, Max and Charlie, noticed that Daryl had a towel pressed against the right side of his head—white, 'cepting where the blood had soaked through it—there it was red. Charlie gasped. It was the last sound out of her for quite a while.

Daryl's eyes had a glazed look, and for the first time Max could remember, Daryl actually looked his seventy plus years; in his state, that shotgun wouldn't do him a bit of good. In the back of the car

Charlie still hadn't calmed down but she was being quiet; which, unsettling in itself, was just as well.

"We are headed to a safe house in the north part of town," spoke Jack to Max's unasked question. "Ellen is already there, along a few folks you know and more that you haven't met before. *Damn*,"—he smacked the steering wheel with the palm of his hand—*"they let me down."*

Max nodded, though he hadn't a clue as to who Jack was referring to; it was obvious that neither Charlie nor Daryl would be of help right now—he gave Charlie's leg a soft squeeze but got little reaction from her … she seemed completely overtaken by events that had yet to unfold.

Unlike the rest of the car's occupants, Max had no trouble finding his voice.

"Christ, Jack, what the hell is going on?"

"If I told you, you wouldn't believe it. I barely do myself and I have seen it firsthand. It has started. Marie tried to warn me of this—poor, prescient, dead Marie—but I would not listen. No one would, no one wanted to believe, no one had their eyes open. Not even him." He jerked his thumb over in Daryl's direction. "Even he never truly believed the worst of his doom-and-gloom predictions. Where we go from here I can't say. I fear the worst, Max, I am afraid that we may all die."

That took Max back a whole bit, indeed sat him back in his seat, looking out the window for phantoms and ghosts in the shadows that whizzed by. They were speeding across town, now heading north, then east; if Jack were trying to shake a pursuit he was doing a good job of it—it was unlikely that anyone could follow their zigzagging route without announcing it to the world with a neon sign.

After what must have been a short while but seemed like forever, they turned and entered a residential neighborhood, coming to a stop after passing a few houses. Jack pressed the garage door opener and in they went, joining the other two vehicles parked within. Max looked around, certainly not what he envisioned when he thought of a safe house.

"This is just a regular house, Jack. How can it be safe?"

Jack made no answer, instead exiting and making his way around the front of the car to help Daryl from the passenger seat. Max shrugged and started to help Charlie from the back, who shook her head in negation and climbed out by herself.

"It isn't safe, really," she began in answer to Max's question, "but it is a place we can hide out for a bit. That is what we are doing, is it not, Jack, hiding out?"

If Max and Jack were taken aback by this change in her demeanor they didn't show it; it was as if her previous disjointed lapse had never occurred—if anything, Jack seemed a little put out by the lack of banter in her query, by her flat demeanor, as if he expected more from her, as if he *needed* her needling him as a jolt of energy, which is exactly what he did not get … instead he replied with a simple, "Yeah."

They entered the house through a door at the back of the garage; inside was a short hall passing a kitchen on the right. At the end of the hall was a door, slightly open, through which could be seen a flight of stairs. They followed them down to a pine-paneled basement; Jack's wife, Ellen, was there with several others Max recognized from Jack's ranch, along with quite a few folks he had met in his travels with Jack and Charlie—too, there were several handfuls of folks he had not met before, there being forty or fifty people in all, maybe more, men and women, though it was hard to be sure of the count … with everyone moving around it was hard to make note of who had been where, in what spot, and whether they had been there before or not. Some seemed bewildered, some angry and agitated, but all seemed to have a sense of purpose about them; though what that purpose consisted of Max didn't rightly know, nor was he sure it was a purpose he wanted to be a part of.

There were no introductions; short, quiet acknowledgments, a slight incline of the head, a pat on the back, or a squeeze of the arm sufficed instead—these people didn't want to be known by people who didn't already know them, and they certainly didn't want to be known by name by anyone other than those whose name they already knew. That seemed just about right; Max himself had no desire to be known by anyone he didn't already know—*he'd fit right in*. A space was made for Daryl on one of the rear cots in the back of the room to afford him some privacy.

"Is he hurt bad?"

Jack gave Max a short, sharp glance; Max wasn't certain but he felt as if he had just been sized up, looked over, and had a check put into the *he can stay* column by his name—of course this probably wasn't really the case, but he could well find himself out on the street with the masses facing whatever awful thing it was that put the fright into Jack. It suddenly seemed that Jack had developed a capricious amount of power over those who he so diligently helped, though what that power might amount to he couldn't rightly say; as it stood, good, bad, or indifferent, Jack's word had somewhere along the line become a law unto itself.

"He wasn't shot, if that's what you're driving at," Jack said, finally deigning to answer. "It was a fall that he took as we were running." Then, as if in anticipation of Max's next question, he added, "The window had been shot out before we took the car."

The imagery was staggering: Jack and Daryl running, perhaps dodging gunfire, keeping low to the ground, sheltering amidst devastated cars; a wild drive through chaotic streets—though at the moment, at least here, the streets were empty and quiet. Jack, in the here and now, was gone; he had left and was involved in an earnest conversation with one of his ranch hands, though about what, Max couldn't catch. Ellen had moved to Daryl's side and was ministering to him, washing the dried blood from his white hair, adjusting his lie so as to make him more comfortable—he was conscious but not terribly so. Charlie, now fully awakened from the trance that Jack's sudden and grim appearance had swept her off to, came over and took him by the arm.

"Come, sweet thing, let's get us a cup of water."

Her playful, sultry voice had returned, yet it was different, as if it were forced. Max didn't know what to make of that.

"Huh? Yeah, water. Where?"

"There's a hall under the stairs. Two rooms are off it, a bathroom and a storage closet—there is a water dispenser in the closet."

"You have been here before?"

"No, I dreamt it," she stated condescendingly.

She pulled on his arm so as not to leave him any choice in the matter. Max smiled, Charlie, pushy, forward, and vulnerable, was back, forced or not, and that suited Max fine; the alternative—well, Max positively did not want to know the alternative ... a catatonic Charlie wasn't something he cared to contemplate.

As soon as they turned into the hall beneath the stairs, Charlie pushed Max up against the wall. He smiled a tad and moved to kiss her.

"No, not now, not here. Besides, we have something else we need to talk about." She stroked his arm to take some of the sting from her voice. "We shan't stay here."

"Oh no?"

Staying, going, it was all the same to him; it wasn't just that he wanted to be with her and would do most anything she asked, it was more—he couldn't honestly trust Jack's judgment over hers … both of them were in over their heads and Max was hanging on for lord knows what the future held. But he did need to know what was behind Charlie's sudden need to depart; standing there, his back against the wall, he gave her the chance to explain herself.

"Why?"

"Because this place isn't safe. Jack thinks that it is, but it is not."

He gave her a searching look, saw confusion and desperation in her eyes masked by feigned indifference, and understood why her nature seemed forced; it was forced because she was out of her element here—Charlie was meticulous, she liked to think things through. Granted she did so in an abbreviated fashion, some would say impulsive; it was more akin to a sky diver who takes in the variables around them and then, on a spur, jumps out of a plane. But they do so after examining the variables in detail, and there was little here that was playing out in a detailed way; Charlie was brave, intelligent, and aggressive, but uncertainty just didn't cut it with her and this day was about as uncertain as one could get. But he wasn't going to acquiesce to her unchallenged.

"We don't know what is going on, *you* don't know what is going on. How can this place be unsafe, unsafe from what?"

Charlie grabbed him by the arms. "There is only one thing that could drive Jack like this, and you know it. If the military is rounding people up, then this house is definitely not safe, no house really is."

"Okay," he said in a softer voice, "if you don't think it is safe here, that's good enough for me. Far be it for me to be the reason that we get picked up because of my intransigence with you about this. Besides, I had a taste of the hospitality of the authorities and don't care to do so again, and will do *anything*." He paused. "Well, almost anything, anyway, to avoid spending time with them again. At my age, their diet is very hard to digest, and I might say it gave me a bad case of the runs."

Charlie looked at him quizzically. It *was* a bad attempt at humor, he had to admit. Maybe he was more out his mind than she was.

"Look, if you want to leave, that's fine. Where do we go?"

"Anywhere but here."

"*Ohkayyy.*" He couldn't hide the hesitation in his voice, but he pressed on anyway. "When?"

"Right now."

Now it was Max's turn to look at her quizzically; what was going on in her head? She seemed to be in a controlled yet frantic state; or maybe a frantically controlled state—no mind, she was focused on this fact, this feeling, and there was no arguing with her … she'd probably go without him if he pushed back too hard.

"We do tell Jack?" he said, more of a question than the statement it was meant to be.

"Of course we do. I'll take care of it," and off she went.

Max considered going with her, but at the moment Jack seemed to have little time for conversation.

His life seemed like a jellyfish caught on a current, hoping no sharp shoals lay ahead, all the while knowing that they did—he had been drifting amidst razor-sharp corral for most of the last year and had the dings, cuts, scrapes, and scars to show for his travels.

She returned a short while later, a small bag slung over her shoulder; she looked like she was off to college.

"Just a few things, *undies* for you and me, and a couple of clean pullovers."

"Shirts?"

"Yeah, and toothbrushes, socks for each of us."

"How?"

"The place is pretty well stocked, and you are a pretty average-size guy. I think that they will fit you. Oh, and some canned food as well."

But have you a can opener? was Max's first thought. He said, "Well provisioned, eh? I thought you said this wasn't a good place to hide out."

"*Well provisioned* does not mean safe. We could eat well here until we die."

Max shrugged his shoulders. "Well, let *me* say goodbye to Jack and we'll go."

"It's not like they're not going to see us for more than a day or so; this will blow over and we will be all lovey-dovey with each other once again."

It was then Max knew she was lying, about telling Jack; she hadn't, and he knew it. What was worse was that she didn't know that he knew she was lying and that really concerned him; she was doing such a bad job of lying and for her not to see it—what was really going on here?

Why did she want to go so badly?

Twilight

Hour 2

Jack was desperately trying to get everyone out of the house; it was imperative that they move now. The scope of the roundup was large—they were essentially taking everyone … from blocks to entire neighborhoods. This was beyond food rations and work brigades; what he was witnessing was the beginning of a slave army. In the land that was once of the free and the home of the brave, Marxism had come full circle; from each according to his ability, *take it all*, to each according to his need, *give them nothing*.

Now he was trying to get his charges out of harm's way, and he could not find Charlie and Max; from Charlie he had expected as much, she was such a flake, or could be at times, but Max—Max should have told him he was going … very poor form, that.

Convinced they were not in the house, Jack gathered the rest of those whose life rested in his hands, including a small array of women, children, and old men. Charlie *was* right about one thing, no house was truly safe, and Jack was not so careless as to believe otherwise.

Charlie and Max were making his job of saving his meager charges more difficult; Jack was under no illusions—Charlie had cracked and Max, well, Max was in love with a girl almost half his age and prone to bad decisions. Choices had been made, actions taken, and Charlie and Max were beyond Jack's help now; it would do no good other than to forget them for the nonce. He silently wished them well and to stay out of harm's way.

He had always known that Charlie was fragile; that was why she hadn't known that *this* house was not the *real* safe house. The house they were in now was where everyone knew to come in the event of an emergency, like the emergency that was taking place all around them; clueing Charlie in on the existence of the "house behind the house" never even occurred to Jack.

The military was about a quarter mile up the street; many of the doors broken down this evening were but sad remnants of homes that were long empty. The remaining families, hearing what was in store for them in the very near future, tried to flee; but making a run for it was like putting a pack of wild dogs on the trail of a hare—on the open plains, with no significant cover to be had. Tonight it just wouldn't end well.

Under the cover of darkness and by the light of an argent moon, Jack quietly led his group out the back door, abandoning their gathering point, the "safe house ruse," and over to the entrance of the real safe house, a block farther east and a bit to the north; he certainly hoped that is was a real safe house, but never having had to use it he couldn't be sure.

Jack fumbled for a minute with the key and, once inside, he led Ellen and the rest of the troop down to yet another basement, then down an old hall, to a room beautifully paneled with real wood; shame they wouldn't be here to enjoy a truly lovely house with lush woods and voluminous trim, dating from the 1920s. *This* safe house was not really that either; this safe house was but another step along the path of escape.

The mechanics of his plan hadn't changed since conception, some seven years ago; it had taken Jack two years to make the plan viable—and tonight it was paying off with life. His plan often reminded Jack of the layers of an onion, or perhaps like those wooden Russian dolls where one doll lived within another, within another, and so on. There was a name for them, the Russian dolls, though Jack thought it might just be that, Russian dolls; he couldn't quite remember.

Anyway, the plan, *his escape plan*, was like that.

On a hot summer night, on the east side of Tucson, Arizona, in a large room at the end of a long hall, Jack removed two pieces of trim, one in the floorboard and one set in the crown molding. Beneath the trim were pins which, when removed, set a panel in the wall rotating and opened a passage leading to a large room … the third layer, though not the final one in the plan. Once everyone was inside the room, Jack replaced the trim pieces on the outer wall to hide the hinges and stepping across the threshold, swung the panel shut, locking it in place with the pins from the inside, shutting it forever until opened from the inside, which would hopefully be never.

It was a large, narrow room crafted from roughhewn pine boards reinforced with studs and strung with a line of electric lights—bright enough to see by, yet dim enough to make the place uninviting, which was just as well, as it was not a place intended for a long-term stay, in this plan certainly not more than an hour at most. At the far end of the room was an opening that led into a tunnel seemingly without end.

The time for moving on had come; now couldn't be soon enough. There were shelves in the room and they began to sort things out. Flashlights came on, allowing the outfitting to proceed at a pace; the sound of water draining from jugs into smaller water bottles echoed softly off the walls—rucksacks were handed out and stuffed with everything from toilet paper to candy bars. Some had managed to bring enough of their own garb, while for others there was a large selection of outfits abandoned by the gentry during the recent evacuations to the coastal areas.

It wasn't long before sixty some odd pairs of eyes crowded around watching *him*, Jack, and waiting for him to speak.

When had this come about? About forty others were to come later; Jack and his band of hundred. But who these hundred were and what were they up against, none really knew.

"The way is long, with naught but these flashlights to guide us, so we will use half now and half should it take us longer than I hope. Spread amongst you are shoulder bags with food, water, matches, TP"—that got a small smile out of some of them—"and a variety of other essentials. Supplies such as these we will be carrying, but there will be more, much more, and clothes too, where we are going."

No one spoke, no one questioned. Sixty-eight pairs of eyes blinked.

"All right, let's go."

He took his wife's hand and led her through the doorway and into a small tunnel; it was the start of a dangerous journey, but it was dark no longer—the way ahead was illuminated by a crazy patchwork of flashlights bouncing off the walls, the ceiling, the floor.

Fifty yards more brought them into the abandoned sewer system that long ago had been dropped from the system for newer lines that flowed to different destinations, newer destinations. They had not been used for over a hundred years and not been listed on any map for almost half that many years again. Jack sincerely hoped that he was the only one living who knew of its existence and the existence of the sealed garage into which it led.

One thing was for sure, he would find out the answer to that question soon.

Twilight

Hour 3 Till Morning

Max held tight to Charlie's hand; delicate yet strong—a microcosm of the tomboy that she was … and at the moment it was sweaty as hell. Her hand was also the only thing keeping him grounded and not off in a shell of a devastated building howling his mind out.

He guided her through the rubble-strewn street while orange plumes, flashes of yellow, and bursts of blinding white slashed across the craggy purple evening.

They were making their way *back* to the house they had started from less than four hours ago. At the moment they were sheltered between a row of hedges along Broadway Boulevard, one of the city's major east-west thoroughfares.

Leaving had been a big mistake, a huge mistake; now they were caught in a fire fight between the most violent of the opposition groups and the army—Jack's petty band of resistance fighters paled against the ferociousness of these hard-core oppositionists … now Charlie and Max were caught in a fight to the death, for only death awaited those who were taken alive on either side. This was an opposition which seemed as much bent on destruction as it did any type of success, for their chances of success were lodged between lousy and impossible. The night was messy and it was ugly, and above all it was violent; deadly as well, if the bodies strewn on the street were any indication of the destruction each side was raining down on the other.

Of all the things he could think of at a desperate moment such as this, Max remembered a warm summer night many years ago when his wife was still alive. It was late and both Karen and Kate were sleeping. Max sat gazing from the front porch of his house—it was monsoon season and lightning was exploding in the sky close above him. The night was a deep, dark purple broken only by window-rattling crescendos and blinding flashes of light; at the time, he thought it looked like a war zone.

Well, it did and it didn't. Missing from the monsoon's fury was the sense of terror; the acrid smell of things—metal, wood, rubber, *flesh* burning, the cries for help … and the fear for one's life. Tonight it was bombs bursting in midair and rockets' red glare; exploding, literally, at their feet—shattering the concrete where it lay and pounding the earth that it laid barren … creating a state of affairs unrivaled by even the most violent of monsoon storms.

Max took a deep breath, closed his eyes, and said an old Hebrew prayer silently; where it had come from and why he chose to bring it forth now was not a mystery but certainly not expected—*and then they ran* … ran as fast as he could, his firm grip never faltering on her lithe, strong, sweaty hand.

They ran down the street, alongside the twisted metal of what had once been cars, ran alongside the still-exploding grenades that slammed into buildings just behind and before them, ran hoping that no one could see them in the dark night, for everyone would have shot at them. Charlie was, for the most part, physically unscathed by the evening's atrocities though her face was puffed and swollen on the left side and the area around her cheekbone was purple; he wasn't sure but he didn't think the bone was broken—as for him, blood ran down his arm from a wound around his shoulder that he did not feel.

Broken bones or not, her spirit didn't lag; her strength of character was evidenced by her determination and perseverance to go on—gone was the craziness of yesterday eve … just like that, as if someone had flipped a switch in her. It was as complete and confusing a turnaround as could be imagined, and it all happened in the space of a single breath.

Literally.

He realized he might not know her at all.

They moved through the wreckage of things that had once made up the lives of the people who had lived here. They moved now in pursuit of her friends rather than away from them; what drove her yesterday to abandon those who over the last five years had become her family, she couldn't say—indeed she at first refused to believe her role in the events leading up to their being on their own in this jungle of despair … having eventually accepted her role as the instigator in their rapid departure, she laughed and scoffed at Max's half-proffered suggestion that it was to spend more time with him. But *that* response from her was good, in fact it was perfect; humorous disdain of his affection was normal for her and coexisted in harmony with her affection for him—she frequently expressed herself through a compilation of opposites ... it was one of the reasons he loved her, or fancied that he did. Love had been one of those things that Max had never quite figured out nor expected to find again in this life; the only love he truly understood was the love of and for his daughter Kate. She was never out of his thoughts, like a pot of boiling water meant something in the future—soup, tea, or pasta, it made no difference. Boiling water represented a potential in the future; he hoped that finding his daughter would be as certain as boiling water becoming tea.

But all of that, the boiling water, his Kate, everything else, everything other than what was happening right now, was a future and Max could spare no more thoughts for it. The immediacy was on getting across the street and up to the second story of what remained of a building that once occupied a small piece of real estate on this thoroughfare running across the city. The building itself was of no particular significance other than it looked to be a good hideout where Max and Charlie could catch their breath and plan their next action; and *that* was a future *that* did interest him—finding a way to live and to go on doing so. He was focused on how he was going to survive right here, right now; the why of what was going on around them he hadn't a clue—as to the *what* that he was going to do in the future, that didn't even exist.

They crossed the street during a lull in the shelling, at least he assumed it to be shelling; it could very well have been rockets or bombs, but for some reason these explosions had a different feel, a harder concussion than the previous ones, so he assumed them to be from shelling; he knew that the earlier explosions were from rocket-propelled grenades—he'd seen them fired and had heard their high-pitched screams as they raced across the night. Be that as it may, Max was unsure just who it was that was being shelled, if it was shelling, or why they were being shelled; that the army was bringing its explosive power down on someone was clear, but as to who it was, neither Max nor Charlie could say. At first Max had thought for sure that Charlie would know, but when asked, her shoulders, beneath a worried face, simply shrugged; *"Jack would know"* was about all she could fathom in terms of an answer—*Jack would know* was an answer he could have come up with himself ... and as Jack was not around,

Max was left with little in terms of understanding and a lot in terms of concern and fear.

Having safely reached the other side of the street they made their way through a large window framed in jagged glass and into the storefront behind; it had been a clothing store at one time. Max had thought that they should look for money in the drawers, but that didn't seem right. Besides, what would they do with it? Money was worthless here, now, and they had enough on their plate without the worry of being shot as looters. They did that, he was fairly sure, shoot people for looting, since they seemed to be shooting people for just about anything. Then Charlie mentioned something about getting a change of clothes. Max started to argue against it; stealing didn't seem right, regardless of the store's dilapidation and the general lawlessness around them—then again, the store owner's livelihood had been stolen long ago ... if the proprietor of this shop still lived, it was unlikely that he would ever ring up a sale here again.

In clean garb resembling what they had just discarded—people really were creatures of habit—they staggered up the stairs to the second floor; it had been blasted open on three sides and only a slight lip of a wall remained abutting the street—its bombed-out appearance oddly reassuring Max ... the ruined wooden beams and studs and a jumble of broken brick looked incompatible with human life, which somehow made it seem incalculably safe.

They huddled against one another beneath a long winter coat they had found on one of the clothing racks; the night didn't require it—indeed, in an odd contrast to the evil which stalked the land, it was a balmy night ... yet there was something embryonic in the sense of cover and security the coat provided.

"We can talk now or not."

"No, now is fine." Charlie pulled in closer to Max. "If they are not at the safe house, and truly I don't see how they could have stayed, given what is happening in the city right now, I really don't know where they could have gone, or I do but I don't know where."

Max sighed wearily. "And what does that mean?"

"Well, Jack always said that he had a super-secret hideout that was so good that one couldn't get to it by conventional means, so I imagine they went there."

If they still lived.

"Quiet, a vehicle is coming."

They slouched down closer to one another. Her breath came hot on his neck, and he pulled her closer, his mouth finding hers—it was crazy yet in the midst of their danger he felt the heat rising; in himself as well as her—his tongue found her neck and for the moment they were about to … but they never got there. The sound of the jeep motored off and their passion with it, almost as if it had been fueled by the approach of the vehicle; Max shuddered to think what might have happened had the jeep stopped at their little hideout with the motor on—their passion might have gone all the way, *oblivious to what was around them* … no doubt they would have been shot while consummating the act, *oblivious to what was going on around them*. Max shook his head; he was going crazy from fear, or from love—he couldn't say which … perhaps it was from the fear of love.

They had to get back to the safe house, *that* was the starting point, the point from which it all began, from which they could begin to reclaim a sense of direction; it was the point from which they could move on and find their friends, or so he hoped.

Charlie and Max rested for perhaps another twenty minutes and then made their way back down to the street and peered out through the ruined storefront. It was all quiet now; the battle, or shelling, had moved on and was now a quieter echo in a more distant reality—they started off amongst the ruined and smoldering stuff. Charlie, her face swollen, hopelessly smudged with dirt and streaked with sweat, her shoulder-length hair all tangled, took the lead; Max was certain he looked no better as they gingerly picked a way forward. She set a quick pace that kept them close into the façade of the buildings along the south side of the street; heading back east, the way they had come—eight miles, they had covered yesterday evening on the way out, and they had made up most of that without food or sleep.

In spite of the danger around them Charlie began humming a tune which Max didn't recognize; that really was no surprise—so much of what passed today for music was only so much noise. But this had a different melodic content to it.

"What song is that?"

To say the question sounded odd, breaking the silence of the landscape, was an understatement.

"Oh, it is nothing much. You probably haven't heard it before, it is an old song."

Old? thought Max. *Old, probably as in all of twenty years or so, at most.*

187

They reached the street, or more precisely, the exact block, on which the safe house sat; up and down the street all that remained were husks of what were once houses. No more; there was no longer a safe house.

"Shit," Charlie said, "I told Jack the house was not safe, but would he listen to me? No. Now the bastard probably has gone and got himself killed."

Max gave her a steady look and a raised brow. "We don't know, Charlie, maybe they got out. Hopefully, they did."

"Oh, I am sure they did. We are talking about Jack, remember? He might be too stubborn to admit that he fucked up the decision as to where to hide, but he wouldn't get caught with his pants down. No way." Charlie looked out from the small plot of trees they had sheltered in, careful to keep herself well hidden, "Well, there is only one way to find out, we got to go in. With all the folks who were in there when we left, well, if they had still been in there when the place came down, there will be body parts."

Max grimaced but said nothing. Again he was reminded as to who the revolutionary was in this relationship; a true revolutionary he was not cut out to be, even as he played the role of one, albeit on a minor scale.

Still, Max was the man in the duo so he needed to lead; he had to, and they both knew it. Charlie offered no resistance when he held her back by the shoulder for a moment so that he could get ahead. Keeping to the shadows as they had done all evening, they made their way down the street. Max was fairly certain he remembered which house it was, though in the purple darkness just before the dawn the skeletons of what were once people's homes all seemed to look pretty much the same, like skeletons of what were once people's homes.

Picking their way through the rubble, they were relieved to realize that there were no, as Charlie so succinctly put it, *body parts* among the wreckage. It was good, very good, of course, but it did not ease the sense of loneliness that Max felt; here in his home town, he felt very much the stranger—almost as if someone had come in and switched towns during his period of incarceration in the Flagstaff mining camp. Pah, he needed to get past this feeling. Jack and the others were *apparently* alive and that is what really mattered. But were they alive and on the run or alive and captive, soon to be slaving away with the other hundred thousand souls who had once made up the free population of Tucson? Max wasn't sure how they were to determine this, not sure at all, but he did feverishly hope that Jack and his minions were still alive and on the run.

"No matter," Charlie piped up as if reading his thoughts, she tried to sound light and upbeat, but it didn't work when one was standing amongst ashen beams, smoldering insulation, and melted glass; what had happened here? Why was the destruction so complete? Why had it been so necessary to … to … to do what? To insure that no one would ever live here again?

Charlie was talking again; her voice cracked with exhaustion, but her eyes sparkled with the light of those who have a secret that can finally share, a good-news secret.

"Jack wasn't as tactful as he would have others believe; he thought he had secrets, and I am sure that he did, many indeed. But it is hard to keep things from *me*. Especially when it is on paper." She shot Max an evil grin. "I am *way* too nosey to be left out in the cold when it comes to details that are of interest to me. You see, I know where Jack's ultimate hideout is. If he is alive and free, I know where to find him. And you're going to get me there," she said with a sly smile.

Max smiled too; a robust, honest smile—he smiled for the first time that evening, and maybe longer than that … Charlie and he were not dead, not cut off from the rest of humanity. He was not going to spend the last days of his life straggling willy-nilly behind a half-sane little harlot after all. Though he probably would not have minded if he had.

No, things were going to be better now, of that he was sure; better might be only until the morning came, or for a day or a week. Regardless, after a night of confusion, deceit, and downright terror, Max had come to a conclusion. He really did love this gal.

Veracity

Kate finished her hair with a flip of her finger, adding a curl to the strands on her left and slipped into her tight blue jeans and plain T-shirt she had selected for her afternoon rendezvous; she nestled her tiny knife in its sheath—fitting snuggly between her belt and left hip.

It was a thin blade and sharp; just over three inches with a thinly taped handle—the ideal defensive weapon for someone who was attentive to her environment and fast with their hands ... and fast with her hands she was. She could have the blade out and between the ribs of her assailant, or anyone else of her choosing, within the time it took to say hello. She had been practicing; she was fast—she was good.

Dressed just so and stealthily armed, she headed out into the streets; truly they had gotten more dangerous of late, almost as if there were a plague creeping into the city– tens of millions living outside of the city and just this side of poverty. There was no lack of folks who would be happy to bring violence and crime to the well-heeled and take home some of that finely polished shoe leather. Crime now ran rampant and the government seemed at a loss to stem the flood of criminal activity—that, or it hadn't the desire to curb the assaults by the criminally inclined ... it didn't hurt to also throw a little intimidation and government dependency the way of the well-heeled. Allowing the criminal element leeway to run riot left the government's hands clean of the foul deeds while at the same time allowing it to swoop in to the rescue and further the reliance on the government. Someone had been doing their homework, creating the need to secure law and order while placing more restrictions on the people for their "own protection."

Doffing a wide-brimmed, light-colored hat and soft calfskin gloves, Kate looked the very epitome of the well-heeled. She couldn't shake the unease at which she embraced the level of comfort and luxury her life afforded her; nine in ten people lived a life barely above that of subsistence living, and she couldn't help but revel in the luxury of the Socialist elite. Unlike Jared, unlike Jambi, she had no real idea why she worked for "the cause," but having a full stomach and calfskin gloves definitely played a part in it. Sure, she felt compassion for the impoverished, but it was not her responsibility to fix that; besides, it wasn't as if she didn't have her own oppressions— they were different, yes, but oppression, well, she had a pretty good fill of that too.

It was difficult for her to say who she was now. She had left Tucson, vain, ignorant, and more than a little selfish; what was she today? The vanity was gone, wasn't it? Well, she *did* have the affection of two men; well, the affection of one man and the lust of another— or actually she was being *used* by one man and abused by another. *Shit*, she thought, *best to drop this line of reasoning, and fast*; it was getting her nowhere.

Yet ….

She was on her way to meet Jared, more than willingly; she didn't trust him, and yet she did—it was like she trusted him day to day to be there, to listen to her, comfort her and love her, physically, yet it was just that, a day-to-day trust. Beyond that there was nothing; certainly there was no reason for Jared to abandon her, but realistically her long-term survival was no less based on Jared's good graces than they were on Guy's; she was young, female, a nobody in a cruel city dominated by ambitious men—it wasn't easy, it certainly wasn't pretty, and it was in no way safe.

Kate wanted to go home, to her real home; she wanted her father, and she wanted her mother too—but the latter was dead and the former might as well be, for all the likelihood she had of seeing him again.

She had reached the Hotel Diplomat; a name strangely apropos to her and of those whose lives were connected to her.

Jared sipped his scotch and drew on a cigarette; she would be here soon, she was rarely, if ever, late—so punctual a spy she was … though she wasn't really that, a spy, that is. Kate had no professional training and no real skill; she was an informer, a source, nothing more—even that was leaving her … she wasn't really any good at this. Her abhorrence for Guy got in the way of her being able to be truly successful. A time would come in the not too far future, when there would be a new girl on Guy's arm, a girl who wanted to please him, from selfishness or love it mattered not; Guy probably would not even know the difference, but adore him she would and where would that leave Kate?

Dead, probably; unless of course a change could be made—a change that might well have to begin today.

Kate arrived in the lobby as agreed, precisely on time; she felt calm and collected, more so than she had felt in weeks or longer. The elevators were across the lobby and she stepped into the left one and punched the number eleven; Jared really liked this floor for some reason that Kate couldn't fathom, not that she'd ever asked; regardless of room number, north side of the building or south, they met always at this hotel and on the eleventh floor—the view on either side was bracing ... looking out over the nation's capital for miles in any direction was nothing to snicker at. Anyway, floor eleven; a lucky number in some game of chance that Jared mentioned he played from time to time—of the name, all she could remember is that it was related to excrement somehow ... she shivered. Men, all different yet so much the same.

She got out when the elevator stopped on the eleventh floor. She had her large over-the-shoulder bag, stylish as befitting her clothing, bearing a single strap; that was out of the ordinary. Perhaps Jared will notice this, perhaps he will not; he liked to think of himself as observant. But Kate already had the advantage of being out of character and knowing it, while Jared would not know what to expect other that what he had gotten in the past; Jared would be expecting Kate, the Kate he knew—what he would get would make all his prior experience with her of little consequence ... it might as well not even be Kate coming to call at all.

A rap at the door, then another, then three short, sharp shocks. In her mind she saw Jared rising and putting his ear to the door, silent, or almost, he was very careful, resting his hands against the glossy paint of the door; he would have his eye up to the peephole and would see Kate standing there. Quiet; no more than that, *silent*— Kate herself was rarely quiet with her slight, nervous little habits ... a trait that Jared found amusing, loveable, and annoying all at the same time. Frowning, she hadn't expected that thought at this time.

He opened the door.

When she passed him on the way in he noticed a hard glint to her eye, but then nothing—had he seen it?

"Scotch?"

"Yes."

This was not good, thought Jared; she usually announced her displeasure for the fiery drink in no uncertain terms as soon as it was proffered—indeed, their first meeting was the one and only time they had imbibed together, at least on scotch … his own penchant for savoring that fine liquor with people he cared for notwithstanding.

His usual retort to her disparagement of his drink of choice was choked in his throat. He let the whole thing lie, and didn't open the bottle. Something was very wrong here.

For the moment he drew her a glass of water and dispensed with the glass of wine he normally gave her at the end of their bantering; the tension in the air was palpable but not dominating—someone who did not know them, or her, might not even pick up on it. But he did, and his reaction was stronger than he had hoped; his hand shook slightly and a rasp of anxiety ran across his skin, a tingling from his wrist, up his arm, over his shoulder, and then down his back—taking a quick breath, he settled himself. *Going crazy,* he thought.

"Have a seat," came out.

Kate stood there not moving, looking vulnerable as ever; she was so beautiful right at this moment.

"Kate, I—"

"Not now," she said. "Shh … listen."

She held her finger up to his lips as if to ward off his words and to draw attention, with slightly cocked head, to a sound in the background.

"I don't   "

"Nooo." She moved up closer to him, sensual, not meeting his eyes.

"Kate, I … "

"Love me. Yes, I know."

Jared swallowed; Kate put her hand on his hip and slid it around to the small of his back, leaning her head into his neck, her hair tickling his cheek.

"You do love me." Not a statement, not a question, but more.

Jared didn't answer; by now he knew that something had happened, was going to happen—he found himself in a new game and he didn't know rule one … and he was far from positive that this was a game he could win.

"What's the matter, Jared."

Soft and sultry, she placed a kiss on his neck.

At that moment he decided to act; he found his footing in the disorienting space in which his head was spinning and reasserted what he considered to be his dominance in their relationship—he was right about that.

He pushed away, untangling himself from her embrace, and pushed her back some more; sensing more than seeing the hostility in her eyes, he chose to ignore it for the nonce.

"Kate, why are you doing this? Have I ever said I love you? Have I ever said that I don't? C'mon, if it is more affection that you want …."

"What, you'll give it to me? Kill off whoever's in your way?" Sarcastically, she pushed him a bit farther away from her.

Jared scratched his day's growth of beard; this was getting interesting—she had never challenged his behavior before. He kind of liked the spunky new Kate, but was it safe?

"So you think that is what I do? What I did? That I killed Guy's father, killed him to move Guy, and by virtue of association, you, up the social ladder? A good observation, but not terribly perceptive; it took you all this time to see what was lying around in plain view for you to see."

"Oh yes, I know," said Kate. "You are very good at leaving things out for people to see, only what you leave out in plain view is what you want a person to see. You answer, *'Do you love me'* with *'I have never said I didn't love you,'* which is not only no answer at all, it doesn't even mean a thing. You're playing with me. You misdirect the truth in such a way as if you didn't even say *it*; not the truth, not a lie—you say nothing … or something. The listener hears what it is they want to hear out of the choices you present them. You play to their mental image, you take the meaningless, clothe it in a truth of sorts, and use it to speak to people's desires.

"Yes, killing Guy's father; that was an answer to a question that was always there to see, but *you* know that I want to think well of you, so you misdirect the nasty question of killing someone to the more positive one of your honesty—you tell a truth when asked, but not to the question asked of you."

Damn, she was good, she was very good. Jared had been playing people, all sorts of people, just like this for years, just as she said; playing to

194

their doubts and to their needs—taking what needed to be said and shaping it around what he knew the listener wanted to hear. He attributed his ability to do so successfully, to his uncanny ability to read people, read people on many levels; from their cultural avocation to their political affiliation, from their interpersonal relationships to their personal moral values, Jared had the ability to read it all from the smallest encounter, take it all in from a glance, a handshake, a chance conversation—people wore so much of their inner nature on their sleeve for those who knew how to see it, to read it … it was a skill that Jared loved, practiced, and enjoyed, practicing it for its own sake as a pianist plays both for profit and love.

But all skills are only as evil or as good as the use they are put to; this inner sense of his, his ability to read people so easily, so thoroughly, actually made him more compassionate—Jack found it hard to be able to read people so well, what they were going through, what they lacked in their life … and to try and provide for them what he thought they needed.

Compassion was the driving force in *his* life; it was the why of his involvement in *the cause*—his involvement in almost any cause that would bring back the free and democratic America of his youth … or at least his younger years. But Kate saw his ability to so easily and clearly read people as a *skill, and* there is a difference between an ability and a skill. An ability is a gift, something which one is born with and entitled to use as one sees fit. A skill is not natural; it is developed by its user and in part is a responsibility to its developer—how it is used and to what ends.

"Okay, no misdirection, then," Jared said. "But I won't be pressed into answering any question that I don't want to answer."

Kate shot him a hard glance but didn't respond. For the moment of silence, Kate took in their redeveloping relationship.

"You had Guy's father killed," she stated matter-of-factly.

"Yes."

"So that I could spy on … higher-placed people?"

"Yes."

Something suddenly occurred to her and Kate deviated from the line of questioning she had intended to pursue. "How did you know that he would move up?" she asked Jared quizzically, for the moment all confrontation gone from her voice.

"That part was easy, really. We have moved to a despotic society. For the first time in this country, ever, positions of power, nonelected ones to be sure, but even elected ones to some extent, have become hereditary. People, they retire, they die, or just plain move on, whatever, and their heirs, family members, or just plain cronies oftentimes as not, step in to fill the role or post just vacated. Usually the father, but sometimes the mother, brings their son or daughter into the organization at a low level. Over time they move up, usually taking a leap forward when the parent vacates the scene.

"Guy actually did better than I thought he would. He moved up many steps. True, it is more of an administrative role than a policy role. Even the dorks in our government can see what a disaster it would be if Guy were making decisions that affect all of us. So they make him big, they make him important, and slough him off as some type of bean counter on steroids. Only, he has a whole cadre of people who count the beans for him; what does he do, Kate?"

"Nothing."

"Correct, he does nothing. He is a nothing with a big title. All he does is sit in a really fancy office talking sports crap, or women crap, or any crap at all that has no point to it, and then he goes to the crapper and takes a crap. He is the ideal bureaucrat, thinking that the world couldn't get along without him, when actually neither he nor anything he has or does is what the world wants, let alone needs."

"Well, that sure says a lot," Kate said with a sneer. "You and Jambi manipulate people. You kill people and then you put incompetent asses in charge of things, which really make people's lives miserable."

"No. You can't. You can't talk about miserable because you don't know miserable."

He took a seat on the edge of the bed, his pants showing a day's worth of wrinkles; he hadn't been to sleep since yesterday—an untouched scotch had ended up in his hands and untouched it remained … without a thought given to how it had ended up in his hands.

"Yes, yes. I know," he said, "you are miserable with Guy, and he does treat you miserably, but that is not what I mean." Then kinder, gentler, he said, "All those things you say about me are true, I do all of them. But when was the last time you were in a coastal city, and I don't mean our little section of 'material heaven on earth' here in the capital. All cities are about ten percent elite. When was the last time you were in a coastal city outside of that ten percent?

"Two, three families in a tiny, rickety apartment. Families in one room only, with a bath at the end of the hall. No, you won't find that in Washington, DC, or in Tucson, Arizona, pitiful as that place may be. You haven't seen anything miserable because you haven't been where the truly miserable things to see are.

"Crime through the roof and parents afraid to let their children out. The children disappear and no one does anything about it. People die in the streets literally every day, and not all who do, meet a violent end. Nutrition is terrible there, and some die from lack of it. Many, many homes are surrounded or built amongst environmental hazards. There are almost no doctors or hospitals and there is little infrastructure of any sort. Lots of people are dying, Kate. Killing Guy's father will perhaps one day, maybe, reduce the rate of death on the other side of the tracks."

"Yeah, well, maybe."

She was quiet again; alarmingly so—Jared felt her drifting off from a point of complacency, felt the hostility rising in her again, directed at him and not at him ... generalized, random, angry. She was dangerous right now, Jared wasn't sure how, but he knew she was and that was enough. They were going to pick up the conversation where they, no *she*, left off, of that Jared was certain; he braced himself—whatever had brought her to this point was bound to be big, and big from Kate was bound *not* to be good. In the final analysis Kate wasn't a team player, so there was no telling what she'd do.

"Tell me, Jared, what is your aim, your goal, your *big* plan? Do you mean to topple the government? Bring back the freedom, prosperity, and the pursuit of happiness thing?"

Jared hesitated, sensing a trap here; he knew he was being drawn into a game of her design, a game wherein she held all the cards and knew all the rules—against his wishes and better judgment he felt compelled to answer.

"Yes. No. I mean no. I mean ... I don't know. I mean, yes, to what you said, ah, in a general sense."

Kate snickered. "And I am a part of this unknown effort of unclear goals."

"Now wait, the goals are clear. Don't ever say that," he protested, a note of hostility creeping into his voice. "We, Jambi and I, the Conservatives, IsPal, all America's old allies and friends, we are all pushing for a return to a free, prosperous, and compassionate America. But no, I can't say how we get there, beyond trying, that is. We are fighting back."

"You have soldiers then, in your army?"

"Yes, no, sort of." Well, this was going extraordinarily shitty. " 'Soldiers' is more of a euphemism than an accurate term for who we are. I don't actually command anyone. Jambi and I work together, and we hire out the messy parts. We know a few other folks who work with us, alongside of us. They also work on their own on, on matters outside of our purview. But it is getting done."

"How long have you known that Guy had my father arrested?"

Oh, she was good, she was very good; Jared was so caught off by this question that his very silence was all the affirmation she needed that he had known, and that he had known for quite some time. Moments passed, many moments, and as time slipped by, more time slipped by; for each passing moment Jared's ability to extricate himself diminished ever further.

"I have known for a while, but not prior to when you asked me to check into what had become of your father. But before that, no, I did not know."

"Oh Jared, you are consistent, predictable. Even now you seek to turn this conversation to your advantage; this whole exercise is a chance to put you in a positive light. You didn't know before I asked you. How very neat. You didn't know before, so you couldn't tell me, and you became aware of it only because I asked you to check into it, so you were noble in your efforts. The fact that somewhere in all of this you kept information from me that I deserved to know is neatly swept under that table. Why, I ask myself. Was it to spare my feelings?"

Kate paused and looked at Jared head on, her face contorted in a sudden rage. She slapped him across the face, a hard, stinging slap that rang his ears and dazzled sparkles before his eyes.

"You bastard, you let me lie next to the vermin who may have had my father killed. *You!* You let me fuck a man, a horrible man, who had done horrible things to me; you had me fucking him, and then you were fucking me, for what?"

Kate brought her left hand up as if to slap him again, only this time with the back of her hand. Jared, his ears still ringing, readied his hand to block her blow and grab her wrist—but no, she didn't strike him.

Slowly she turned her hand over, and stuck it out, extending her arm as in a gesture of, of what, greeting? It looked sort of like that.

He didn't liked this, an odd gesture, aggressive in a calm, quiet way. There was a tangible danger in this room; trouble had caught up with him when he least expected it—the source catching him completely unawares. The room seemed to close in on him, but it was surprisingly cool; he had always imagined that people in these types of situations sweated profusely.

"So, now you know." His voice sounded both strange and strained to him, and the worse part about it was that was the most clever thing he could think of to say; for once, this prince of words was left without anything to say.

"Yes, now I know. But—"

She stopped in mid-sentence and moved in toward him, running her hand over his chest. He wore a heavy cotton shirt, but he could clearly feel her press and the warmth of her hand—calm she was, moderate in her delivery … but the sense of her presence was that of someone who would not compromise, especially when it came to matters that concerned her. Her needs were strongly felt by her—and by all those around her.

"Yes, but what?" he said.

Kate laughed and, stepping back, she pulled her hand off his chest and reversed the motion that had brought it there; her hand returning to her left hip.

"But I killed him. And now, what he did makes no difference at all."

Jared raised his eyebrows but did not twitch; if the thought that Kate had killed Guy surprised him, he hid it well.

"Makes no difference? How can you say that? He had your father arrested, your father who is still held captive."

"No he's not. You said so yourself. You said it is unlikely that he is incarcerated now. With his disappearance from the labor camp, you said he was probably on the run."

"Alright, so maybe I did. But the fact is that he has been uprooted from his life, his daughter has been taken from him, and he has been abused and enslaved for most of the last year and he is still out there. Don't you see? You have to find him, or what has become of him. You need to help him."

Kate gave him a level look. "I don't know, Jared, why you say the things you do. I wouldn't believe you, no matter what you said. You know what I am left with? I am left with a man who maybe loved me, but probably not. A man who used me, and let other men use me. Tell me. If I poked you in the eye and told you to come back the next day, and I made you a pair of glasses so that you could see better, wouldn't you think the whole thing to be odd? Yet that is exactly what you do, exactly who you are. You send people up the river and then sell them a paddle to get back home and tell them that you are doing them a favor."

"Stop. That isn't true and you know it. Yes, I do use people, but I give them a choice. You could have left anytime, but you chose to stay. Why? Well, in part for warmth and security. Like an anchor in a stormy sea. But you stayed on also because what you were doing was exciting. Too, I use people because they let themselves be used, because they are too stupid, uninterested, or unconcerned about what is going on in their lives. And you know what? I am bettering, or at least trying to better their lives. I know it sounds condescending and self-serving, but I am doing it for their own good, as it certainly doesn't do me any good personally, directly, any of this. I live a dangerous existence that could cost me my life on any given day. I am using people to improve their own lives because they damn won't help themselves."

Kate pondered this for a moment. "No, I suppose they won't. But not all. Some do help themselves."

She quieted down for a moment, and then came the words he had not expected to hear, the words that he didn't believe that she had in her.

"I slit his throat, ear to ear, completely, under his chin. Did you know that? I sat on his chest, I don't remember how we got there, and I slipped this"—in a flash her hand drew the finger-sized blade from where it had been so secretly ensconced on her hip—"and calmly ran it across his neck in one smooth stroke while looking him right in the eye."

Another flash and her knife was only inches from Jared's chest.

This is it, this is the end; never would he had believed that he would meet his end this way. Overpower her easily he could, but he felt trapped, mesmerized. The moment was Kate's—he was powerless to move, and oddly enough, it was by his own volition … he would not move even with his life in the balance. The choice was hers.

Kate moved the blade up to his throat; a smirk, an insane look in her eyes—thumbing the handle mere inches from Jared's neck. She leaned in until her lips were as close to his ear as the blade was to his neck.

"I will kill you, you bastard," she exhaled hotly on his cheek. The smirk became a grin and the blade moved ever so slightly, inward, touched his skin and a spot of wetness spread across a point low on Jared's neck. "But I won't, I can't. And it's not because you don't deserve it, it's because I am weak and stupid and I love you."

Kate backed up and dropped her arm to her side, the blade in her hand falling against her thigh.

Jared exhaled; *she would not have killed me.*

But he knew that was false; not that she wouldn't have killed him, that might well have been true. What was false, and he knew it, was his belief that he knew she would not have killed him. He hadn't really known. But what he had known, and perhaps for the first time had really known, was fear. He had been really and truly afraid.

Every move of his, all of the time, was calculated, or at least he liked to think so, wanted to believe so; he did not suffer from the malady of the normal man, the inability to control one's inner self, to control his fear and self-doubt. Jared did not live for the moment, far from it; Eastern mysticism held no mystery for him, it was vain and indifferent—but he could not deny the detour his linear mind had taken mere moments ago. Instinct was a very powerful force to be reckoned with, and not simply instinct of the mind … instinct of the mind he understood, but uncontrolled reflex of emotion, that was something until now he didn't want to admit that he had.

Jared made to reach for her, a surprisingly instinctive move, as was Kate's reply.

"Stay, away, from, me," she said coolly, coldly; quite unexpectedly her hand with the knife found its way between them. Kate looked at the knife for a moment as if she didn't know what it was, how it had gotten there; then, without thought, lowered her hand and glared up at Jared.

"*Understand,* Jared, *that 'love you' does not mean I want to be with you. I do not want you touching me again, I am not staying here with you,* and *I never want to see you again.*"

Jared examined her quietly, thoughtfully, as if seeing her for the first time; not as an equal, for he could not permit such. The things he did were by strength of will alone; he managed to move from one day to the next by sheer focus and determination. But he did not fool himself. He knew that he was not infallible, that he would not win forever; every victory was but a victory for the day only—he had always won, yet someday he would lose and it would be ugly. But today was not that day, and Kate was not his equal.

"I can understand that. I guess. Where will you go?"

"Well, that is a good question, isn't it? I imagine they will look for me."

"Imagine?"

He laughed and she smiled. It was okay, he guessed.

"Of course they will be looking for you."

Kate could have made Guy's death look like an accident and make all the plans from here forward unneeded, but such went unsaid; somehow he knew that premeditation and pretense were not what she was about—she had wanted to murder Guy irrespective of the consequences, and she had wanted him, both of them, Guy and Jared, to know that … Guy no doubt had understood this very clearly as the steel cut through his throat while her eyes pierced his soul. But her own death was not necessary to complete her retribution.

"Come on. We've not much time to make you disappear."

"Disappear?"

"Off course. I am an ambassador and it is my job to make people appear and disappear. It is one of the things I do best. Actually, it is what Jambi and I do best. You'd be surprised at the number of things the two of us can do. He is, after all, Palestinian."

Kate shook her head. These IsPal folks were one odd lot. She flinched when he took her by the elbow, but let his hand stay. It was the right thing to do and it was okay, she guessed.

Yes, he was losing her, he was losing an asset *and* a lover. True, he may not have loved her in the traditional sense, in the sense that Kate wanted to be loved. But Jared would have given his life for her, even if it had meant letting her take it herself.

If that wasn't love Jared, had no idea what love was.

Sea Animals

The snow fell with abandon.

Children … acted like little kids.

Adults … well, acted like children.

It had been many years since a snow like this had blanketed the city. Of late, winter was stark trees, bitter cold, colorless gray skies, and a dampness in the air that one could never shake—today the air was light, frigid, dry … yet still it snowed and snowed.

Little Jamie was four years old, his face and nose a cherub red, ruddy from playing in the cold and wind. His little body, bundled layer upon layer with garments to protect him from the cold, came bounding up to Kate on the snowy park bench; his sister, Jasmine, was already there as if waiting for him, which she was not—she waited for no one, leastwise not for her brother … she had bolted from the womb first only to have Jamie follow some two years later. It was Jasmine that that was always out front, always in the lead, ever the one to take chances first, to cross the line that separated what had not been allowed with what was now allowed. Jamie and Jasmine, two peas in a pod but not twins; as similar and as different as two children could be—as two children ought to be.

Now she played in the snow at Kate's feet, sitting there in the cold and wet without a care in the world. Really. For Jasmine it was not cold, it was not wet, it was not winter, not summer; it was nothing at all but fun. Jasmine loved Kate, loved being with her, loved Kate as only a six-year-old could.

Kate watched them with an attention beyond responsibility; an attention of love, for she did truly love these two little ones—grow they would, in their own mysterious ways, and as children will do, they would raise her as well … she would never be the same person she had been even as recently as a month ago. Murder, mayhem, sex, abuse, none of it would leave an imprint on her as strong as what she felt now. For now, in spite of all that had happened, Kate could honestly say that she loved life.

Gone were all her immodesties and false modesties, dropped were all her self-centered urgings and yet she managed to focus on herself as she had never been able to before. She had two children, a dog; she was—home.

But it wasn't her home and they weren't her children either, nor was the dog hers; Kate was, for lack of a better word, a nanny. Granted not a very old nanny. She was only twenty-five, but a nanny she was, and to a good family; well, at least a *well-off* family—her moral judgment she kept to herself ... needed to keep to herself.

Jamie and Jasmine and the dog Jasper surrounded Kate, laughing and flinging snowflakes at and on each other; a single snowflake, two armloads of snow, an avalanche of snow. The snow swirled, caught by the wind and lifted in small tuffs off the ground. It whirled off on a drifting, spiral course; sometimes it drifted to the side and sometimes it even drifted back up the way it came—sideways or up, it drifted all the same. The children flicked their wrists, the snow flew its course, Kate got a face full and laughed out loud.

Rosy cheeks, a good strong laugh, a full figure of life. But in close examination she was very much the woman that carried the haunting of having killed two men. The killings did haunt her, as did the predators themselves; their faces, their laughs, their hatred of what was female about her—the first predator, the man who had so selfishly over time decimated her life ... the second predator, a stranger who had tried to decimate her body in but a matter of seconds.

Both now lay dead.

She had opened both their throats and left them for dead.

If it had been snowing then, the ground would have run red.

The sun had started its journey downward toward the horizon, giving the day that warm reddish glow in spite of the chilling air. Evening was coming. Kate got the children home, fixed them some hot chocolate, something in her past life she would never have done; now this was a typical day—after a day at the park, or the zoo, or if it were a school day, Kate would bring them home where, after a snack, they would read picture books or watch a show on the monitor, Kate didn't care.

Then it was time for dinner.

This part was a little fuzzy for her. When she had been young, even after her mom had died, they almost always had a sit-down family dinner, even if it was only her and her father; usually it included one or more members of their extended family—who in actuality were a few but close friends.

But for the Briners, it was different. They were important people; part of the ruling elite.

The people she had known in the capital were part of the government: politicians, bureaucrats, military leaders, and the like. They took a near limitless share of the wealth collected by the government in the form of fees and taxes; the elite were a different animal altogether—it was they who systemized the government's collection of wealth, with a *large* cut for them off the top, and it was they who allowed society to function.

The government had no mechanism to get food to the people, to get housing built, or roads to the factories and schools. These services and products could only be built by the highest strata of all: the retail moguls, the construction apparatchik, the medical combines—they were the ones who allowed society to function in the sense that they controlled the resources that allowed society's infrastructure of roads, courthouses, and hospitals to be built … and the resource they controlled was obviously money, and the share they took for their livelihood was over and above any redistribution of income.

The government took in money in the form of taxation and fees; in compensation the people had a standard of living provided to them in the form of government stipends and services; but it was the ruling elite, the Socialist bosses, who really took for themselves—and they were very, very wealthy … their Marxist ability was never taxed and their Marxist needs knew no bounds.

The Briners were just such a family, just such a couple.

With such an accumulation of wealth there were six "kept" people at the Briners', servants in the old sense of the word. There was Kate, who had the role of the nanny; Ghdzeke, the cook who was as big as the meals she whipped up, and whipped was the operative word here, as in butter—a better cook than Ghdzeke Kate had difficulty in conjuring, but she had to be careful around her … Ghdzeke would ruin her figure in days if Kate didn't constantly keep an eye on what the old biddy cooked, how she cooked it, and how much she herself ate. There was also Illian, the gardener, from somewhere to the south, as in way to the south; Illian was from Argentina, or so Kate believed—which left Nick, the driver … and

Roberta, who cleaned. Last but certainly not least, for he watched over them all, was Gus, a bodyguard, for lack of a better word—a bodyguard who managed a second staff of hired hands ... a private protection service of sorts. These hired hands were not *servants* of the Briners, but contracted labor who supplemented Gus on an as-needed basis; it was Gus to whom the responsibility for the safety of the Briner family empire was entrusted, seven by twenty-four—it was Gus who wasn't around that fateful night beneath the pier of the Briners' oceanfront property on the majestic Virginia coast.

That night a struggle for life silently battled back and forth in a small spot of sand before the softly churning sea.

The new Kate went nowhere unarmed, and here on the beach she managed to extricate herself from his strong grip, a position in which she first found herself after he had grabbed her from behind. She twisted to the right and slammed her palm into his chest, pulling herself free. He lunged and grabbed her around the waist, butting his head up under her breast. His hair was greasy, she noticed. Her knee found his gut above his groin; she was trying to hit his balls, but missed and the impact drove the air from his lungs.

Kate spun, stepping outside of his arms and beyond the reach of his hands. Without rising he lunged for her again and Kate's knee caught him in the face, causing him to step back and stand up. She reached across her waist and pushed the handle of the knife down below her belt and grasping it in her right hand, swept it out and across her antagonist's throat—he fell back clutching at his throat and looking down at the life flowing through his fingers ... and soaking into the sand at his feet.

Kate stood there, her chest heaving from the concerted effort it had taken to fight off and kill a man twice her size. She felt no compunction about killing the man; he would have most certainly raped her—and might well have killed her. But Kate killed him first, one month to the day after she had been hired by the Briners.

The incident on the beach had happened two months ago. Now, with the children settled, Kate turned to her room. Mrs. Briner would be in soon; she actually was attentive to her children to a point, when she was around—tonight she would be ... she would see them to dinner. Kate would take toast and soup in her room, as was her want when her duties did not include dinner for Jamie and Jasmine; her own time she spent reading or sitting quietly, thinking, in a comfortable chair by the large window with a view of the garden behind the house. She would read the controversial, and probably now illegal, books she loved; it had taken her some time to amass a new, albeit smaller collection, following her displacement from Tucson—she had found several used bookstores in the capital, and after careful surveillance to make sure that they were safe, or at least appeared safe, she would go in and browse, hiding books behind other books, until she felt comfortable enough to go in and buy a half dozen or so at a time. She would try not to return once she had made a purchase, but there were only so many stores; after two or three months she might return to a particularly well-stocked store, well-stocked in the "old" books, that is—in this way she had managed to accumulate sixty-seven books which she had boxed up when Jared moved her down to the Briners ... Guy had never suspected her hobby in this regard, and if he had, he'd have never understood the nature of what it was she was collecting, anyway.

Too, she spent her private time writing in a journal; she hoped someday to write a book of her own and have it published—if that type of thing ever occurred in the United States again.

Such as it was that Jared made his appearance at the park where Kate took the children; she had always known that he would come— it was the when that had eluded her, not the if ... and it had taken longer than she had expected. Three months now she had been with the Briners and in that time she had received only a short card letting her know that he was okay and that he hoped she was well. The letter left her feeling a wide range of emotions; guilty for having, in a sense, betrayed Jared by killing Guy—it was a rather odd, somewhat twisted sort of guilt that took a while for her to arrive at, but arrive she did ... she saw it as a selfish act, though one that definitely needing doing. There was this as well: despite the fact that Jared had used her, he had not coerced her—Kate had stepped onto that stage willingly, knowing fully what she was doing, what she was getting into ... she knew the price for failure, and while she had not failed, she had not exactly carried through on her end of the bargain. Though just what the bargain consisted in would remain unclear, perhaps for the rest of her life.

Then, too, she felt both the twinge of attraction and revulsion; she longed for his physical presence, yes, in bed, in part, but also for the excitement she found in his presence, his hard-driving lifestyle of resistance—use her he had, but deceive her he hadn't. She stepped into all of it knowing what the terms were from day one.

It was a cool, overcast day, though warmer than it had been for most of the month; much of the snow from the previous week had melted and the sky held a cool gray of a colder than normal November day; the sun was too weak to impact the earth on any but the most cloudless days. Jared simply approached and took a seat beside her to her left on the bench; the view from this bench took in the entire playground and Kate could watch her two charges as they roamed the play area of swings and slides and jungle gyms. Typically this was one of Kate's favorite times of the day; she could watch the Briner children without having to concentrate on watching them— they were like a salve on her consciousness … grounding her physically while letting her mind drift.

Kate was on fire, she always was these days; to the casual observer and to those who didn't know her well, she still was the docile young girl with a mop of sandy hair who had arrived on the Virginia coast some three months ago. But she couldn't hide the intensity from Jared, who pretty much had an exclusive on knowing her, and she couldn't hide from Jambi, perhaps, either, with her unrealized affections for him circling like a bird waiting to land and to see what the ground would support. Kate loved Jambi, who had always intuitively understood her; it was as if she was with her brother, a brother she never had, and ofttimes as not they would laugh at some long-kept secret. Only they hadn't known each other long, and they had no long-kept secrets; but it was like that, like being with a close brother and laughing at inside jokes. Kate knew that it sometimes annoyed the oftentimes dour Jared, but that just made them want to do it all the more; but in the end, during the six months they had been together, they were like a family, or the closest thing to a family she'd had aside from her early childhood and her mysterious relationship with a father who never actually trusted himself to be himself—so at least she felt.

However, there was one who she had to be careful of; Mr. Briner had come to understand Kate quite well and had taken an interest in her beyond that of his apparent usual lecherous interest in younger women—Mrs. Briner seemed more proper, but that was no indication of her fidelity. Mr. Briner suspected, no, knew, that Kate was not the dull, disinterested spinster she appeared to be; between that and his casual body contact, and the definitely *not* casual glances he directed toward her—well, she was glad she had a room on the other side of the house with a thick oaken door.

"Things are not going well. I am hanging on by a thread, we are all hanging on by a thread. But how would you know of it out here, out of the city."

It was as if they had been in the middle of a conversation. It was his way; he was embarrassed with the common courtesies in conversations between friends, lovers, associates.

Kate kept quiet; she didn't trust herself to break the silence— nothing would come of it, nothing nice. Her incriminations, fears, passion; none of these emotions could produce a casual inquiry into Jared's life.

"IsPal is considering breaking relations with the United States. It is a dilemma, especially for us in the diplomatic corps. What are we to do? Our human rights record sucks, and there are more economically sound countries than us to do business with. IsPal owes us, to be sure, but their debt is not to the current generation's administration and they have grown weary waiting for things to change. They aren't like our European allies who revel and join in our misfortune. But IsPal will not save us, no more than we saved the Israelis and the Palestinians from each other. We must save ourselves, soon too, and not just for IsPal's allegiance."

That was a lot of "us's," but Kate knew how to sort them out. Jared held dual citizenship between IsPal and the United States, so there were always two *us's* for him when talking about his work. But it was plain; the United States never did solve the Israeli-Palestinian conflict—and it was probably best for IsPal that they never succeeded … by solving it on their own, by strength of will and a true desire to be friends, they became the economic big boys on the block and a world leader in human rights. Now it was the United States that needed saving, saving from itself. IsPal could help those who wanted to bring the country back from ruin, but it was still a tiny country and could do nothing directly, nothing overtly. However, if the Social Democrats grew any more domineering in their hold on the United States, well, there would be little that anyone could do for many years to reverse that tide; the once grand stallion of world peace and prosperity had the real potential to become as bad a bear as the Soviet Union had ever been.

Jared looked at the Briner children with recognition. It was evident that this was not the first time he had seen her at this park. Kate sighed; he had been spying on her, of that she was sure—Jared looked at her with eyes raised but didn't have a clue what she was thinking … and she wouldn't tell him what was on her mind.

"What does Jambi think about all this?"

"He doesn't."

"He doesn't what?"

"Huh? Oh, Jambi. … He is not involved in the diplomatic corps any longer."

"Oh." She didn't think to ask why.

"Kate, this isn't a social visit."

How dare he. He wasn't here to see how she was doing, she had suspected as much all along, but somehow she couldn't adjust herself to the fact that Jared had traveled all this way not to see her but to, well, use her again; to invite her back, which was one and the same.

Jared watched her. He knew what she was thinking. Kate had always been so incredibly easy to read; it was part of her, all of it—the passion, the pride, the wearing of her emotions on her sleeve … how clearly she could see, yet how little she understood.

"Kate, I didn't come here to ask you to come back. But neither did I come her simply to see you, to see how you were getting on. There is a reason for this visit and unfortunately the reason for it is not good, it is bad. Kate, you're in trouble, deep trouble."

She knew it. No one killed two men and didn't pay for it one way or another in the end; but somehow the two were so deserving of death that she thought the great wheel of life, the great equalizer, God, or whatever it was, would let her off the hook—at least part of the way … and perhaps it had, at least for one of them. How could anyone know of the other?

"It's Guy, isn't it?"

"No, actually it is not. You managed to keep that one under wraps, albeit with help from a pro." He smiled and lightly touched her hand. It lingered and she did not pull away, but then he removed it. "It is the other one, the predator who went after the wrong fish."

It should have surprised her that he knew about *that*, and it would have surprised her had it been anyone else but him; Jared *knew* things—if there was one thing that she had learned in Washington, DC, it was that Jared knew more than anyone … more than anyone

210

had a right to know. He carried a wealth of information in his head like so much small change, and that small change added up to large sums of knowledge that he could distribute as needed. He knew, and Kate wasn't surprised; she just shrugged.

"He would have raped me, he might have killed me. He has probably killed before. He deserved to die."

"Bingo! That is it, you know, the trick, the talent. *Killing those that deserve to die.* The world is full of petty assholes and ignorant schmucks. But most of them don't deserve to die. It is so much easier when the bad guys decided for us, by their own actions, who is to live, who is to die, and who it is we get to kill. Sometimes they even fix it so they kill themselves."

There was a pause and for a moment Kate thought the topic was done.

"You are right, you probably did save your own life and quite likely other lives as well. Or leastwise saved another woman from having her life ruined for good. If they manage to live through the ordeal. In this particular case, you did most likely save your life. The man you killed, Walter, was a particularly nasty piece of work. He *has* killed before, several young girls, as a matter of fact. Leastwise, he has been the prime suspect in the disappearance of several young girls that later turned up dead."

"And why hadn't he been picked up?"

"I don't know." Jared leaned forward, adjusted the left cuff on his pants, and brushed off a smidgen of snow. He sighed. "Who is to say the mind of the police? Maybe they didn't know he was the one, maybe they just didn't care, or didn't want to take the time to figure it out. Who is to suffer? The poor, the wretched, the nobodies that assholes like Walter prey on? What difference does it make, and to who? This is America today, the home of the rich who are not so free and not so brave.

"Do you know how they would handle Walter's misbehavior in the Arab world? No? Jambi could tell you. He's told, tells me, all the time. Let's just say that they usually dispense justice as they're removing body parts. A man guilty of rape and strangulation … well, I wouldn't want to have such a body myself and live. Death would be a much preferred alternative. In a way, you did Walter and everyone else, a favor when you killed him."

Jared sent Kate from intrigued to ill-tempered in a heartbeat; all this time and again with the misdirection, again he sought to bury her question in an answer designed to bury her question.

"Quit changing the topic and tell me why you're here. Will I be needing yet another new home?"

"Home? You call this home? This is no home. This is a tenuous existence in a hostile land. And you have made it that much more tenuous."

He rounded on her now verbally. She had done this to herself so she might as well hear it now from him.

"What are you, a fool? Where is it that you think you live? That you can write a book, a book so politically overt that even a child could see your disdain and hatred for the government."

Again, how did he know? How did he, or anyone else, for that matter, know what she was writing. But she wouldn't even ask how, what difference would it make. Her blood boiled and her anger overflowed and she was not about to waste her time and energy on pointless questions.

"Well, you hate our government too. Look what you do."

"It is not the hate that is the issue here, nor any other emotion, *nor what I do*. It is your carelessness, your certainty that you know how to play at a game whose rules you don't understand. A game in which you don't even know what a winning hand looks like."

Kate was silent. Just what was he talking about?

But Jared didn't let up. "Jambi is dead, you know."

Kate stumbled, physically, right there; her heart stumbled, her resolve stumbled. "How did he die?"

"He was arrested. He died under interrogation."

"Interrogation? Arrest? I don't understand. What was he arrested for?"

Jared drummed the right arm of the bench with his fingers. He had already said more than he had intended, broached a topic he had decided in advance he wouldn't discuss.

"He was arrested for not talking about things he knew. Come on, get your coat on, we're leaving."

"Going where?" she said, but thinking that he hadn't answered her question about Jambi.

"Your journals have been read by people—no, not people, they can't be referred to as people—have been read by those that will have

212

you arrested. If not today, tomorrow, if not tomorrow, then soon, someday.

"You think Guy was the only bastard in the house? That everyone else of the high and mighty is not some kind of creep? They weed all the good ones out, the *unjust* who profit the most from this system make sure the *just* are not around to rock the boat.

"Why do you think IsPal is turning its back on the United States? Because we are no democracy, not anymore. You read those books, write your analysis, but you see nothing, you know nothing. Economic inequities, media censorship, racial exploitation … they are but the bulwark behind which the true horrors exist. Now they are coming after you, so now you have to run, and run fast.

"Your journals are enough to put you away all on their own, but they won't stop there. They will make the connection as to who you were, and quickly too. I made you disappear, I didn't make you invisible. And now,"—he took her by the arm, helping her to button her jacket, which she had begun with uneven and trembling fingers; he had gotten through, made his point—"and now," he said again more softly, "it is time to make you disappear again."

"Where are we going? I have to go back and get my stuff."

"Yes, and you do have the two of them." He motioned toward the children. "But tonight is the last. Tomorrow you will be on your way someplace else. Where is it you want to go?"

"*Home.*"

There was a pause as they both weighed the significance of that word for this girl who suddenly seemed very shy for her twenty-five years.

"Yeah." It was the only thing he could think of to say.

They stood on the spotted, greased-stained gravel in the rail yard, just off from the main platform where the train sat to take her west. The sky was overcast; there was a scattering of snow nestled among the black sludge of yesterday, and yesteryear's oil drippings and waste; Jared had not wasted any time—when he had said she would be on her way tomorrow, he had meant it.

Her decision to return to Arizona had rattled him a little and sent him scrambling a lot; there was much to be done and little time to do it. To begin with, she couldn't travel without cover; it was a long way to go—questions would be asked and documents would be checked. She couldn't travel suspiciously, either; hiding in the back of a truck or in the bowels of a freight car would just get her shot if she were found out—and heading into that part of the country there was a good chance that 'get found out' she would.

The idea was that she would travel openly, on a *"governor's passport,"* as the saying went; she would travel as a government employee from the diplomatic corps—on a cross-country sojourn for a posting to the West Coast. She would detach at cities along the way to deliver diplomatic pouches; there was a small call for diplomatic activities in the country's interior, enough to send her on a ten-city excursion, anyway. But Kate would do only seven of her ten stops, melting away in Tucson; how clever—how convenient.

It would have been more convenient still if he could have arranged an actual posting for her in Tucson, but a posting meant a real job, and a real job required a real background, something that Kate couldn't have; Jared was good but he wasn't that good—he could shuffle people on the sly here and there, but he hadn't the resources to maintain ongoing fraud ... he had friends who did, for sure, but he wasn't going to call in a marker on a girl who wouldn't be saving anyone but her own skin. Besides, he didn't want to part permanently from her, anyway.

But he didn't want her to stay, either.

She was compromised beyond any redeeming value as an operative; but he did like having her around—she was fun ... more than that, she was important to him. But to keep her here, now, was well beyond dangerous; it was probably deadly.

"You've the pouches?"

"Yes."

"Good, I do need them delivered, you know. You can't simply throw the bag out into the first river crossing you come to."

"Of course not. How you would berate me when next we met!"

"*Next*, huh. It is a big country. You don't see this separation as forever?"

"What, you mean me leaving? Why should it? Be forever, I mean."

"Because that is usually what these kinds of moments in life amount to."

"Jared, I didn't know you cared."

He gave her a searching look; this was more than just bantering. "No, you didn't know I cared, why would you? I never really gave you cause to. When did I ever imply that ours was more than a relationship of convenience?"

"There were times, you slipped up. But directly? I guess not."

"No, and you wouldn't stay even if I asked."

"Goodbye for now, Jared."

They walked over to the platform without speaking. She lightly ran her hand over his cheek and climbed on the train. Jared turned and left; Kate looked back at him. Another chapter in her life was closing and, wait, she had forgotten; it was too late now, she would have liked to have closure on Jambi—he was one of the few people she had met that she had thought of as a friend, even if they had met irregularly, and always under the oddest of circumstances. Why had he been taken? Why had he been killed? She frowned. The excitement she had felt at this new phase of her life tasted sour in her mouth. She *should* have asked; it was one of those questions that would nag at a person, at her, for the rest of her life. She just knew it.

Jared hadn't told her and he hadn't done so on purpose; he found it difficult to tell Kate that Jambi, his best friend and partner in crime—a husband, a father, and perhaps the only person that Jared had truly loved—that Jambi had died *protecting her* … protecting her from the search that had been undertaken for Kate in retribution for Guy's murder.

Why had it been Jambi who had been singled out for this interrogation? Jared didn't know; choosing Jambi as the object of the interrogation and torture had also insured that Jambi died protecting Jared, *his* friend, *his* partner in crime.

Now Jambi was gone; now Kate was gone too.

Jared was alone; alone and standing in the frozen slag of a railway yard that should have been mothballed years ago.

Precursor

Jack shifted his weight; the rock on which he was lying was uncomfortable, all the more so with his handgun digging into his gut—unexpectedly his knees banged hard against the granite every time he adjusted his positioned …just when he thought that he had figured out how to lie comfortably on this perch he had selected to observe the humanity in motion below.

He didn't care much for the aches and pains in his body; they made him feel old, more than the thirty-seven years he carried—Jack cringed at the thought of getting really old, like Max or, god forbid, Daryl … though he acknowledged that each seemed spry for their age. But what truly was meant by *spry*? When was spry used other than when referring to someone who was already old? Granted it was better to be old and spry than old and moribund. Best not to get old at all. Best of all not to end up like those he was spying on.

Jack looked at the valley through his compact binoculars; he had come on his own—he needed to see firsthand what was going on, and he needed to do so without concerning himself how others might react to what he saw or seeing firsthand how he reacted. He had left the safe house before the crack of dawn and by bicycle traveled the nine miles west to the fringes of the deep desert, taking the byways and low ways, coming the last half a mile on foot. The sun was not yet high in the sky and he would wait till dusk to head back, a long wait; but once he returned to the city it would be best if it were dark—he so much did not want to end up dead … or worse.

He lay there thinking; there was really no danger of being discovered on this secluded jamb of rock. He thought of all those now gone, all those whose love had been lost to him and so many others; so many gone, so many dead, so many changed from who they had been, what they had once believed. Max and Charlie, drifted in and out of his life like phantoms, and like phantoms they killed with impunity, quietly, successfully. It had not become frequent, not yet, but they were hanging out now with those who were involved in a macabre street war with the government; remnants of those who had battled the military, independent evangelists for freedom, and plain 'ol violent drifters; from these came guns, bullets, small bombs, and food—from Daryl they got fewer of the bombs and guns, but he was a dangerous leader of a different sort.

In this life, Daryl endured, and his age did not slow him down; he too egged Jack on—kill, that had become his common refrain, kill all the sons of bitches. How odd it all sounded coming from the lips of one who had seen some seventy plus summers ... but endure he did and stronger he seemed to grow. He saw it as his job to help others endure, and to kill; he no longer talked of evolution or revolution—it was pure justice and retribution with him. Daryl had become an avenging angel of death, he called himself that, lashing out without quarter; a vigilante, he would go on any mission, lay any trap, destroy any unsuspecting agent of oppression. Daryl had truly morphed into a culmination of his literary pursuits. His novels, had he still been writing, would have been *about him*, not *by him* about *someone else*. He had become a historical figure, a character of historical necessity; he had devoured himself with his writing and he had become a story line.

Jack was truly going to miss him. One never returned from historical necessity. Historical necessity simply devoured its own.

Where to go from here; that was the question, *the* question. If he was going to lead he needed to lead; no longer would it be sufficient for him to say *we are here, we are alive, we are safe.* Leadership demanded action; he needed to reassert a sense of direction over his small group before this group disintegrated into lost individuals—for it was only as a group that any of them would survive ... alone, each was doomed, much like a single stalk of corn in a field exposed to the harsh elements of sun, drought, and wind—that is why there are corn*fields. Blah,* this was crazy talk and he knew it.

He looked at the ants hard at work below in the copper mine, working their fingers to the bone; he alone owned the choice to be made, and none of the options were particularly attractive—the opposition, including his small band, couldn't win ... not with all the oppositional groups combined. To be sure, some spoke of an independent Tucson, as did the folks in Albuquerque talk of an independent—*what? Nation? City-state?* As if any of that could come to pass, be allowed to come to pass; never. The opposition could win every battle but they could never win the war; not without the entire population rising against the government.

217

But what was the likelihood of that?

Little to none.

The government was smart, Jack had to grant them that—they had proactively set up an opposition *to any opposition* … young versus old, government employees vs. private employees, *rural versus urban*. The Social Democrats swiped the disaffected into resistance armies of its own. The last stroke, pure genius, knelling the death in advance of any possible popular uprising; the urban population was being supported by the rural economy, primarily through the use of forced labor, any pretenses which had previously demanded a free and democratic nation fell by the wayside. The city folks hadn't reached the point of openly supporting this new totalitarianism, but they were close; the rural land was being squeezed so as to expand the prosperity of the urban folks. Under such circumstances, why would the city rise to fight for the country? They were now of two completely different stripes—they weren't even of the same family anymore. The population of Tucson, indeed all the remaining heartland population centers of any significance, mined, farmed, and manufactured for populations living on either coast on a scale of forced labor unprecedented since the economic policies of the Soviet Union.

If there could be no victory and surrender was impossible, what remained was endless fighting; fighting for honor—or fighting because it was fun.

Such were the choices which Jack could lead, and so far he had balked at choosing one; no wonder he had been overtaken and passed by a stream of desperate impatience—most of the other opposition groups had taken to killing anything with a uniform on and expropriating as much food as they could … the small band he now led was moving closer to that model every day. The decision was being made for him.

But there was an alternative, a desperate one, as if everything wasn't already desperate in this day.

There was the alternative of escape; escape by an independent village—a village that might make it, a village that might flourish under the radar … at least for a while.

This was the direction that Jack's thoughts had taken lately, *this* was a stand he could take and hoist upon its ground a banner, although in this case the banner would be on the move, far away, on the run, to the deepest country, the darkest forests one could find. This village would be fraught with dangers, not the least of which was success; success meant growth and, if anything, it would be size that gave them away in the end—so they would need to keep their exiled community small … but that was a concern many miles, obstacles, and potential lives down the line. Just getting to that point, of needing to manage such growth, would be victory in and of itself.

"You think to flee? Escape? Turn *coward*, I say."

"What about wanting to live, to love, heck, even to fight another day, a better day, what about that is cowardly? And to top it off, we cannot win."

Daryl snorted derisively.

Jack continued. "Let's say that we do beat them here in Tucson. What then? Do they let us set up shop as the Free Country of Tucson? Of course not. There is no reason for them to do so. What's to keep them from simply flattening the city and squelching our insignificant spark of freedom?"

Charlie, filthy from a day of crawling about in the dirt and running house to house, smelling of sweat and gun oil, smiled. It was a light-hearted sad smile; she had ever been more than a friend—and losing a good friend could be as hard as losing a love, only Jack hadn't lost her friendship, or had he? For so many years he had been her confidant, and now it seemed as if he were her confidant no longer and he sorely missed that.

Max came up beside her, as lean as Charlie, having spent the day in *her* world, crawling, clawing, most likely killing. But Charlie looked energized, flushed, ready for a fight; Max seemed listless, tired—*he is too old for this kind of thing*, thought Jack … yes, there he was, slugging away with Charlie, who seemed to have become almost sadistic in the weeks since that bloody night she and Max went off.

"A pittance for you, Jack," Daryl said. "I created this scenario, at least on paper, before you were born. I knew this day would come, I warned the world."

He took a step forward and shook his finger in Jack's face; Jack swatted it away and shook his head in open disgust; niceties would get one nowhere here. This was going poorly; Charlie, Max, and everyone around were listening attentively to an exchange that could only end up poor to middling—he had no upside in this. And without these three … well, he didn't claim the same respect he did with them.

"Yes, Daryl, you did," Jack spat through gritted teeth. Then in a softer voice: "Yes, Daryl, you did foresee this, you wrote about it, and you warned us all that Socialism, virulent Socialism, is the culmination of Liberalism."

Jack paused, taking a breath, before saying, "You were right, no doubt about it, only we didn't take note—but you are wrong in this. We cannot win and it is wrong to die trying."

The flame from an oil lamp shifted the shadows on the concrete walls; everything seemed out of time, like an argument in the caves of old—there was very little twenty-first century going on here … it was more akin to the days of desperation when there was no law in the land, for there was none here.

"Can't win? What, then, are you proposing? Losing? Hide in the mountains, live a life of fear, maybe on the run? *And you* call that victory? I want something more."

"You want to die."

Yes, that was it; why hadn't he seen this before—everything made so much sense with this realization.

"At my age? What is wrong with that?"

"Plenty. You are not that old. And *we* are not as old as you."

"Revenge, then," growled Daryl.

Silence.

"You want to hurt them. Is that it?" said Jack softly.

"Yes." Equally soft.

Quiet settled over them, all of them; they were in the lowest level of the long-abandoned underground parking garage—forty people, forty feet below ground, the entrance to the surface long since bulled over. *This* was the ultimate hideout that Jack had found, accessible only through eight miles of abandoned sewer tunnels. The hideout was, as far as hideouts go, safe, secure, secret. But no secret was safe if more than one person knew of it, and the hundred or so living here now, and for the past several weeks, all shared in the secret; with all the comings and goings of late, all it would take is for one of them to be caught and the gig would be up. It was much too hot a place to stay in much longer, safe and secure for the moment as it was.

With the toe of his boot, Jack scuffed at the dirt on the concrete floor.

"I know, Daryl, I want to hurt them too. But you also want to die, and that is just plain wrong. It is wrong for you, and especially it is wrong for them." He nodded in Max and Charlie's direction. "Do *you* want to die, Max? You, Charlie? Why so silent? You think you can go on killing them and not get killed in the end? You think this is a game that you can't lose?

His gaze rounded the room, taking them all in.

"We must live. Hurt them, yes, that is good. I love hurting them too. Lord knows they have hurt us plenty and more. But I don't want it to be my last act on this earth, and I don't want to get consumed by my hate, which admittedly is strong.

"We must leave, and do so tonight. Every moment we remain puts us in jeopardy. We have grown soft, we have grown lazy. Lax in our own defense. The enemy could already be on his way here. We must assume that he is, or we will never be ready when that time comes, and it will come at a time not of our own choosing."

"Leaving has its own risks, too," Max stated matter-of-factly, though not strongly.

Jack knew he had them then. They were listening now, considering the alternatives; the childish need, the emotional greed, was gone—in their minds they were working out the risks of leaving, which Jack knew were not as great as the risks of staying, and knew he could convince them of this. He glanced at Daryl; he didn't appear to be won over, but he was remaining, thankfully, quiet.

"We can travel at night, take the sewer lines as far as we can. We can travel light. Get behind the Catalinas where there is an abundance of ways to shelter oneself and eat; where there are abandoned homes and rangeland that hasn't been hunted in years. We can make it there … if we can make it there."

Jack saw desolate resolution on their faces; this was not easy nor would it get easier—to be an outlaw, a renegade for life. To go from a life that had been whole and fulfilling; of a nation of prosperity, though fifteen or more years ago, to where they were today—killers and outlaws … in a land where days were darker than night. They were good folks; they had been teachers, doctors, plumbers, and the children of such—the life they had once known and lived was now gone … never to come back, not in their lifetime nor in their children's.

Max ran his thumb down the side of his nose; the smudge it left spoke about the here and now.

"I'll go," Max said flatly.

He pulled Charlie close to him. Her dark hair, tangled and matted, fell in ringlets around her face. For the moment Jack saw her as the queen of beauty, tragic beauty.

"We will go, but not to escape. We are done fighting, done killing, but neither will we leave, not yet, at any rate. We will accompany you as far as you need, to the mountains if such is the case, and see you off. But remain here I must. I have to stay and wait for Kate. I have to wait for Kate or find a way to go to her, but I cannot run off without her."

Jack looked at Max, he looked at Charlie, and then nodded in the affirmative or understanding, it amounted to the same thing. Jack didn't demean the man by asking what he would do; he knew what Max would do, for it was the same thing that he himself would do— he would work to build a home for the two of them … he would keep his head down and find a way to reach out to his daughter.

"But," he said as he pulled on the automatic weapon hanging over his shoulder, "we go with these, and god help anyone who gets in our way. And, when it is the three of us, then we will come to you. Just be prepared to feed me again."

"With pleasure. After all, as you once reminded me, I got you into this mess …"

"And now you got to feed me," they both said together.

"Well, I will go too," Daryl joined in. "You need someone to keep you safe and sane, and what is a village without a school? Yes, I think I will start a school in this new rinky-dink village or yours, be the first employee and whatnot, and yes, I think that is it. We will name the village Rinky-Dink. That sounds right." And he walked off as he muttered to himself.

With Daryl on board and Max and Charlie willing to help out, most of the rest fell into line pretty straightforward. Some would remain behind for reasons of their own, either to keep fighting with guns or to fight the brutality with compassion. Not all would go, but enough would. A village, Rinky-Dink, if that is what it was to be, would be born.

They gathered up their gear; food, clothes, weapons, some tools—it would be so much easier if they could drive … and deadlier too. On a recent outing Jack and a couple of the others got a firsthand glimpse of the perils of vehicular travel; all military vehicles were stopped, searched, identities and ranks of the soldiers thoroughly checked—those were the military vehicles—all nonmilitary vehicles were destroyed on sight, their occupants shot on the spot … evidently, traveling was now a felony.

So it was that they walked out of the dark and seemingly secure sanctuary of more than two months and worked their way into a system of long-unused sewer gutters, some large enough to ride a truck through, others so small that one could not walk without stooping. The trek through the sewers, until they exited in the desert, would be some twenty miles, all told. The tunnels were dry; Jack and his band were still in an area of long disuse—they followed the line north and west. Jack had a map of the entire underground waste transport system from modern times to ancient settlement aqueducts. Without it, it is doubtful they could make it more than a few hundred yards without getting turned around. They took a branch heading due east and then after half a day, followed another line east by north.

Conserving food, battery power, and sleeping in turns, two days later they arrived at a short spur which opened into the riverbed. Water rarely, if ever, flowed through the steep concrete-lined embankment; it was wide, it was dry, and it was dark—as dark as dark could be on a night where the stars boasted of a new moon. They had covered twenty or so miles from the abandoned garage to this point on the outskirts of town, and they had traveled, thankfully, undetected and underground; occasionally the best-made plans did bear fruit and this was one of those infrequent but happy times.

Jack had point on exit, followed by Charlie, Max, and Daryl, and a dozen or so fighters; Ellen was back with the "social element, the women, children, and old men—and behind them were the rear guard, five heavily-armed men … there were about seventy people total. The balance, about thirty or so, had elected to remain in the garage.

Jack had his people spread out in a thin line on the sandy riverbank; their dark clothing was all the more pronounced by the light from the stars wheeling overhead—there was no moon. This was a hazardous moment for the team; they needed to exit the drain, get out of the dry riverbed, and melt away into the flat of the desert without being seen. Though the lighting was minimal, the dark figures stood in stark relief against the lighter dirt and sand—a patrol crossing the bridge would have little trouble discerning the dark shapes floating across the riverbed. As to where they should head once they reached the flats above the riverbank? Well, that was the rub; where exactly were they to go? Suddenly their route, which had seemed so assured in the relative comfort of the previous morning, seemed ghastly and unsure in the twilight before dawn; a group of people, and not a small group at that, huddling along the banks of the city's major riverbed could hardly be considered discreet and stealthy—a chance patrol and it was all over. Jack looked back, considered the option of moving everyone back into the drain, and dismissed it out of hand; there was no purpose to such a move and, besides, that option posed risks of its own, none greater nor less than the ones he was facing now. No, it was best to move on, move out, and get the thing over with. Still to be decided was how to cross the main road running just north of the wash, and beyond that, where to go to from there. But he really couldn't spend time considering future options; he was way too exposed where he sat in the here and now.

In the end, as was usually the case, it was more a matter of doing it rather than considering it; Max and Charlie went up top first to set a perimeter and to keep the group low, keep it together, and keep the first folks up and out of the way of the folks cresting the bank behind them. Max was turning into a real asset, so different from the bumbling professor Jack had saved eight, nine months ago? Ha! That was a good one; saved from the hell into which Max had been cast for the hell he now found himself in.

He turned instead toward a gray-haired man next to him; he and Jack went back many years, almost to Jack's childhood—Jack's father had employed him and when he died, the man's services seemed to fall naturally to Jack.

"Yes, Alfred, it is right up this embankment. I know that it is a bit of a clamber, my old friend and caretaker of my vines, but you can manage it." Jack smiled as he said such.

"I don't suppose that we will be doing much vineyard business when we get to wherever it is we are going, will we, Jack?"

This last brought him up short; took the wind right out of his sails, as they say. They really had broken with their past—no more ranch, no more vineyard, no more home. Even if they did find a place, a quiet place where they could learn how to catch their child a dream, it would never again be a place they could call their own; Jack had *owned* a ranch, they couldn't take that away from him, though they could and probably would take the ranch—what was to become of it now? What was to become of them all?

He looked back up to the crest of the riverbank. Max and Charlie were making their way down to the wash to reenter the tunnels and return to the route that had brought them here. He clasped Charlie in a warm embrace; a goodbye to the daughter he never had, the lover who never was—he, a good friend who would always be … the very good friend.

To Max, their parting began with a handshake and then became an embrace; a short embrace and mutual word of encouragement—and then the two were on their way.

They crossed the threshold and stepped into the tunnel, not looking back as they did so, not looking back the whole time it took for them to disappear into the dark, and then the light from their flashlights was swallowed up by the darkness as well.

Jack turned his back on it, tuned his back on it all; Max, Charlie, the tunnel, his past, their past, the past. One foot in front of another, he began his climb into the future. He and Ellen, Max and Charlie, Daryl, a host of others.

And God led Moses and the Israelites out of the land of bondage and into the wilderness beyond in which flourished the promised land.

Tucson

Max looked around; he took a step backward and up onto the curb behind him. He wasn't watched, at least so he thought; the nearest guard, about thirty yards upstream from where he stood, was watching the flow of slaves filing past—channeling past was more like it, between rows of barbed-wire fencing eight feet in height and twenty-five feet wide.

This dirty, ragged mass of humankind flowed and churned the three miles from the barracks to the copper mine. Meals were eaten at the mine; hundreds of slaves, sitting, squatting, in the dirt—the fine dust mixing with the thin, watery soup. It was copper mine seventeen at which this particular herd of slaves toiled; all other menial human needs were accommodated here as well, right at the face of the mine—the showers, the latrine, the medical facilities, such as they were, or not … the morgue. They came back to the camp every evening at dusk, bellies more empty than full, to fitfully sleep off another day of toil.

He looked again left and right, making sure that he wasn't being watched. He looked across the street; through the barbed wire and past the matted hair dangling in front of her eyes—to the girl in the faded dress and the dirty face … it *was* her and he had no idea what to say. He stood still, staring at her as discreetly as one could, though hardly anyone could notice what one particular slave was up to, and wondered if she still held the flat they had shared for six weeks; if her father's moderate position of authority still shielded her—he thought not, but he couldn't be sure. Yet there she was, free and better fed than most; she had yet to develop the famished look common among the prisoners and the free people not in the employment of government.

A half-dozen steps forward and he reached out to stroke the hand clasped tight and taut around the wire; he uncoiled her grasp one finger at a time—he had thought it lithe and strong once … now it was neither. With his touch, she noticed him for the first time, though she had been looking at him all along.

"Charlie."

He stopped; he couldn't go on. What to say? What could one say? What did the dying say to the near dead?

"Charlie, go home. Go home to your father. Leave this place." Then, hardest of all: "Leave me."

"But," she said, and looked steadily into his eyes, her gaze firming; it was perhaps her most steadfast gaze in weeks. "I love you."

"And I you. That is why you must go, don't you see?"

Then he hit on it. "I will need someone to take care of me when I get out. I will come to you." Yes, this was good. "I will come to you and you will heal me, but you need to be strong, not wasting away here."

"Oh, Max," she said, stroking his gray-stubble cheek through the wire, "you know nothing, Max Stein. You know nothing."

But Max knew all too well, he knew that he had lost. He had lost not only Charlie and Kate, he has lost everything and everyone that had ever mattered to him since the beginning of time. Life seemed like a nightmare with intermittent illusions of happiness; he had lost his wife, his new friendship with Jack, and his old friendship with Daryl—he had lost Charlie in spite of their protestations of undying love … he was losing his memory of his wife, and, worst of all, he had not only lost Kate but he was losing his memory of her as well. He was, in short, losing that which had made a man; he was losing himself and he was losing his last shreds of humanity.

"No."

It was Charlie speaking, but to whom? Max couldn't tell; it was as if she read his mind—or had been thinking along the same lines as he.

"No, Max. I will go, yes, I will go home, to our flat,"—*ah, she had it still*—"I will clean it and clean myself up,"—she waved her hand down the length of her body—"and I will be here for you. I will not die and neither will you. We will be together."

With that, she cupped his weather-beaten chin in her hand and piercing the veil of barbed wire between them, laid a kiss on his cheek; several moments later she vanished in the crowd as it moved and churned—a sea of people that soon clouded Max's sight and mind.

Spring has long been sung as a time for hope, of life renewed, a thaw in the hard cold; for Kate it was a time to return home—her real home … the home she had not seen for almost a year and a half.

The month-long excursion that Jared had sent her on was soon to take a dramatic turn, of that there was no doubt; the only question was the direction the drama would take. Kate looked out the train's window; this part of the rail carried the train on a straight path through open flatlands where desert scrub grew right up to the tracks. At one time, diligence had been employed in keeping the area around the tracks free of debris, but that was years, even lifetimes ago; now, occasional cattle or drifting sand brought the line to a halt—farther back, when they were winding through the southern Appalachians, cattle had crossed the line, bringing the train to a stop. They stopped for them at least once a day, or so it seemed, in an effort to convince the dumb beasts that life was better alive on the side than dead on the tracks; it seems that the beasts were no brighter here in the West than they had been back East.

It was all fine with her, the delays and whatnot; she had nowhere to go, and was in no hurry to get anywhere other than away from the trials that had dogged her during her stay back east; it had seemed an eternity, but now with the place physically behind her, the days didn't seem such a burden to her soul—indeed it seemed just yesterday that Guy was intimidating her all the way to the airport at the start of what she had thought was to be her new life of … what … servitude? Death? No matter, she had outplayed him, much as she had expected, and she had outlived him as well, which had not exactly been expected, but in retrospect seemed absolutely how things should have been from the start, 'specially since it was her hand that had killed him. She had out played them all and was going home.

They were passing through Texas Canyon, a mysterious rocky place of tall red spires of rock and jumbled boulders strewn about the base of the spires. Kate couldn't understand what this steep ravine, filled with the entire spectrum of geometry of *rock,* had to do with the bland and dismally flat Lone Star State of Texas—what was up with that, anyhow … the *Lone Star* State?

Having delivered the packet that Jared had entrusted to her, Kate decided that she wasn't going to stay in Tucson; the city was not the city she remembered from her youth, or even the city she remembered when she left it over a year ago. Jared had probably known this when he had sent her on her excursion westward; he had said absolutely nothing when she mentioned that after getting her father she would probably stay on in town and try and find work—indeed, his silence spoke volumes of knowledge.

Now it was a blackened, empty city; the university had closed down, the population had all but fled or was scattered to the remote fringes in the form of compulsory labor brigades or "free enclaves" of workers and their families—it was a depressing and probably dangerous place … not necessarily for her, but it could be.

Kate traveled as the assistant director of the Internal Passport Control Office—an office and director no one had heard of because it didn't exist—it wasn't the most secure of covers, but it also wasn't a cover that needed to hold up very long … just long enough for her to get into Tucson unmolested and then disappear once she had what she had come for. Jared and Kate had considered creating a permanent position for her as an official of the federal government in Tucson, but such a *created* position would need to withstand a deep investigation and not hold out for very long; eventually she would be found out—it was best not to fall victim to convenience but rather to understand her position from the start and approach life accordingly. So it turned out she wasn't going home after all; her real destination would be anonymity in SoCal City, where she would take up with contacts that Jared had there, laying low while he worked on establishing something more permanent for her.

As such, Kate had about three days to find her father and get him out of whatever jam he might be in. Few enough in this town had someone to get them out of a jam—but Max did … quite possibly on the way to being Jared's father-in-law.

But how to find him? While Tucson held only a fraction of the population it once did, those remaining were spread over a wide area; there was little in the way of records and lots in the way of suffering—Kate had little in the way of resources or time, no knowledge of the layout of the population, and no one to turn to for help. It was a crummy, brutal world she had entered, and no one would be extending the hand of friendship to someone as undesirable as an outsider, even an outsider with her pedigree.

So she began. First she had to assume he was in a compulsory work brigade; it wasn't definite, but it was likely—so he was one of the approximately thirty thousand conscripted workers. Not very good odds to start with. Complicating matters further was that, as an escapee from the northern labor camps, it was unlikely her father would be able to go under his own name.

But there were other ways she could limit her search; her father had no skills, so he would most likely be put to the most general labor, which accounted for about four of five jobs available for assignment; that parameter cut the number of conscripts she would need to search to about twenty-four thousand—still too big a number to indiscriminately ask to see them all. Besides, on what basis could she make such a request?

With time ticking she placed a call to Jared, who stealthily communicated to her a user name and password allowing her access to the local system, but only for a day. The log-in would be detected during the night security sweeps and disabled; Jared knew it, Kate knew it, and so did the people who designed the system's security. It was intended that intruders who were not stopped at the castle gate would only be able to pry for a day if they penetrated the outer systems.

Kate was able to deduce that one of eight labor camps was for women only, eliminating one whole camp and another four thousand inmates from her search. A more significant find was that in each of the other seven camps there were a small number of laborers who had been picked up for having a lack of or improper documentation—they had been picked up for not having an internal passport, as it were ... these prisoners were housed in a separate group altogether.

This would work; it fit right in with her cover, with her being a representative of the Internal Passport Department—talk about the value of hindsight and all that ... talk about luck.

Kate would start with the hardest labor camps, those dealing in mining; Kate would either find him and somehow get him out, or at least make sure that he wasn't in the most direst of conditions, at least not at the moment.

The rest was pure courage and all bluff—from one camp to another she made her way, asking under various guises to see the list of undocumented and conscripted workers in each camp she visited. She needed to, for some odd reason, having to do with the issuance of new internal passports. Why the dying and those sentenced to work till they were dead, needed a passport was never covered in much detail. Time was running out; in a short while they would be looking for a tall, brown-haired woman with pale skin, posing as an employee of the State Department; she moved fast, moved with an air of confidence and brutality—it was the right combination for the environment ... she bullied one clerk after another but found nothing. More than once she noted the person she had been haranguing with picking up the phone receiver even as she was departing; Kate couldn't hear what was being said, she didn't need to—the phone calls were going out, and she needed to hurry.

In the end she found him, bruised, battered, and malnourished; he almost didn't recognize her—it has been so long since he had seen someone he knew and cared for, someone bright-eyed and rosy cheeked ... but then he did, he recognized her.

"I need to save you." The only words he initially could say, and he said them weakly and but once.

"Yes, Dad, I know."

But it was she who saved him, holding tight to this man who was her father and who weighed less than her. The only man who had ever really mattered to her. She took him in her arms and half-walked him, half-carried him to her chauffeur-driven vehicle. Tears streamed down her face unchecked, tears like she hadn't had since her mother had died; but she kept herself quiet—he was unconscious, near death, or so it seemed, skin roughened, battered and bruised ... but it wouldn't do for him to see her cry like this.

The driver said not a word; he had managed to keep his job, and his head, by ignoring everything he saw but the road, everything he heard but the traffic.

She saved *him*, but *he* saved Charlie; before they boarded the train that would take them finally to SoCal City, Max made her pluck a numb and disoriented Charlie from a filthy apartment where she sat in the dark, barely eating and almost never going out—even as they coddled her out the door she went on mumbling about waiting for Max, a man named Max ... she was but twenty-nine and acted all of eighty-eight. Max could only hope that her derangement was temporary; there were many who would never recover from the past year's brutality.

On the last morning of the third day, the number of days that Kate knew she could safely stay in Tucson, the three of them boarded the train; they were running again, *the trains*, that is—Max remembered, what seemed lifetimes ago, the trains had stopped running when this initial horror had begun … now, for him it was ending and the trains were running again. How wonderful.

Kate had come full circle all on her own, returned in strength where she'd left in weakness, grabbed what was left of her family, the old, and evidently the new, and started them on their way to their new life. Kate sighed and looked at her family sleeping next to her on the train as it darted west at a truly amazing speed, wondering just what it was that her father intended to save her from; well, not really—she already knew, for she already had saved herself … but there was no need to tell him that.

About the Author

J. D. Levy was born in Las Cruces, New Mexico in 1957. Mr. Levy graduated from Northern Arizona University with a Bachelor of Science in Philosophy and holds Masters Degrees in Computer Science and Education. He currently lives in Tucson, Arizona with his family and enjoys hiking and most any other activity that takes place in the quiet outdoors.

Mr. Levy has extensively researched the American and Russian civil wars, being of the mind that such profound historical events determine the 'Historical Necessity' of people for decades and generations to come.

Currently an instructor of Computer Science at a Junior College, Mr. Levy believes that it is up to each of us to do our part to make the world a better place for all of mankind; and that the best way of doing so is to build a world based on inclusiveness, freedom, and prosperity – the very values that have made America the leader among the free nations of the world.

www.ingramcontent.com/pod-product-compliance
Lightning Source LLC
Chambersburg PA
CBHW070616130626
46556CB00001B/382